"NAIL HIM!"

The tyrannosaur strode from the pines with a hacking challenge.

"Christ, he's looking for us," the pilot said. The carnosaur slammed aside the ribs of its kill like bowling pins. Its nostrils were flared, and the sound it made was strikingly different from the familiar bellow of earlier occasions.

"If you'll stand over here, Adrienne," Vickers said, stepping to the back rail of the platform. The client followed with brittle quickness. "When I say shoot," Vickers continued, "aim at the middle of the chest."

Washman had put the platform in an arc toward the tyrannosaur. The big carnivore lunged forward with a series of choppy grunts like an automatic cannon. The pilot rotated the platform on its axis, a maneuver he had carried out a thousand times before. This time the vehicle dipped. It was a sickening, falling-elevator feeling to the two gunners and a heart-stopping terror to the man at the controls who realized it was not caused by clumsiness. The platform began to stagger away from the dinosaur, following the planned hyperbola but lower and slower than intended.

"Nail him," Vickers said calmly.

TIME SAFARI

DAVID DRAKE

BAEN BOOKS

TIME SAFARI

Copyright © 1982 by David Drake

A Baen Book

Baen Publishing Enterprises
260 Fifth Avenue
New York, N.Y. 10001

First Baen printing, March 1989

ISBN: 0-671-69812-5

Cover art by K. W. Kelly

Printed in the United States of America

Distributed by
SIMON & SCHUSTER
1230 Avenue of the Americas
New York, N.Y. 10020

Part II of this novel was published in somewhat different form in *Destinies*, © 1981 by David Drake.

DEDICATION:

To Ralph H. Eisaman, MD
Hunter, shooter, friend.

ACKNOWLEDGMENTS:

Among the friends to whom I owe personal debts for help given me on TIME SAFARI are: Jim Baen; Bernadette Bosky; Jase Valentine; Karl Wagner; and my wife Jo, who is indeed a friend. They are not responsible for the mistakes, for the questions I didn't ask and the advice I didn't take; but bless them all for what they freely offered.

Part I

CALIBRATION RUN

The sabertooth sprang from cover just as Vickers bent to pick up the partridge he had shot. Holgar Nilson had been dynamiting rock samples a hundred yards away. He shouted as he leveled his Mauser. The blond Nilson would have had an easy shot—except that Vickers' own body blocked the Mauser's line of fire.

The thud of the cat's paws crossing to leap again warned Vickers an instant in advance of Nilson's cry. The sandy-haired guide was holding his shotgun at the balance, not ready to fire—and not that bird-shot would have affected the 500-pound killer.

The cat swung down its lower jaw, locking out of the way everything extraneous to stabbing with its six-inch upper canines, as it made its third and final leap. Its bared palate was white as bone.

Vickers flung himself backwards, trying desperately to raise the shotgun. The sabertooth's hide was mottled brown on black, its belly cream. As it sprang, its forelegs splayed and the ten black claws shot out of the pads. Every tense muscle of the cat's body quivered in the air. Its weight slammed Vickers' torso against the stony ground while the blast of Nilson's rifle rumbled about them.

The cat's eyes were a hand's breadth from Vickers' face as they glazed and the life went out of them. A shudder arched the creature's back, rocking the serrated fangs downward. Vickers screamed but the points were not piercing his chest, only compressing it, and the thrust itself was a dying reflex. Blood had been spurting from the cat's throat where the Brenneke bullet had entered. Now the nostrils drooled blood as well and the cat's muscles went limp.

Holgar Nilson ran to the linked bodies, cursing in Norwegian. Vickers could not breathe. The carcase sagged over him like a bag of rice, pinning him so tightly that he could not move his index finger enough to put the shotgun on safe. The weapon was pressing against his right leg. It would blow his foot off if it fired now. Nilson tugged at the sabertooth ineffectively, his panic little less than that of his partner trapped under the cat. The big Norwegian was waving his Mauser one-handed while his eyes scanned the brush in quick arcs. "There was another one," he gasped, "the male. But it ran off when I fired."

"Here, let me help," said Linda Weil, dropping the first aid kit to seize one of the sabertooth's fangs. The curved inner edges of the teeth could shear flesh with all the cat's brutal strength behind them, but they did not approximate real knife blades. In any case, the fangs were the only handholds available on the slack carcase. Weil was a short, broad-hipped woman. She twisted, using the thrust of her legs against the passive weight of the sabertooth. The great, brown-and-black body slumped away fluidly, Its haunches still covered Vickers' calves. Nilson stopped groping blindly and looked down. He gripped a clawed foot and rotated the cat's hindquarters away from his partner.

Vickers was sucking deep breaths. His face and tunic front were covered with blood. He put the shotgun on safe and cocked an arm behind him to help him rise.

"No, no," said the dark-haired woman, touching the guide's shoulder with a restraining hand. "Just wait—"

Vickers lurched upright into a sitting position. "I'm all right," he wheezed. Then, "It was my fault. It was all my fault."

"The buckle," said Nilson. "Look at your pack buckle." The Norwegian's composure was returning. His left index finger touched one strap of the pack Vickers had been wearing to hold small specimens. The steel buckle was warped like foil against its padding where it had blocked the thrust of the sabertooth's fang. The brushing contact of Nilson's finger caused pain to stab Vickers.

"Damn," muttered the older guide as Linda Weil helped him off with the empty pack and unbuttoned his tunic. The blood that sprayed Vickers was the cat's, but he knew from the pain that he might well have a cracked rib of his own. The female paleontologist's fingers were cool and expert. She had been chosen as an on-site investigator for the Time Intrusion Project as much for her three years of medical school as for her excellent series of digs in the Sinai with a University of Chicago team.

A square mark larger than the buckle's edges was stamped in white above Vickers' left nipple. "I don't hear anything grating," Weil said. "We'll strap it. Maybe when we get back to Tel Aviv they'll want to drain the hematoma."

"It was waiting for me like I was a goddam antelope," Vickers said. He was a stocky man of thirty-five who usually looked as calm as a fireplug. Now he rubbed the back of his hand over the sockets of his pale eyes, smearing the splotches of tacky blood. "Holgar," he said, "I wasn't ready. I wouldn't have had a snowball's chance in Hell except for you."

"Holgar, we'll want the skull and limbs of this macheirodont when you have a chance," said Linda Weil, pointing toward the sabertooth as she stood. She looked back at Vickers before she continued, "And frankly, I think that if anyone's error can be said to have led to this—problem, near disaster—it was mine. Both of you are used to animals that've had hundreds of thousands of years to learn to fear man. That's not the case here. As you said, Henry, we're just meat on the hoof so far as the bigger carnivores here are concerned. *I'm* the one who should have realized that."

Vickers sighed and stood up carefully. He walked over to the spur-legged partridge, ten feet away where he had dropped it when the cat struck. Raising the heavy bird, he gestured with it to Weil. "It's a francolin like the one we got in the snare two days ago," he said. "I thought I'd roast it for dinner instead of keeping it for a specimen."

The dark-haired paleontologist nodded back. "After I get you bandaged," she agreed. "I think we could all do with a meal and a chance to relax."

Hyenas had already begun to call in the sullen dusk. Time spent in the African bush gave the ugly, rhythmic laughter a homely sound to the pair of guides, but Linda Weil shuddered with distaste.

Holgar Nilson laughed. He patted the paleontologist on the thigh with a greasy hand. "They are only predators like ourselves," he said. "Perhaps we should invite them to join us for dinner one night, yes? We have so much in common."

Weil switched the francolin drumstick to her left hand and squeezed Nilson against her thigh with her right. "I don't question their right to exist," the woman said. "It's just that I don't like them." She frowned, scientist again. "We could use a specimen, though. There's a good enough series of hyena fossils known Topside that fresh examples ought to be more datable than most of what we've gathered."

"You know," said Vickers, speaking in a conscious effort to break out of the shell of depression that surrounded him, "I've never quite understood what use the specimens we bring back were going to be. For dating, that is. I mean, taking radiation levels from the igneous rocks should give them the time within a few thousand years. And if I understand the Zeiss—" he gestured with his thumb— "its photographs ought to be down to the minute when they're compared to computer models of star and planet positions."

The 200 mm reflector bolted to the intrusion vehicle was lost in the darkness, as was the normal purr of the motor drive that rotated it by microns along the plane of the ecliptic. As Vickers gestured the mechanism gave one of its rare clicks, signalling the end of an exposure as the telescope reset itself to lock on another portion of sky. The click might have been that of a grenade arming for the level of response it drew from Holgar Nilson, though the younger guide kept the edges of his anger sheathed in bluff camaraderie. "Come, come," he said, "machines fail. Anyway, the sky could have been overcast for months, for years, for all they knew Topside. And for the rock dating to work, they must compare the samples we bring back with samples from the same rock a million years in the future. How are they to be sure of that, hey? When they only *think* so far we are inserted into the same place, with latitude and longitude changing as the continents move."

Vickers nodded, realizing why his partner reacted so defensively. "Sure," he said, "and the more cross-checks, the better. And I suppose the astronomical data is going to be easier to correlate if they've got a fair notion of where to start."

"Besides," said Linda Weil harshly, "I don't think anyone quite realized how useless anything I came back with would be for the intended purpose. Oh, it'll have use—we've enormously expanded human knowledge of Pliocene life-forms. But as you say, Henry, for dating—"

She paused, looking out over the twilit hills. They had been fortunate in that their intrusion vehicle, an angular block of plates and girders, had been inserted onto high ground. During daylight they had a good view over the brush and acacias, the short grass and the beasts that lived there. Now the shadows of the trees and outcrops had merged with the greater shadow of the horizon, and the landscape was melding into a velvet blur. "The whole problem," Weil said toward the darkness, "is that we've got an embarrassment of riches. Before—when I was Topside—a femur was as much as you were likely to get to identify an animal, and a complete skull was a treasure. We decided what the prehistoric biomass looked like by reconstructing a few fragments here, a few fragments there . . . ." She chuckled ruefully and looked back at her male companions. "And here we are, in the middle of thousands and thousands of animals, somewhere in the past I've been studying for years . . . and I'm nowhere near being able to accurately place the time we've been inserted, the way I've been hired to do—because I can't swear that a single species is one that we 'know' from fossils. I feel as if I've spent my working life throwing darts at a map and convincing myself that I've travelled to the places the darts hit."

"Well, you've travelled here, for certain," said the blond man, "and *I* at least am glad of it." He raised his hand to Weil's shoulder and tried to guide the woman closer to him for a kiss.

"Holgar . . . ," the woman objected in a low voice, leaning free of the big hand's pressure.

"I'll get a couple hyenas tomorrow," Vickers said morosely. The fire he stared at glinted from his face where grease from the bird smeared him. "Unless I screw up again, at least. Christ, Holgar, maybe I'd have been better off if you were a second slower with your shot. Hunting's about the one thing I'd decided I could handle. If I'm no good for that either, then I may as well be a cat's dinner." Unwatched, the shorter guide's hands turned and turned again the section of francolin ribs from which he had gnawed only half the flesh.

Nilson looked disconcerted. He lowered his hand from the paleontologist's back and resumed attacking his meal. Absently, Vickers wished that one of the three of them had had the skill to make gravy to go with the mashed potatoes, freeze-dried and reconstituted.

"Ah, Henry," said Linda Weil, "I think that's just shock talking. You aren't incompetent because of one mistake—it's the mistakes that make us human. The planning for this, this expedition, was mostly yours; and everything's gone very well. Except that all I can really say about the time we're at is that we're a great deal farther back than the round million years they intended to send us."

"You see, Henry," Nilson said, "what you need is a wife." The Norwegian gestured with the fork he had just cleared of its load of canned peas. "You have no calm center to your life. Wherever I go, I know that my Mary is there in Pretoria, my children are growing—Oskar, Olaf, and little Kristin . . . do you see? That is what you need."

Vickers looked at the bigger man. Nilson had jarred him out of his depression as Linda Weil had been unable to do with her encouragement. The paleontologist's complexion was dark, but it was no trick of the firelight that led Vickers to see a blush on her face. She looked down at her hands. "Maybe I've been looking in the wrong places," Vickers said dryly. "Your wife is British, if I remember?"

Nilson nodded vigorously as he chewed another mouthful of peas.

"Both of mine were Americans," the older guide said. "Maybe that's where I went wrong." He turned his face toward the night. His profile was as sharp and thin as a half-worn knife. "The sporting goods store I tried to manage was in Duluth," he continued, "and the ranch was in Rhodesia. But I could hunt, that I could do. Well." He looked at Weil again. In a normal voice he added, "Well, I still can. I'll get you a hyena in the morning."

"Actually," said Weil, visibly glad of the change of subject, "what concerns me more is that something's raiding our box traps. Several of those to the west had the lids sprung when I checked them this morning. The rest were empty. Probably *was* a hyena; I don't think a mongoose would be strong enough. But apart from being interested in whatever's doing it, I'd like to have the damage stopped."

"We could lay a sensor from the intrusion alarm under one of the traps," Holgar said. His enthusiasm rang a little false. It was a reaction to the embarrassment he finally had realized that his earlier comment had caused. "Sleep close with the shotgun."

"I've got a three-bead night sight on the Garand," Vickers said, the problem reflecting his mind away from the depression that had been smothering him. "I can sandbag the gun and the spotlight a hundred yards away. That ought to be far enough we won't disturb whatever it is." He frowned and turned to Linda Weil. "Thing is, I can't make sure of something at night unless I give it a head shot or use soft-points that'll blow the body apart if it's small. What's your preference?"

The paleontologist waved the question away. "Save the skull if you can," she said. "But— we've just seen how dangerous the predators here —now, that is—can be. Are you going to disconnect the warning system around us?"

"Just move one pick-up," Nilson said with a laugh. His left fingertips caressed Weil's cheek playfully. "Otherwise you might get a closer and sooner view of a hyena than you expected, no? And what a waste that would be."

Vickers noticed that his hands were still trembling. Just as well the administrators Topside hadn't permitted any liquor among the supplies, he thought. Though usually it wouldn't have mattered to him one way or the other. "It's all right," he said aloud. "I probably won't be sleeping much tonight anyway. Holgar, let's rig something now while there's still enough daylight to work with."

They were forced to finish moving and resetting the nearest of the traps by lamplight after all. When the door mechanism was cocked and the trigger baited with nuts and fruit, Vickers made his own preparations. His rifle was an M1 Garand, modified by a Marine armorer to accept twenty-round BAR magazines. He rested it on a sand-filled pair of his own trousers, its sights aligned on a point just above the center of the trap. The variable-aperture spotlight was set for a pencil beam and also aimed at the trap. The light should freeze the trap-robber long enough for Vickers to put a soft-nosed .30-'06 bullet through its chest.

Around 2 AM the alarm rang. It was a hyrax which had blundered into the trap in search of the nuts. The Hyracoidea had been driven to holes and the night by the more efficient grazing animals who followed their family's Oligocene peak. The little creature in the trap wiggled its whiskers against the electric glare. Vickers switched off the spotlight, hoping the live bait would bring the robber shortly. But to his own surprise, he managed to fall asleep; and it was dawn rather than the intrusion alarm that awakened him the second time.

Vickers' neck was stiff and his feet were cold. A sheen of dew overlay his nylon parka and the flurocarbon finish of his rifle's metal surfaces. The fire was dead. Hot coffee was the only reason to kindle another fire: the sun would be comfortably warm in an hour, a hammer in three. But hot coffee was a good enough reason, God knew, and a fire would be the second priority.

The flap of the tent which Linda Weil shared with Nilson opened while Vickers was still wiping the Garand with an oily rag. It was a habit ingrained in the hunter before steel could be protected by space-age polymers. Caring for the rifle which kept him alive was still useful as a ritual even if it were no longer a practical necessity.

"No luck?" asked Weil as she pulled on her jacket in the open air.

"Well, there's a hyrax," Vickers replied. "I guess that's to the good. I was about to put on a pot of—"

The intrusion alarm pinged. The hunter looked by training at the display panel, even though most of the sensor locations encircling the camp were in plain sight in the daytime. The light indicating the trap sensor was pulsing. When Vickers flicked his eyes down-hill toward the trap, the paleontologist's breath had already drawn in.

The guide rolled silently into a prone position, laying his rifle back across the makeshift sandbag. He looked over but not through the Garand's sights, and his index finger was not on the trigger. Weil was too unfamiliar with guns to appreciate the niceties which differentiate preparations from imminent slaughter. She snatched at Vickers' shoulder and hissed, "Don't shoot₁"

The guide half-turned and touched Weil's lips with the fingertips of his left hand. "Are they chimps?" he mouthed, exaggerated lip movements making up for the near soundlessness of his question. "They don't look quite right."

"They're not chimps," Weil replied as quietly. "My God, they're not."

The tent passed Holgar Nilson with a muted rustle and no other sign. When the intrusion alarm rang, the Norwegian had wasted no time on dressing. Neither of the others looked around. They had set the trap where neither trees nor out-cropping rocks interfered with the vantage, and where most of the mesh box itself was clear of the grass. The blade tips brushed the calves of the three beasts around the trap now. They were hairy enough for chimpanzees, and they were only slightly taller than chimps standing on their hind legs; but these creatures stood as a matter of course, and they walked erect instead of knuckling about on their long forearms like apes.

Vickers uncapped his binoculars and focused them. The slight breeze was from the trap toward

the humans up the slope. The beasts did not seem
to be aware they were being watched. Their attention was directed toward the trap and its contents.

The hyrax was squealing in high-pitched terror
now. The top of the trap was hinged and pegged
closed so that it could be baited and emptied without reaching through the heavily-sprung end-gate.
The traps that had been raided the day before had
simply been torn apart. This one—

The tallest of the—hominids, it didn't mean human, the word was already in all their minds—
the tallest of the hominids was a trifle under five
feet in height. His scalp was marked by a streak of
blond, almost white, fur that set him apart from
his solidly dark companions. He was fumbling at
the latch. Without speaking, Vickers handed the
binoculars to Linda Weil.

"My God," she whispered. "He's learned to open
it."

The hyrax leaped as the lid swung up, but the
hominid on that side was too quick. A hand caught
the little beast in mid-air and snatched it upward.
The hominid's teeth were long and startlingly
white against the black lips. They snapped on the
hyrax's neck, ending the squeals with a click.

The other black-furred hominid growled
audibly and tried to grab the hyrax. The white-
flashed leader in the middle struck him with an
open hand. As the follower sprang back yelping,
the leader turned on the one holding the hyrax. Instead of trying to seize the prey directly as the
lesser hominid had done, the leader spread his
arms wide and burst into angry chattering. His
chest was fully expanded and he gained several
inches of height by rising onto the balls of his feet.

The smaller hominid's face was toward the
watchers. They saw his teeth bare as he snarled
back, but the defiance was momentary and itself

accompanied by a cringing away from the leader. He dropped the hyrax as if he had forgotten it, turning sideways as he did so. As if there were something in the empty air, the follower began to snap and chitter while the leader picked up the hyrax. The mime continued until the white-flashed hominid gave a satisfied grunt and began stalking off northward, away from the human camp. The other hominids followed, a few yards to either side of the leader and perhaps a pace behind. The posture of all three was slightly stooped, but they walked without any suggestion of bow-leggedness and their forelimbs did not touch the ground. The leader held the hyrax by its neck. Not even the binoculars could detail the position of the hominid's thumb to the paleontologist.

"That's amazing," said Holgar Nilson. He had dressed while watching the scene around the trap. Now he was lacing his boots. "They didn't simply devour it."

"Not so surprising," Linda Weil said, the binoculars still at her eyes. "After all, there were more traps in the direction they came from. They're probably full." She lowered the glasses. "We've got to follow them."

"Look at the way they quarrelled over the coney," Nilson protested. "They're hungry. And it's not natural for hungry animals not to eat a fresh kill."

Vickers eyed the sun and shrugged off his parka. If they were going to be moving, he could get along without the insulation for the present so as not to have to carry the warm bulk later in the day. "All right," he said, "they seem to be foraging as they go. It shouldn't be too hard to keep up, even without a vehicle."

"They should have sent a Land Rover with us," complained the Norwegian guide as he stood, slinging his Mauser. "We are bound to make some changes in the environment, are we not? So how can they worry that a Land Rover would be more of a risk to the, to Topside?"

"Well, we'll manage for now," Vickers said, stuffing a water bottle and several packets of dehydrated rations into his knapsack. Despite the bandage, it felt as though his chest were being ripped apart when he raised his arm to don the pack. He kept his face still, but beads of sweat glittered suddenly at the edge of his sandy hair. "I think it's as well that we all go together," Vickers added after a moment to catch his breath. "There's nothing here that animals can hurt and we can't replace; and I'm not sure what we may be getting into."

The three hominids were out of sight beyond one of the hills before their pursuers left camp. Both men carried their rifles. The paleontologist had refused the autoloading shotgun, saying that she didn't know how to use it so it would only be in her way. Weil and the younger guide began pressing ahead at a near run through the rust and green grass. Vickers was more nervously aware than the others of the indigenous predators lurking in these wilds. Aloud he said, "Don't be impatient. They're not moving fast, and if we blunder into them over a rise, we'll spook them sure." Nilson nodded. Linda Weil grimaced, but she too moderated her pace when the guides hung back.

At the looted trap, the paleontologist herself paused. Vickers glanced around for sign, but the ground was too firm to show anything that could be called a footprint. Dark smudges on the otherwise dew-glittering grass led off in the direction the hominids had taken, but that track would stand less than an hour of the sun's growing weight.

Weil turned from the trap. "What's this?" she demanded, pointing. "Did you bring this here when you set the trap?"

Nilson frowned. "It's just a piece of branch," he said.

"Holgar, there's no tree within fifty yards," said Vickers quietly. To the paleontologist he added, "It was pretty dark when we set up the trap. I probably wouldn't have noticed it anyway. But I didn't see any of the—others—carrying it either. For now it's just three feet of acacia branch, broken at both ends."

Weil nodded curtly. She uncapped her neck-slung camera and took several exposures of the trap and the branch lying beside it. She did not touch either object. "Let's go," she said and began striding along the dim trail again at almost the pace she had set at the start.

When they crested the next rise, even Vickers felt a momentary concern that they might have lost their quarry. Then he caught the flash of sun on blond fur a quarter mile away and pointed. They watched through their binoculars as two, then all three hominids moved about the trunk of a large tree.

"They're trying to dig something out of a hole at the root of the tree," Vickers said, "and I'll swear they're using a stick to do it." Then he added, "Of course, a chimpanzee might do the same thing . . . ."

"Linda," said Holgar Nilson, "what are these creatures?" He rubbed his forehead with the back of the hand holding his binoculars. His right thumb tensioned the sling of his rifle.

Linda Weil at first gave no sign that she had heard the question. The blond guide's eyes remained fixed on her. At last she lowered her glasses and said, "I suppose that depends on when

we are. If we're as far back as preliminary indi-
cations suggest we are, those are ramapithecines.
Primates ancestral to a number of other primate
lines, including our own." She would not meet
Nilson's stare.

"They're men, aren't they?" the younger guide
demanded.

"'Men' isn't a technical term!" snapped the
paleontologist, raising her chin. "If you mean,
'They belong to the genus Homo' I'd have to say
no, I don't believe they do. Not yet. But we don't
have any data." She spun to glare at Vickers. "Do
you see?" she went on. "What a, what a laughing-
stock I'll be if I go back from my first time intrusion and say, 'Well, I've found the earliest men
for you, here's a smudgy picture from a mile
away'? They drove Dubois into *seclusion* for find-
ing Java Man without an engraved pedigree!"

Vickers shrugged. "Well," he said, "it isn't anything that we need to jump the gun about."

Licking their fingers—the leader still carried
the hyrax—the hominids wandered away from the
trees again. Weil snapped several photographs,
but her camera had only a lens selected for close-
ups of animals too large to carry back whole.

The landscape itself was beyond any camera,
and the profusion of life awakening with the dawn
was incredible. Vickers had been raised on stories
of the great days of African hunting, but not even
Africa before the advent of nitro powders and
jacketed bullets could equal the animate mass that
now covered what some day would be Israel.
Standing belly-deep in the grass they cropped
were several species of hipparion, three-toed
horses whose heads looked big for their stocky
bodies. The smallest of them bore black and white
stripes horizontally on their haunches. When the
stripes caught sunlight at the correct angle, the

beasts stood out as candid blazes. The horses were clumped in bodies of twenty to forty, each body separated from the others by a few hundred yards. These agglomerations could not be called herds in the normal sense, for they mixed hipparions of distinctly different sizes and coloration.

Indeed, antelopes of many varieties were blended promiscuously among the hipparions as well. Vickers had vaguely expected to see bovids with multiple, fanciful horns during the intrusion. Linda Weil had disabused him with a snort. She followed the snort with a brief disquisition on the Eurasian Cenozoic and the ways it could be expected to differ from the North American habitat which the popularizers were fonder of describing.

Oryx had proven to be the most common genus of antelope in the immediate area, though the region was better-watered than those Topside which the curved-horned antelopes frequented. There were other unexpected antelopes also. On the first day of the intrusion Nilson had shot a tragelaphine which seemed to Vickers to differ from the rare inyala of Mozambique only in its habits: the lyre-horned buck had stared at the rifle in bland indifference instead of flashing away as if stung.

The hominids were moving on; the human trio followed. Weil was leading as before but Holgar Nilson had begun to hang back. Vickers glanced at the younger man but did not speak. In the near distance, a buffalo bellowed. The guides had scouted the reed-choked bottom a mile away, beyond another range of undulations, but they had not actively hunted it yet. Earlier, the dark-haired paleontologist had commented that a sampling of bovine skulls and horn-cores might be helpful in calibrating their intrusion. Vickers nodded toward the sound. "On our way back," he suggested, "if it's late enough that the buffs have come back out of the reeds after their siesta, we might try to nail you some specimens."

"For God's sake, let's not worry about that now!" snapped Weil. She stumbled on a lump of exposed quartz which her eyes, focused on the meandering hominids, had missed. Vickers had guided tourist hunters for too many years to think that he had to respond.

The clumps of grazing animals seemed to drift aside as the hominids straggled past, but the relative movement was no more evidently hostile than that of pedestrians on a crowded street. Still, when one of the hominids passed within a few yards of a group resting under a tree, up started a 400 pound antelope of a genus with which Vickers was not familiar. After a hundred yards the antelope turned and lowered its short, thick-based horns before finally subsiding beneath another tree. A jackal might have aroused the same reaction.

The hominids had skewed their course twice and were now headed distinctly southward, though they still gave no evidence of purpose. "Reached the end of their range and going back," Holgar Nilson said. He spoke in a tone of professional appraisal, normal under the circumstances, and not the edged breathiness with which he had earlier questioned the paleontologist. "Do we still follow them?"

Linda Weil nodded, subdued herself by embarrassment over her outbursts at the two guides. "Yes, but I want to see what they were doing at the base of this tree first," she said, nodding toward the acacia ten yards away. She unlimbered her camera in anticipation.

Vickers stopped her by touching her elbow. "I

think we can guess," he said quietly, "and I think we'd better guess from here. Those bees look pretty peeved."

"Ah," Weil agreed. The dots flashing metallically as they circled in and out of the shade crystallized in her mind into a score or more of yellow-bodied insects. Fresh dirt of a pale reddish tinge had been turned between a pair of surface roots. The stick that had done the digging was still in the hole. Up and down it crawled more of the angry bees. "Surely they aren't immune to bee-stings, are they?" the woman asked.

Vickers shrugged, wincing at the pressure in his chest. "I'm not immune to thorn scratches," he said. "But if I'm after an animal in heavy brush, that's part of the cost of doing business."

The hominids were almost out of sight again. "We'd best keep going," said the paleontologist, acting as she spoke.

While they walked uphill again, Vickers swigged water and handed his bottle around. The water was already hot from the sun on his dun knapsack, and the halogens with which it had been cleared gave it an unpleasant tang. Neither of Vickers' companions bothered to comment on the fact.

"This is where we got the horses two days ago," Nilson said, gesturing toward the low ridge they were approaching.

Vickers thought back. "Right," he said. "We got here due west from the bottom of the trapline. We've just closed the circuit in the other direction, is all."

They heard the growling even before they crested the rise. Nilson unslung his Mauser. Vickers touched Linda Weil to halt her. He knelt to charge his Garand, using the slope of the ground to deflect the sound of the bolt slapping the breech as it chambered the first round of twenty. The paleontologist's face was as tense as those of the guides. "All right," Vickers whispered, "but we'll keep low."

In a swale a quarter mile from their present vantage point, Vickers had dropped a male hipparion. It was large for its genus; a good 400 pounds had remained to the carcass after the hunters had removed the head and two legs for identification. Hyenas are carnivores no less active than the cats with which they share their ranges, but virtually no carnivore will refuse what carrion comes its way. A pack of hyenas had found the dead horse. They were still there, wrangling over scraps of flesh and the uncracked bones, as the hominids approached the kill. The snarls that the intrusion team heard were the warning with which the hyenas greeted the newcomers.

"We've got to help them," said Nilson.

Vickers glanced at the junior guide out of the corner of his eye. He was shocked to see that Nilson was watching over his electronic sight instead of through his binoculars. "Hey, put that down!" Vickers said. "Christ, shooting now'd screw up everything."

"They'll be killed!" the Norwegian retorted, as if that were an answer.

"They know what they're doing a whole lot better than we do," Vickers said, and at least on that the men could agree.

There were six of the shaggy carnivores. Two of them paced between the remains of the hipparion and the hominids who gingerly approached it. "I'd have thought they'd be denned up this time of day," Vickers muttered. "When you don't know the animal, its habits don't surprise you . . . . But those'd pass for spotted hyenas Topside without a word. Damned big ones, too. They ought to act like the hyenas we know."

At the distance and through the foreshortening of the binoculars, it was impossible to tell for certain how near the hominids had come to the kill. The foremost of the brindled hyenas was surely no more than twenty feet from the hominid leader. The carnivore turned face-on and growled, showing teeth that splintered bones and a neck swollen with muscles like a lion's. Holgar Nilson gasped. His hand sought again the pistol grip of his slung rifle.

The white-flashed hominid jabbered shrilly. He squatted down. The hyrax was still clutched in his left hand, but with his right he began to sling handfuls of dirt and pebbles at the hyena. To either side, the other hominids were also chattering and leaping stiff-legged. One hominid held a rock in each hand and was clashing them together at the top of each jump.

The pelted hyena only snarled back. Its nearest companion retreated a few paces to the scattered carcass, it's brushy tail lifted as if to make up for the weakness of the sloping hindquarters. The other four members of the pack were lying on their bellies in a loose arc behind the hipparion. One of them got to its feet nervously.

The empty-handed hominid suddenly darted toward the carcase. He almost touched the ribs, streaked white and dark red with the flesh still articulating them. The nearest hyena leaped up snapping. Its jaw thumped the air as if a book had been slammed. The hominid jumped sideways with a shriek to avoid the teeth, then cut to the other side as the foremost hyena rushed him from behind. Sprinting, the hominid retreated to his starting position with the snarling hyena behind him.

The hominid doubled in back of his leader, still squealing. The carnivore skidded to a halt. The

white-flashed leader had dropped the hyrax at
last. He hunched with his head thrown forward
and his arms spread like a Sumo wrestler's. Each
hand was bunched around a heavy stone, held in a
power grip between the palm and the four fingers.
Unnoticed by the watching humans, the leader had
prepared for this moment. The angle hid the hominid's bared teeth from the watchers, but his hissing snarl carried back to them on the breeze.

Only the one hyena had followed through on its
rush; now it faced the three hominids alone.
Snarling again to show teeth as large as the first
joint of a man's thumb, the carnivore backed
away. The white-furred hominid hurled a rock
that thumped the hyena in the ribs. The beast
snapped and snarled, but it would neither attack
nor leave its position between the carcass and
the hominids. Its powerful shoulders remained
turned toward its opponents while its hind legs
sidled back and forth nervously, displaying first
one spotted flank and then the other to the watching humans. Making as much noise as a flock of
starlings, the hominids also retreated. At a safe
distance from the hipparion carcass and its pro-
tectors, they turned and resumed their leisurely
meander southward. The hominid with the pair of
stones continued to strike them together occasionally, though without the earlier savage insistence.
Chips spalled from the dense quartz glinted like
sparks in the air.

Holgar Nilson let out his breath slowly. Linda
Weil lowered her binoculars and said, "Holgar,
what's gotten into you? I *know* why *I'm* so tense."

The Norwegian scowled. Vickers glanced at him
and then raised his glasses again. He did not know
how personal the conversation was about to become. "I—" said the blond man. Then, "Hyenas
are terrible killers. I've seen what they can do to

children and even to a grown man who'd broken his leg in the bush."

"Well, we're here as observers, aren't we?" said the paleontologist. "I don't understand."

Nilson turned away from her gaze and did not reply. The woman shrugged. "We need to be moving on," she said. Her face, like that of the younger guide, was troubled.

The hyenas had disappeared back into shallow burrows they had dug around the site of the kill. The humans skirted them at a distance, knowing that another outburst might call the hominids back from the rise over which they had disappeared. "Sort of a shame not to bag one now when we know where they are," Vickers said regretfully as he glanced toward the hipparion. The ribs stood up like a beacon. "I'd expected to be stuck with a night shot . . . and nobody's as good in the dark, I don't care what his equipment is." Neither of the others made any response.

No unusual noise gave warning as the intrusion team neared the next crest, but Holgar Nilson halted them with a raised hand anyway. "They turned their direction to go where they knew carrion was, the horse carcass," he said. The senior guide nodded, pleased to hear his partner use his flawless sense of direction. "But if they are making a large circle, so to speak, and they have been looting our traps west of the camp, then we must be close to where they started."

Nilson's logic was good; all three made the obvious response. Both men tautened their rifle and binocular straps and got down on their hands and knees. Since the grass was thick and over a foot high, there was no need to go into a true low crawl with their weapons laid across crooked elbows. The paleontologist looked dubious, but she followed suit. Her camera finally had to be tucked

into the waist band of her trousers. The ground,
prickly with grass spikes and flakes of stone,
slowed their progress more than did concern over
security.

The hominid camp was in a clump of acacias
less than 200 yards down the next slope.

"Oh, the lord have mercy," whispered Nilson in
Norwegian as his eyes adjusted to the pool of
shade on which he focused his binoculars. It was
hard to tell how many of the hominids were
present; anything from a dozen to twenty was possible. Clumps of grass, shadows, and the emerald
globes of young acacias interfered with visibility.
The three hominids which the intrusion team had
been following were standing. The white-flashed
leader himself was the center of a clamoring mass
of females and infants. Vickers noted that
although many hands were stretched out toward
the leader and the prey he carried, neither was
actually touched by the suppliants.

Much of the confusion died down after a few
minutes. The small hominids made way or were
elbowed aside by additional males. Their external
genitalia were obvious, though the flat dugs of the
females were hidden by their fur. Most of the
males were empty-handed, but one of them was
dragging forward what could only be the femur of
a sivatherium. The bone was too massive even for
the molars of the great hyenas; in time it would
have been gnawed away by rodents, but nothing of
a size to matter would have disputed its
possession with the hominids. Vickers frowned,
trying to imagine what the latter with the relatively small jaws expected to do with a bone which
was beyond the range of hyenas and the big cats.

But the troop's first order of business was the
hyrax. It provided a demonstration that the jaws
and limbs of the hominids were by no means

despicable themselves. The leader gripped the little animal with his teeth and systematically plucked it apart with his hands. One of the males reached in for a piece. The leader cuffed him away and dropped the hyrax long enough to jabber a stream of obvious abuse at the usurper. With something approaching ceremony, the leader then handed the fleshy hind legs to two males. Despite the confusion, Vickers was sure that at least one of them had been a companion of the leader during the morning's circuit.

Dignity satisfied, the white-flashed hominid continued parcelling out the hyrax. The leader's motions were precise; each twist or slash of nails that still resembled claws stripped away another fragment. As each hominid received a portion, he or she—a foreleg had gone early to a dun-furred nursing mother—stepped back out of the ruck. There was some squabbling as members of the troop bolted their allotments, but Vickers did not notice anyone's share actually hijacked.

"Nineteen with him," Linda Weil counted aloud as the leader stood alone in the widened circle of his juniors. Every member of the troop—Vickers found he had an uneasy tendency to think 'tribe'— every member of the troop had been given a portion of the hyrax. The leader held only the head and a bloody tendril of hide still clinging to it. With a croak of triumph the leader bent and picked up the lump of quartz he had carried since the encounter with the hyenas. He rotated the hyrax head awkwardly with his thumb, then brought his two hands together with a resounding *smack*. Dropping the stone again, the leader began to slurp the brains greedily.

"God damn it, you know they're men," Holgar Nilson whispered hoarsely.

"It's nothing more than sea otters do," the paleontologist replied, but she kept the glasses to her eyes and would not face her lover.

Vickers looked from the one to the other, Weil tense, Nilson angry. "I don't think otters share out meat like that," Vickers said. "I don't think I've ever seen animals share out meat that well. Maybe wolves do." He paused before adding, "That doesn't mean they're not animals."

The hyrax was a memory, though a memory that had provided each hominid with a good four ounces of flesh in addition to whatever protein individuals might have scavenged for themselves during the morning. Now the females were bringing out the results of their own gathering: roots and probably locust pods, though it was hard to be sure through the binoculars. Females appeared to be approaching males one on one, though the distinguishing marks of most hominids were too subtle for immediate certainty. The dun-colored mother and an adolescent female whose pelt was a similar shade stood to either side of the leader, cooing and attempting to groom his fur as they offered tubers of some kind.

But the males had not completed their own program as yet. The leader barked something which must have been more in the line of permission than a command. Two of the males responded almost before the syllable was complete, squatting down and chopping furiously with rocks gripped in either fist.

"I can't see them!" Linda Weil said.

Vickers looked at her. Grass blurred all but the heads and flailing arms of the squatting hominids. The *crack!* of stone on bone denser than teak ricocheted up to the watchers. "Ah, they're breaking up the giraffe thigh with rocks," the guide said.

"I know that!" snapped the paleontologist. "Of course they are! And I can't see it!"

Long flakes of bone were spitting upward, catching stray darts of sunlight that made them momentary jewels. The remaining hominids surrounded the activity in a chattering circle, the nuts and tubers forgotten. Occasionally one of the onlookers might snatch at a splinter of bone which would quickly be cast aside again after a perfunctory mumbling.

Linda Weil stood up, holding her camera.

The motion drew the eyes of one hominid. His chirp focused every head in the troop. It was the minuscule whirr of the camera that set off the explosion, however. The hominids fanned forward like a rifle platoon, the half-dozen adult males serried out in front while the young and females filled the interstices a pace or two behind. Even at a distance, their racket was considerable. Each throat was snarling out a single, repetitive syllable as loudly as the lungs beneath could drive it. Some of the females threw handfuls of dirt. It pelted the backs of the males, only the wind-blown dust carrying any considerable distance toward the humans.

The males were not throwing anything. For a further icy instant, Vickers studied their hands through the binoculars. Then he dropped the glasses onto their strap and unslung his Garand. One or both fists of each male hominid bulged with a block of stone. The whole troop was beginning to advance.

"Holgar," Vickers said without taking his eyes off the hominids, "you and Miss Weil strike for camp right now. I'm going to follow just as quick as it's safe. *Right now!*"

Both Nilson and the paleontologist turned to speak, so it was the senior guide alone who saw the rush of the sabertooth from the instant it burst from cover. Dirt flew as the cat's paws hit, its legs doubling under as its spine flexed to fire it along on another leap. In motion, the sabertooth's mottled body looked so large that it was incredible that it could have sheltered behind the small acacia from which it had sprung. Even more amazing was the fact that it had reached the acacia, for the grass to a considerable distance in every direction seemed sparse and featureless.

Despite their noise and apparent concentration, the hominids saw the sabertooth almost as quickly as Vickers did. They had reacted to the humans as if to a territorial challenge; the response evoked by the big cat was one of blind panic. The orchestrated threats dissolved into patternless shrieking. The individual hominids, even the leader, blasted away like shot from a cylinder bore.

The sabertooth was only a leap from its victim, the dun mother. Nothing the troop could have done at that point would have made the least difference.

Nilson's Mauser was fitted with an electronic-bead sight, awesomely fast for a shooter trained in its use. The rifle was up and on and as suddenly wrestled away as Linda Weil lunged at it. "No!" the paleontologist shouted, "No! *Don't—*"

The dun hominid knew she had been chosen. She plucked off the infant which clung to her with all the strength of its tiny arms. The nearest member of the troop was the adolescent female, possibly an older daughter. To her, poised between love and terror ten feet away, the mother hurled her infant. Then, at the last possible moment, the mother cut against the grain of the charge with an agility that could scarcely have been bettered.

It was not enough. The macheirodont twisted. It was unable to flesh its teeth as it intended, but its splayed forepaws commanded a swath six feet broad. The right paw smacked the hominid in the middle of the chest. Four of the five claws hooked solidly and spun the light hominid into the path along which the killer's momentum carried it. The jaws crunched closed. One of the long canines stabbed through a shoulder blade to bulge the dimple at the base of the victim's throat.

The surviving hominids had regrouped and were scampering away westward like wind-scud. Vickers retrieved his binoculars. The adolescent had already passed her burden onto an adult female without an infant of her own. The males were bringing up the rear of the troop, but the looks they cast over their shoulders as they retreated were more anxious than threatening. The leader still carried the block of quartz he had found near the hyenas. All the rest had dropped their weapons in the panic. The leader continued to call out, his voice a harsh lash driving the troop. Behind them, the sabertooth had begun to feast noisily.

"If you'd shot," Linda Weil was shouting, "it'd be the last time they'd let us get within a mile of them! They're *smart*, I tell you. Smart enough to connect a noise we make with things falling dead!"

The big Norwegian had wrenched away his rifle too late to shoot to any purpose. He stood with the Mauser waist high, half shielded by his body as if he expected the paleontologist to snatch at the weapon again. "It's all right for *you* to frighten them!" the guide shouted back. "When I want to save their lives, what then? You scream, you prevent me! Look at that—" he waved toward the blood-splashed grass beneath the acacias, the muzzle of his rifle quivering as he released the fore-end to gesture. "That could be the end of our race down there!"

After a quick glance at his companions, Vickers had resumed giving his attention to the scene focused in his glasses. Neither of the humans appeared to be immediately dangerous, and the big cat certainly was. It was ripping its prey apart by mouthfuls, pulling against stiff forelegs which pinned the small carcass to the ground. The hominid's bones affected the killer no more than a sardine's bones affect a hungry human. The cat was obviously aware of the humans watching it, but for the moment it had food and did not feel threatened.

"We aren't here to save animals," Weil said, pitching her voice normally in contrast to the shouts she had exchanged with Nilson a few moments before. "We're here to observe them. Those, ah, primates reacted to me as they would to another troop of primates—display, threats—warnings, that's all. They'll continue to let me come close enough to observe. But if you'd shot, from then on they'd have reacted to us the way they did to the macheirodont—and I damned well doubt any of us can stalk the way that cat did!"

Holgar Nilson's face was red beneath his hat brim. He turned and spat, knocking dust from the heads of brazen oat-grass. "Observe?" he said. "Meddle! You're going to meddle us all out of existence!"

"It's already been a pretty long day, as early as we started," Vickers suggested with what was for him unusual diplomacy. "I think we've seen about all we're going to see today . . . and if we're going to discuss it, I'd rather it was after a meal and coffee. A lot of coffee."

Vickers led his sullen companions back past the looted trapline. He was not sure whether either of the others noticed that three of the traps were still set, even though the tops of all of them had been unlatched. Since the bait was still there, it meant that the hominids had opened the traps purely for fun.

"All right," said Holgar Nilson, "I'll tell you just what's bothering me." The blond man's concern had not affected his appetite. He gestured with the remnants of his hipparion chop, an experiment which the others were willing to call a failure. "You play games with me with words, but these *are* men we've found. What I am saying is, what if these are the only ones? What if we do something that gets them all killed? Like we did this morning, drawing their attention to something that shouldn't be in this, in this time at all so that they don't see the tiger waiting to kill them!"

Weil raised her hands in frustration. "I couldn't guess within a million years what time we've been inserted into, Holgar," she said. "You know that. The chances of us being landed on exactly the right time and place to find the absolutely earliest individuals who could be called human—that's absurd! Now, I'm not saying the troop we've observed isn't typical of the earliest, well . . . men."

Vickers swallowed the bite of coarse, musky hipparion flesh he had been chewing for some time. "That's fine, what you say about likelihood," he said quietly. "But I suppose there had to be a first some time. It's an open secret, in the Project at least, that the reason some of the brass Topside is so excited about time intrusion is the chance that it *will* turn out to be possible to change the past."

"You're both still looking for the missing link!" the paleontologist said with more acid than she had intended to show. "There isn't any such thing, isn't, wasn't, whatever. There were at least three primate stocks we know about that could have and would have become homo sapiens in time. One of them did—and both the others, australopithecus and homo habilis so called, were thought to have been direct ancestors during your lifetime and mine. They could have been, they were that close; and if it weren't for competition from our own stock, one or the other of them would certainly have evolved into a higher hominid that you couldn't tell from your next-door neighbor."

The younger guide's face was still as a death mask. "That's all very well," he said, "but would they *be* my next-door neighbor? Would they *be* my wife, my children, will there be my farm in the Transvaal as I left it if we upset the, the past that all that grows from? This cosmic viewpoint is very scientific, no doubt, but *I* at least am human!"

Linda Weil swallowed with difficulty though her mouth held nothing but saliva. "I—" she said. Then, "Holgar, don't let's talk about this now. I can see you're upset and I, I'm upset also. This is . . . this is a very big opportunity for me. I shiver when I think how big an opportunity it is."

Nilson looked at her silently, then tossed the rib bone toward the coals. Ash spurted and the rib spun off into the grass beyond. "I'm going to shoot a hyena," the guide said, wiping grease from his hands on the grass. He gripped his Mauser and stood. They had been eating as they always did, beneath a nylon fly. Sunlight now bisected the tall man diagonally. "Or perhaps you want as many as possible carnivores left alive, now, to kill men?"

Weil's forehead scrunched up, but she would not call to the Norwegian as he walked away. Vickers said, "Look, Holgar, hang on a moment and I'll—"

Nilson's head spun around. "No thank you!" he said. "I will take no risks—we are both aware of how dangerous the land is now, are we not? But I will do this thing alone, thank you."

Vickers shrugged. Technically the younger man was his subordinate, but they were several million years from any further chain of command. Vickers' own bad experience the day before did not make Nilson's proposal unreasonable. Only the situation was unreasonable, and that wasn't something Vickers could help the Norwegian with. "All right," he said, "but call in every half hour on the radio."

The blond man nodded but did not turn around again as he stalked off.

Linda Weil cursed in a dull voice. She looked at the forkful of meat she was holding and put it down again. "Vickers," she said, then paused to clear her throat. "Ah, Henry, I'll need a specimen of these primates before we go back."

The guide met her eyes while continuing to chew. "Tell you the truth," he said, "I don't know that I'm ready to shoot anything quite that, ah, anthropoid, without a good reason. What do you need a specimen for?"

"Oh, of course killing one was out of the question," the paleontologist said. Vickers continued to look at her, blinking but not speaking. Touching her tongue to her lips, Weil went on, "The specimens would be for the same purpose as the others that we've gathered, dating . . . . We're probably dealing with an advanced ramapithecus. I think that's the safest assumption. But a careful examination of dentition and cranial capacity, plus the knee and pelvic joints in particular, could . . . well, it's—possible—that the primates we've observed could really belong in the genus homo after all. If we knew that, we'd know as much about when we are as those macheirodont specimens, for instance, can tell us. Among other things."

Vickers' face softened in a tired grin. "So in terms of the task I've been sent to aid you in," he said, "you're justified in ordering me to help gather primate specimens. You can burn me with the administration Topside if I start—having qualms the way Holgar seems to be."

The woman scowled and looked away. "I'm not threatening you," she said. "You're not the sort who needs to be threatened to get him to do his job —are you? I'm just pointing out that it *is* your job, that yes, I *am* the one who has final say over what specimens are to be collected. That's why they sent a paleontologist."

"All right," said Vickers, "but if you had a notion of retrieving that sabertooth's kill, you can forget it." He stood up and walked to the edge of the fly, where he could observe the tiny dots that were vultures a thousand feet above the plain.

"Umm?"

"Our friend treated it just like a cat with a field mouse," the guide explained. "Ate the whole head while I watched it. Its mate would likely have done the same thing with me—if it hadn't been for Holgar." He paused. "You might find the knee joints. I wouldn't count on anything much higher up."

"Oh," the paleontologist said, her careful eyes on the guide's back. "Well, to tell the truth, that wasn't really what I had in mind anyway." After a moment, Vickers turned around. Weil continued, "There's nothing we need to know that can't be learned as well or better from X-rays of a living specimen. Without hurting it a bit. All we have to do is carry one back Topside."

"Jesus," said the guide in disbelief. "Jesus Christ." He spread his hands, then closed them and looked away from the dark-haired woman. "Did it ever occur to you," he said, speaking toward the heat-shimmer above the fire, "that

Holgar could be right? That we mess up this, this *present*, and when we get back Topside there's nothing there?" He jerked his head back to look at Weil. "Or that what is there is as different from us as baboons are from chimps? Does that bother you?"

"It doesn't bother me," Linda Weil said calmly, "because it's absurd. I'm bothered by the realistic problems of completing my task. That's all."

Vickers smiled again. "That's really all?" he asked, letting his eyes brush Nilson's empty camp stool.

The woman blushed, a dark rush of blood to a face already as tan as Vickers'. "That's neither here nor there!" she said. "Now, how can we capture a specimen?"

"Oh, there's ways," the guide said. He put his hands in his hip pockets and turned away once more. For a moment he whistled snatches of "Blue Water Line" through his teeth. "Yeah, there's ways," he continued, "although it'll be a lot easier if we can get Holgar to cooperate."

"He'll cooperate," Linda Weil said grimly. "I'm going back with my specimen. His choice is whether it comes aboard in a cage or gets packed in sealant like the rest."

"I got two," Nilson said, thumbing toward the bloody tangle on the collapsible sled he was drawing. "A male and a female, I wanted. But when I dressed them out, both were pregnant, so I just left the other with the offal."

Vickers glanced at what was left of the hyena. For specimen purposes and the need to pack it in alone on the titanium sled, Nilson had used a heavy-bladed knife to strip the beast to head, spine, and limbs. The ribs, hide, and the whole abdominal cavity had been abandoned at the kill site as useless; and for that matter, this was about the first use Vickers had heard of for any part of a dead hyena. "Just about impossible to sex a hyena, even after you open them up," he agreed. "I know people to this day who'll swear they're hermaphroditic, that if you shut two males in a cage for a week, one'll change so they can screw." Vickers' eyes, but not the Norwegian's, flickered toward the intrusion vehicle where Linda Weil occupied herself with a microfiche catalog of the Pliocene specimens known Topside.

"Well," said Nilson. He dropped the tow line and walked toward the frame-supported drum which stored their water. It was pumped through plastic line from the stream a thousand feet east of them. The spigot could be adjusted to dribble sun-heated water in an adequate shower. The younger guide leaned his rifle against the trestle set there for the purpose, out of the splash but in easy reach if occasion demanded it. Vickers nodded in approval. The Mauser chambered powerful 9.3 by 64 mm cartridges. Needlessly big for hyena, perhaps . . . but both the hunters were of the school that used what worked for them; and if their tastes were radically different, then they were alike in their scorn for purists who could not hunt without a battery of a dozen guns.

"Ah, Holgar," the senior guide said, knowing that he had to be the one to broach the subject but increasingly uncomfortable with his role, "I think we have to talk about this hominid business."

"I don't want to talk about it," Nilson said, unzipping his filthy trousers and hanging them on the trestle.

"Well, I don't know that I do either," said Vickers, "but I guess that isn't an option." He picked up the sprayer he had filled when Nilson approached the camp. It was Vickers' task to seal the speciman since his partner had done the even messier job of dressing it out. More important, the work gave Vickers something to do with his hands. The stripped carcass was already black with flies, but the sealant would suffocate those it did not drive away. Vickers began to pump. Raising his voice to compensate for distance and the spatter of water, he continued, "While you were getting the hyena, we rigged a net trap down by our water supply. There's a grove of locust trees there, and when we knew what to look for we found plenty of sign that the, the hominids were gathering pods. Maybe the troop we saw, maybe another one. It's hard to guess what their ranges are."

"We ought to leave them strictly alone," the younger man said distinctly. "We ought to get out of here at once, go back on the intrusion vehicle before we do irreparable harm. If we haven't already done irreparable harm." He twisted off the spigot and stepped barefoot away from the muddy patch under the tank.

Vickers set down the sprayer but did not immediately turn the specimen over to cover the other side. "Yeah," he said. "Well. Look, Holgar, we're not going to hurt anything, we're going to capture one ape to study." The sandy-haired man did not at the moment mention Weil's intention of carrying the speciman back Topside. "You know goddam well yourself from baboons that we could take a lot more than that on a one-shot basis and you wouldn't be able to tell the difference in five years time."

Nilson was toweling himself off without speaking. Vickers noticed that Linda Weil, a hundred feet away, was no longer even pretending not to be watching the men from the platform. Sucking on his lips in frustration, Vickers went on, "I cut a section off the end of the drive net we used for small animals. We've got it sprung between a pair of trees; and it's command-released so there's no

chance of it being tripped by a pig or going off
when the, the hominid we want's in a position to
maybe get hurt. But that means that one of us has
to be watching it in the morning when the foragers
are out."

The younger guide left his bloody, sweat-stained
clothes hanging and padded back toward the tent
and his footlocker. "Holgar," Vickers said, trying
to control the tremor in his voice. His skin
prickled on the inside with the dry anger he had
not felt since his second wife left him. "I'm talking
to you. Don't walk away like that."

The Norwegian turned at the tent flap, rolled up
during the day. "You haven't said a thing that touch-
es me, you know," he said. "Not a damned thing."

"The *hell* it doesn't touch you!" the older man
shouted back. "Somebody's got to watch the trap,
and somebody's got to squire Linda around
tomorrow. She wants to poke through their old
camp and see if she can locate the new one . . . .
And that's her *business!* Now, you can do whichever you want, but if you think you're going to
pretend you're nowhere around—look, buddy, I
wouldn't have to be a lot madder than I am before
I'll put a soft-nose through the chest of one of the
goddamned animals and get a specimen that way.
We've got jobs to do, and sulking like a little kid
who didn't get the bike he wanted for Christmas
doesn't cut it!"

The bigger man slung his towel to the ground between them as if it were a gage of battle. "That slut
up there," he shouted, "she has everything to gain
from meddling, does she not? And you—I know
you, I've watched you—you have nothing to lose,
that's your trouble. But what about me and all the
people like me? When we get back Topside, will it
be all right for us if everything is the same—except
the people all have purple skins and tails?"

"Holgar, you've heard the options," Vickers said in a voice as hard as a gunlock.

"All right, I'll mind the trap!" Nilson stormed. "You didn't really think I'd go off with her, did you?" Still nude, the Norwegian snatched up his sleeping bag in one hand and his foot locker in the other, dragging them out of the tent. "And may God have mercy on your souls!"

"Yeah," said Vickers tiredly. "We all need a little mercy." He walked away from the half-prepared hyena, scanning the horizon. He wished he saw something there that he had an excuse to kill.

"Will the macheirodus still be at the camp site?" Linda Weil whispered in the near darkness.

"Possibly," Vickers said, more concerned with his footing than he was with the question. Early morning had seemed a likely time to observe hominids revisiting their former camp, so the guide and paleontologist had set out as soon as there was enough light to shoot by. "Frankly, I'm a lot more worried that it may be somewhere between here and there."

"Oh," Weil said. Then, "Oh—*that's* what you meant when you said we couldn't leave before you could see to shoot."

The guide looked over his shoulder. "Good lord, yes," he said in amazement. "You didn't think I was planning to shoot one of *them*, did you?"

There was more sky-light now than there had been only minutes before. The paleontologist stepped around Vickers and a thorny shrub without pausing. "I don't interfere with the hunting decisions you and Holgar make, you know," she said. "The animals I've worked with all my life are bones that can't hurt you unless you drop them on your foot. Or you let them lead you to an assumption that makes your colleagues say you're a fool—that can hurt too."

"I'd better lead," said Vickers after a glance behind that assured him that the sun was still below
the horizon.

There were several minutes marked by the whispering of grass against leather and the occasional
clack of stones slipping under a boot sole. At last
the guide said, "That hominid can't have gone
more than eighty pounds on the hoof, so to speak.
Dressed out, maybe half that . . . and that's counting a lot that that sabertooth eats and you and I
wouldn't. Now, I've seen lions gorge forty pounds in
a sitting, and they were a lot smaller than our
friend. Still, it was a good five days before a lion
that full even thinks of moving on . . . . All things
considered, and assuming that the sabertooth kept
eating the way it started yesterday while we
watched it, I'd expect to find the fellow snoozing
under the trees where it made the kill."

"Oh," said the paleontologist. "Ah, do you think
—I'd still rather call them primates—do you think
they'll come back even if the macheirodont is
gone?"

Vickers laughed. "And do I think there's life on
Saturn? Look, how would I know?" By using
common sense, the right half of his brain told him.
It was always easier to plead ignorance,
though . . . . "All right," the guide said slowly,
"there was nothing permanent about that camp.
The troop probably roams the area pretty widely.
And they dropped everything when they took off,
but everything wasn't—anything, really. We saw
some of them carrying rocks, but they were as like
as not to drop them. And the roots and such they'd
gathered, that wasn't anything they were storing,
just a day's supply and as easy to replace as re-
cover. So no, I don't think they'll come back."

Vickers missed Weil's muttered response, but it

might have been a curse. "You mean," she said more distinctly, "that the chances are we won't be able to get near the campsite because the cat's still there; and even if the cat's gone, there won't be any real chance of seeing living hominids there again."

"Well, don't worry about the sabertooth," Vickers said, smiling at the term 'hominid' which the other had let slip. "I—" his expression sobered. "Look," he went on, "I blew it bad the other day and let that cat almost get me. That doesn't mean I can't nail one if it's sleeping in a place you want to look over."

Weil nodded, though the guide in front of her could not see the gesture. "How is your chest?" she asked.

Vickers shrugged. "It hurts," he said. "That's good. It reminds me how stupid I can be."

They were in sight of their goal now, though the paleontologist did not yet recognize the clump of acacias from this angle. The anvil tops of the trees, forty feet in the air, were already a saturated green in the first light of the sun. Vickers touched Weil's shoulder and knelt down. The dark-haired woman crouched and studied the scene. At last she recognized the swell of the hill to the right from which they had watched the camp and the kill the day before. "All right," she whispered to the guide. "What do we do now?"

"We wait," said Vickers, uncapping his binoculars, "until I've got a clean shot at that sabertooth or I'm awfully damn sure it's nowhere around." With the lenses just above the thorny shrub between him and the acacias, Vickers studied the blurring gray-on-gray beneath the trees.

Vickers could feel movements all around them. A trio of squabbling finches fluttered into the bush inches away from his face, then scurried back again without having taken any obvious interest in the humans. The grass moved, sometimes in sympathy with a puff of wind, often without. The landscape was becoming perceptibly brighter, its colors returning as pastel hints of the richness they would have in an hour.

Over a ridge a half mile south of the humans ambled a family of sivatheres. As they walked, the beasts browsed high among the thorny acacias. The sivatheres were somewhat shorter than the largest of the true giraffes with which Vickers was familiar, but that difference was purely a matter of neck length. The sivatheres were higher at the shoulder and were greatly more massive in build than giraffes Topside. Males and females alike were crowned with a cluster of four skin-covered horns, blunt as chairlegs. "You know," whispered the guide as he stared at the graceful, fearless, creatures, "I ought to be able to get one of those for you if this doesn't pan out ...." The stocky man had done his share of trophy hunting in the past, and the old excitement was back in a rush as he watched the huge animals move.

"Quite unnecessary," retorted Linda Weil. "I've compared their ossicones to those of known species, and there's no correlation. These are a new species; and that's no help at all in the question of dating."

Vickers lowered his binoculars. He was conscious of the mechanism that had caused him to suggest the sivatheres as a target. Despite that embarrassment, however, he said, "But it's the pattern of the teeth, not the horns, that's really diagnostic, isn't it? What you mean is, you're more interested in the hominids than you are in doing your job." The woman looked away, then met his eyes silently. "Look," the guide continued, "I tore a strip off Holgar because he wasn't doing his job.

But if you're going to pull the same crap yourself in your own way—well, we may as well go back Topside right now."

The guide had not raised his voice, but the iron in it jolted the woman as effectively as a shout could have. She touched Vickers' wrist in a pleading, not a sexual, fashion. "Henry, this may not be exactly what they sent us here to find," she said, "but I'm certain in my own mind that even the people in the engineering section will be able to see how desperately important it is. A chance through time intrusion to actually *see* which theories of human nature are true, whether our ancestors were as violent as Chakma baboons or as friendly as Capuchin monkeys. This might be a chance to understand for the first time the roots of the political situation that makes the—men in Tel Aviv so anxious to refine time intrusion into a, well, a weapon."

Vickers shook his head. He felt more frustration than disagreement, however. "The men and women in Tel Aviv," he corrected. "Well, understanding the roots of their problem is fine, but I suspect that they'd trade it for a way to get a nuke into Berlin around '32." He sighed. "But this isn't getting our job done, is it?" Vickers turned his binoculars onto the acacia grove again.

For a moment, Vickers was in doubt about the dark shape at the base of one of the trees. It could have been a root gnarling blackly about a boulder bared by ages of wind and rain. Then the shape rolled over and there could be no doubt at all that the sabertooth had slept where it killed. Vickers let the binoculars hang gently on their strap and lifted his Garand.

Weil's breath sucked in. It was that, rather than her fingers clamping on his biceps, that caused Vickers to slack the finger pressure that would an

instant later have sent a 150-grain bullet cracking
down range. The guide's seated body held the rigid
angle of which the rifle was a part, but his eyes
slanted left to where the woman was pointing. "I'll
be damned," Vickers mouthed. He lowered the
butt of his weapon.

The sabertooth lay 200 yards in front of them, a
clout shot at a stationary target. But a hominid
was quartering toward the acacias from the left,
already as close to the trees as he was to the
watching humans. The hominid was sauntering
with neither haste nor concern, a procedure which
seemed both insane and wildly improbable for any
creature his size when alone in this habitat.
Vickers had the glasses up again. From the hominid's build, from the way his arms hung as he
walked . . . from the whorled grain of his fur that
counterfeited two shades in a pelt of uniform gray
. . . the guide was sure that this hominid was the
one that had made the unsuccessful snatch at the
carcass in the midst of the hyenas. That hominid
had been present when the sabertooth struck—
and therefore he could not conceivably be walking
toward those murderous jaws in perfect non-
chalance.

Weil's camera was whirring. Vickers suspected
that she would learn more through her binoculars
than through the view finder, but there are people
to whom no event is real unless it is frozen. No
doubt many of them worked with bones. The
hominid was only fifty yards from the sprawling
cat. He stopped, scratched his armpit, and began
calling out in a sharp voice. He was facing the end-
most tree in the grove as if someone were hiding in
its branches. Nothing larger than a squirrel could
have been concealed among the thorns and sparse
foliage.

 ⁻ The sabertooth's wakefulness was indicated not

by its movements but by the sudden cessation of all the tiny changes of position a sleeping animal makes. The great head froze; the eyes were apparently closed but might have been watching the hominid through slitted lids. The cat could not have been truly hungry after the meal of the previous day, but neither had the dun female provided so much meat that another kill was inconceivable. The cat grew as still and tense as the mainspring of a cocked revolver.

Vickers made a decision. He started to raise the rifle again. Linda Weil shook her head violently. "No!" she whispered. "It—it's their world. But if none of the other primates are in sight, ah, afterward, kill the macheirodont before it has time to damage the specimen."

The guide turned his head back toward the grove with a set expression. He held the Garand an inch short of firing position despite his anger. But they were just animals . . . .

The cat charged.

Considered dispassionately, the initial leap was a thing of beauty. The torso which had seemed to be as solid as a boulder was suddenly a blur of fluid motion. Vickers could now understand how he had been so thoroughly surprised by this killer's mate; but the recollection chilled him anew.

The hominid himself was not in the least surprised. That was evident from the way he sprinted away from the cat at almost the instant that the carnivore first moved. There was no way that the hominid could match the sabertooth's acceleration, however. When the forepaws touched the ground the first time they had covered half the distance separating killer from prey, and when the paws touched the second time—

It was as if the sabertooth had stepped into a

mine field, and the mines were alive. Vickers had counted six adult males in the hominid troop. The cat's leap after the first had carried it into the midst of the other five. Sparse as the grass and brush had seemed, it had served to cloak the ambush not only from the humans but also from the sabertooth. Murderously intent on its running prey, the cat's upper canines were bared and its claws were unsheathed to sweep its victim in. A pair of hominids leaped from either side like the jaws of a trap closing. If their own fangs were poor weapons in comparison to those of the 600-pound carnivore, then the blocks of stone they carried in their fists were impressive weapons by any standard. They smashed like sledge hammers, driven by the strength of the long arms.

Whatever might have come of the tumbling kaleidoscope, it should have involved the death of the hominid acting as bait. The cat's paws were spread, certain to catch and rend even if reflex did not also flesh the long fangs an instant later. The bait, the Judas goat, made one last jump that would not have carried him free had not the white-flashed leader risen behind the sabertooth and seized the cat's rigid tail.

The hominid's mass could no more have stopped the flying cat directly than it could have stopped a moving car; but 120 pounds applied to a steering wheel can assuredly affect a car's direction. The cat's hindquarters swung outward with the impact. Mindless as a servo-mechanism, the same instinct that would have spun the cat upright in a fall reacted to counter the torque. The claws twisted away from their target. The sabertooth landed on the ground harmlessly, and the thud of its weight was overlaid by the sharper sound of stones mauling its ribs and skull.

The cat had charged silently. Now it screeched

on a rising note and slashed to either side. Hominids sprang away. This was not the blind panic of the previous day. Rather, they were retracting themselves as a rifle's bolt retracts to chamber another round. The leader still gripped the base of the cat's tail, snarling with a fury the more chilling for the fact it was not mindless. When the sabertooth tried to flex double to reach its slender tormentor, the hominid that had acted as bait smashed a rock against the base of the cat's skull.

The sabertooth would have run then, but its left hip joint was only shards of bone. Escape was no longer an option. The cat tried to leap and failed in a flurry of limbs. Hominids piled onto the flailing body. One of the attackers was flung high in the air, slashes on its chest filling with blood even as the creature spun. That was probably the last conscious action the carnivore took. All that Vickers could see for the next several minutes was a montage of stone-tipped arms rising and falling with a mechanical certainty. They made a sound on impact like that of mattocks digging a grave in frozen soil.

"God," whispered the hunter.

Vickers had seen baboons kill a leopard, and he knew of well-enough attested instances of dholes, the red hunting dogs of India, killing tigers that had tried to drive them off their prey. The calculated precision of what he had just watched impressed Vickers in a way that the use of stones as weapons had not, however.

"Oh, I've died and gone to heaven," breathed the paleontologist. "This is incredible. It's just incredible."

Vickers shivered. He peered through his binoculars but kept a firm grip on the rifle with his right hand. He was checking, not wholly consciously, to make sure he could account for all six males of the troop. He had sometimes felt a similar discomfort in baboon country, though never so intense. "I don't think," he said carefully, "that we'd better track, ah, these further today. They're apt to act, ah, unpredictably. Used to be I thought if worst came to worst and they rushed us, one shot'd stop them. Right now, I don't know that would be a good idea."

Weil looked at the guide's thin profile, measuring his mind with her eyes. "All right," she said at last, "we'll go back for now instead of seeing where they—" she nodded—"head. We'll see what Holgar has found. But it all depends on Holgar."

"I hope to God you're right," muttered Vickers as he began the task of backing away without arousing the hominids' attention. They were hooting cheerfully around the macheirodus, surely dead by now. The furry arms still rose and fell.

The closest human-sized cover was 200 yards from the locust trees but that was close enough. Nilson had to admit that his senior had done a masterful job of arranging the trap. The section of netting lay flat. Each pair of corner ropes was slanted across the net to a bent branch on the other side. When the trigger peg was pulled out to release the branches, the net would be snatched upward and rolled shut simultaneously—while still under enough unreleased tension to prevent anything within from escaping unaided. The release line itself led to a patch of brush on a rocky outcrop. It would become unbearably hot by ten in the morning, but by then the hominids should have visited the grove if they were coming at all.

Nilson desperately hoped that the troop had completely evacuated the region in the aftermath of the sabertooth's attack.

The Norwegian morosely fingered the handle of

doweling around which Vickers had clamped the release line. Anyone else would have used nylon cord for the line; Vickers had disconnected the braided steel cable from the winch to use instead. The nylon could easily have taken the strain, but it would have stretched considerably over the distance when Nilson pulled on it. That could be enough warning to send the hominids scurrying away before the trap released. The steel would require only a single sharp jerk with enough muscle in it to overcome the line's dead weight.

Nilson studied the watercourse through his binoculars, for want of anything better to do at the moment. A half-squadron of hipparions dashed up to the bank, paused, and dashed away again without actually touching the water. The nervous horses were ignored by the score or so of antelopes already drinking. From their size and markings they appeared to be impalas; but if so, the species was different enough from those Topside for the females as well as the males to bear horns. There was no sign of hominids.

The younger guide had considered failing to spring the trap or deliberately botching the operation—perhaps managing to frighten them away permanently without capturing one. But even though this was Holgar Nilson's first expedition with Vickers as his partner, he knew already what result such sabotage would bring. If Vickers found the trap had been released at the wrong time, or that it had not been released when there was sign in the grove that hominids had been present . . . well, the senior guide was accurate out to 500 meters with his Garand. There was not the slightest chance that he would not shoot a hominid if he thought Nilson had tried to call his bluff.

The half-light had become true dawn. Even the gray of the bush pig's hide was a color rather than a shade. The sow watched as her piglets drank and stamped at the edge of the water, light glinting on the spikes of her tusks.

Something was moving in the grove.

Even before he shifted his glasses, Nilson knew that the hominids had arrived as he had feared they would. There were three of them, all females. Two were fully adult, each carrying a nursing infant. The third was shorter and slighter, the adolescent who had received the infant from the tiger's victim. Now she was holding a large leaf or a swatch of hide. Fascinated, Nilson forgot for a moment why he was stationed there, forgot also his fear and anger at the situation.

The adult hominids were gathering locust pods from the ground. When each had a handful, she dropped it onto the makeshift platter which the adolescent carried.

Nilson swore under his breath. An incipient basket was a more frightening concept to him than was an incipient axe. They were men, they were ancestors of him and of all the billions of other humans living Topside, who *had* been living Topside before the intrusion team started meddling . . . .

One of the adults moved off to the left, hunched over and momentarily hidden by bushes. The other adult chittered happily. Ignoring the thorns, she began to climb the trunk of one of the trees that armed the trap.

The trap. The adolescent was holding her bundle in one hand and with the other hand was plucking curiously at the nylon meshes on which she stood. Nilson touched the release handle. He did not pull it. Then he had a vision of the hominid as she would look through the sights of Henry Vickers' rifle, the front blade bisecting her chest and the whole head and torso framed by the ring of the rear aperture. Nilson jerked the line.

The whittled peg flipped from its socket and the two anchor lines slashed against the sky. Their twang and the victim's shriek of alarm were simultaneous as the net looped crosswise in the air. It hung between the branches, humming like a fly ambushed and held by a jumping spider.

The two adult hominids and their infant burdens disappeared screaming like children near a lightning strike. The Norwegian hunter could not be sure that the one who had been climbing had not been flung from her perch and killed when the trap sprung. There was no time to worry about that now. Snatching up his Mauser and the sled, Nilson began running through the grass toward the grove. Antelope exploded from the water. Hipparions joined the rout with less grace but a certain heavy-footed majesty.

Nilson pounded into the grove, panting as much from nerves as from the 200 yards he had run. The net was pulled tight enough to bulge the meshes around the captive, though not so tight that it choked off the hominid's helpless bleats. Locust pods spilled from a horsehide apron were scattered on the ground beneath the trap.

"Sweet Jesus," the guide muttered. "Oh, my children, my Mary."

Vickers had planned a safe method of completing the capture single-handedly as well. It proved as effective in practice as the trap itself had. The hominid hung six feet in the air, only eye height for the Norwegian. He flung a second square of netting over the taut roll. Then, through the edges hanging low enough to avoid the captive's teeth and claws, he wove a cord back and forth in a loose running seam. When Nilson had reached the hominid's feet, he pulled the cord and tightened the outer net over the inner one like cross-wrapped sheets. As soon as he tied off the lace, the guide had a bundle which the captive within could not escape even after the tension of the branches was released. Holding the head end of the bundle with his left hand, Nilson cut the anchor cords one at a time, dampening the backlash and ultimately supporting the hominid's weight with his own unaided strength. She mewed and twisted within the layers of net, baring her teeth but unable to sink them into the Norwegian's arm.

Nilson found it easier to think of the creature as a beast now than it had been when he watched her moving freely at a distance. She was small, and small without the softness of a human child of the same size. Her jaw was prominent, her forehead receding, and her nose little more than the bare nostrils of a chimpanzee. Most of all, the covering of coarse brown fur robbed the captive of her humanity.

And the fur was as specious an indicator as the rest of them, which the guide knew full well. The hominid had no more hair than Nilson did himself. Only the fact that the body hairs of later-evolved hominids were short and transparent by comparison to those of the captive permitted Nilson to pretend the captive was inhuman. That did not matter. The fact that Nilson *could* pretend to be dealing with a beast and not an ancestor was the only thing that allowed him to do what circumstances forced him to do.

The big man set his captive down gently. With practiced speed he extended the titanium frame of the sled and locked its members into place. He picked up the hominid again, lifting her off the ground one-handed instead of dragging her as a smaller and weaker man would have had to do. The sled had integral tie-downs with which he fastened his burden securely despite her squirming. It would be to no one's benefit for her to break halfway loose and injure herself. The best Nilson could hope for now was that Weil would examine the hominid briefly and release her. Unharmed, the creature could go on about whatever business she would have accomplished had the time intrusion not occurred.

The guide settled his slung rifle and began trudging toward camp at a pace that would not upset the sled on the irregular ground. As a matter of course, he glanced around frequently to be sure that he was not being stalked by a predator. He paid no particular attention to the brush surrounding the locust grove, however.

Nilson would have had to look very carefully indeed to see the glint of bright eyes hidden there. The eyes followed him and the captive hominid step by step toward his camp.

"I'll put a kettle of water on and do the dishes," Henry Vickers said. "No need for you two to worry about it."

The firelight brought out attractive bronze highlights in Linda Weil's dark hair. It softened the lines of her face as well. "Oh, I don't think that will be necessary," she said with a comfortable smile. "We can carry them Topside dirty and let somebody there worry about them."

Both men turned and stared silently at the beaming paleontologist. The hominid whimpered outside the circle of firelight. She was in a cage, the largest one available but still meant for considerably smaller specimens. Weil ignored the sound. She turned to Holgar Nilson who stared glumly at his hands. "Holgar," she said, "you did a great job today. I know how much you hated doing it, but you did it splendidly, professionally, anyway. Because of that, we're able to return Topside first thing tomorrow and not—not interfere with the creatures living here any further."

Nilson looked up slowly. His face was as doubtful as that of a political prisoner who has just been
informed that the revolution has made him president. "Do you mean," he asked carefully, "that
you're already done examining, ah, it?" A quirk of
his head indicated the cage at which Nilson had refused to look ever since he had transferred his
captive to it.

The paleontologist gave a brief head-shake, a
tightening around her eyes showing that she was
aware of what was about to happen. "No," she
said, "we'll carry the speciman back with us Topside. The sort of testing necessary will take years."

"No," said the Norwegian flatly. Then he cried,
"God in heaven, *no!* Are you mad? Henry—" turning to the senior guide who would not look at him,
stretching out both hands to Vickers as if he were
the last hope of a drowning man—"you cannot
permit her to do this, will you?"

"Look, one cull from a troop," muttered Vickers
to his hands. "Not even breeding age . . . ."

Nilson's eyes were red with rage and the firelight. "I—" he began, but the alarm pinged and cut
off even his fury.

Both men focused on the panel, their hands
snatching up their rifles. Linda Weil was trying to
place the source of the sound. The indicator for
Sensor Five, northeast of the camp, was pulsing.
From the dial, the intruder was of small to
medium size: an impala, say—or a hyena.

The guides exchanged glances. The Norwegian
shifted his rifle to a one-hand hold, its butt
socketed on his hip. He picked up the spotlight.
Vickers leveled the Garand, leaning into it with all
the slack in the trigger taken up. He nodded.
Nilson flicked on the light and slashed its narrow
beam across the arc the sensor reported. Nearby
bushes flashed white as the spot touched them;

further out, only shadows pivoted about the beam. According to the sensor, the intruder was still there, 150 meters out in the night. It did not raise its eyes to give a pair of red aiming points when the light touched them.

"Turn it out," Vickers whispered across the breech of his rifle.

After-effects of the fierce white beam shrank the firelit circle to a glow that scarcely cast the men's shadows toward the bush. The sensor needle quivered as the intruder moved. Vickers fired into the night.

The crack of the .30-'06 made Weil scream in surprise. The muzzle flash was a red ball, momentary but as intense as a bath in acid. Chips of jacket metal spun burning into the night like tiny signal rockets. The sensor jolted, then slipped back to rest position as the intruder bounded back into darkness.

"What was it?" Linda Weil demanded. Her palms were clamped to her ears as if to squeeze the ringing from the drums.

"I don't care so long as it's gone," Vickers said, slowly lowering the Garand. "I've seen a man after a hyena dragged him out of his tent by the face."

"The world might be better off if we *were* killed here," said Holgar Nilson bitterly.

Vickers looked at the younger man. He did not speak. Nilson spat on the fire. "I am very tired now," he said. "I will sleep." He nodded toward the intrusion vehicle, its supporting beams sunk to knee height in the ground. The metal glowed with a soft sheen of oil where rust had not already crept. "There. I wish you both comfort."

The blond man's footsteps could be heard on the steel even after his form had blurred into the night. "I shouldn't care, should I?" said the woman, speaking toward the fire but loudly enough for Vickers to hear her.

Vickers walked to the water tank and began filling the eight-liter cauldron. The stream rang from the galvanized metal until the water buffered itself. "I don't know," the guide said. "If somebody thinks he's accomplishing anything by sleeping on steel planking, I guess that's his business." He set the pot directly on the coals, twisting it a little to form a safe seat.

"After all, I was only recreation anyway, wasn't I?" the dark-haired woman resumed. "What was a twenty-seven year old man going to want with a woman five years older when he got back to a place with some choice? Even if he didn't already have a family!"

"Look, that's out of my field," said the guide. He had already switched magazines in the Garand. Now he checked his pockets to see if they held a loose round to replace the one he had just fired into the night.

"Well, he can *have* his damned security!" Weil said. "*I've* got success that he couldn't comprehend if he had to. Do you realize—" her index finger prodded the air toward Vickers—"just how big this is? By bringing back this specimen, I've just become the most important researcher into human prehistory in this century!"

The guide's expression did not change. Linda Weil pulled back with a slight start. "Well, we all have in a way," she amended in a more guarded voice. "I mean, I couldn't have done this here without you and, and Holgar, of course. But the ... well, it's my *field*, of course."

Vickers laid the Garand carefully across the stool on which he had been sitting. He tested the dishwater with the tip of a thumb. "You know," he said, "I've got some problems about carrying her—" he gestured toward the dull whimpering—

"back with us, too. Look, you've got your camera, and they aren't expecting us back Topside for three more days anyhow. Why don't we stay here, you do your tests and whatever, and then—" Vickers spread his hand with a flare toward the hills, completing the thought.

The look that flashed across the paleontologist's face was as wild as the laughter bubbling from the throat of a hyena. Weil had control of herself again as quickly. "Do you really want to keep her three days in a cage she can't stand up in, Henry?" the woman asked. "And you *know* that we couldn't accomplish anything here, even with a reasonable length of time—which that isn't. Quite aside from the fact that they'd all suspect I'd made the story up myself. A few photos for evidence!"

"Holgar and I are here as witnesses," Vickers said. He lifted the cauldron's wire handle with a stick.

"Marvelous! And where did you do *your* post-graduate work?" Weil snapped. She softened at once, continuing, "Henry, I know my colleagues. They'll doubt, and they *ought* to doubt. It's better than another Piltdown Man. Oh, there'll be another expedition, and it may possibly be as incredibly fortunate as we've been—but then it'll be their names on the finds, not mine. And it's not fair!"

Water sloshed as Vickers shifted the pot. A gush of steam and flying ashes licked his boots. "I don't think she's human," he said quietly, "but if she is, I don't think we've got any business holding her. Not here, not Topside. You know they'd never be able to find this, this slot in time close enough to put her back in it once she leaves."

"Henry, for God's sake," the dark-haired woman pleaded, "we're not talking about some kind of torture. Good grief, what do you think her life span's going to be if we leave her? Five years? Three? Before she winds up in a sabertooth's belly!"

Vickers gave the woman an odd look. "I think both the sabertooths in this range," he said, "have eaten their last hominid."

"All right, a hyena then!" the paleontologist said. "Or until she goes into anaphylactic shock from a bee sting. The point is not just that when we go Topside, everything here will be dead for five million years. The point is that the specimen will live a much longer life in comfort that she'll appreciate just as much as you do. And she'll advance our knowledge of ourselves and our beginnings more than Darwin did."

"Yeah," said the guide. He slid the trio of aluminum plates into the water. "I like modern comforts so much that I spend all the time I can in the bush." He stirred the dishes morosely with the tableware before he dropped that in as well. "Okay, I've been wrong before. God knows, I've generally been wrong."

Five distant hyenas broke out in giggling triumph. No doubt they had just killed, Vickers thought. He spat in the direction of the sounds.

Holgar Nilson swore in Norwegian. He had been doing a last-minute check of his ammunition as they all stood on the sun-struck platform of the intrusion vehicle. As rudimentary as their camp had been, it had taken four hours of solid work to strike it and restack the gear and specimens on the steel. "We can't go yet," Nilson said. "I can't find one of my cartridge cases—we can't leave it out there."

Vickers had already unlocked the vehicle's control panel. Now he took his hand from the big knife switch, but his voice was sour as he said, "Look, Holgar, have you forgotten to count the one up the spout?"

"No, no, it's not that," the big man insisted. "Of course I don't have a shell in the chamber for returning to Tel Aviv." Nilson held a twenty-round ammunition box in his left hand. Twelve spaces were filled with empty brass; four still held live rounds, their cases bright where they showed above the styrofoam liner. Only three of the remaining four spaces could be accounted for by the rounds in the Mauser's magazine. "Leaving the brass here—what will it do to the future?"

"Oh, for Chrissake," Vickers said. "Look, we're leaving the lead of every shot we've fired here, aren't we? And this isn't the first team that's been sent back, either."

Linda Weil stood beside the wire-mesh cage. The hominid hunched within, scratching at the dusty floor, did not look up. She had not eaten anything since her capture, despite offers of locust pods and what must have been to her an incredible quantity of antelope haunch. The paleontologist looked up from her speciman and said, "Yes, and after all, we've been evacuating wastes, breathing, sweating ourselves. I think it's wise at this point to clean up as much as we can, but I don't think we need be concerned over details."

"When I want your opinion, slut, I'll ask for it!" Nilson shouted.

Earlier that morning the younger guide had ignored Weil's occasional, always conciliatory, comments. Now his face was red and the tendons stood out in his neck. The woman's face distorted as if she had been struck.

"Damn it all anyway," said Vickers. "We're about five minutes away from never having to see each other again if we don't want to. Let's drop it, shall we?"

The other guide took a deep breath and nodded.

Vickers reached for the control switch again. Actually, he wouldn't have minded going on further intrusions with Nilson if the big man could get over his fear of possible future consequences. Nilson was hard-working, a crack shot ... and besides, he had already saved Vickers' life once.

"Oh, hell," Vickers said. He dropped his hand from the switch. "We forgot to pick up those goddam rock samples in the confusion. Hell. I'll get them."

Nilson held out a hand to stop the senior guide. "No, let me," he said. Giving Vickers a sardonic smile, he inserted another fat cartridge into the chamber of his rifle. He had to hold down the top round in the magazine so that the bolt would not pick it up and try to ram it into the already-loaded chamber. "After all," he continued as the action snicked closed, "it was I who forgot them. And besides, I don't care to stay with the—remaining personnel."

"Do you think I care?" Linda Weil shrieked. The blond man ignored her, his boots clanking down the two steps to the gritty soil. Far to the west a storm was flashing over a rocky table, but here around the intrusion vehicle not a breath stirred. The grass was scarred by signs of human use: the blackened fire-pit and the circle cleared around it; the trampled mud, now cracking, beneath the shower frame; the notches in the ground left by the sled's sharp runners. A hundred yards away was the outcrop shattered by Nilson's dynamite a moment before his shot saved Vickers' life. Like the other damage they had done to the land, this too was transitory. It only speeded up the process that frost and rain would have accomplished anyway over the next five million years.

Nothing in the landscape moved except Holgar

Nilson, striding purposefully toward the broken rock.

"Something isn't right," Vickers muttered. His eyes narrowed but they saw nothing to justify what he felt. Reflexively, he charged his Garand. The bolt rang like an alarm as it stripped a round into the chamber.

"What's the matter?" Linda Weil demanded.

"Stay here," Vickers said. *"Holgar!"*

The Norwegian turned and waved. He had almost reached the outcrop. He continued walking.

Vickers swung over the stairs, his left hand locking to the rail while his right controlled the weapon. "Holgar!" he shouted again. "Stop! There's something—"

When the younger guide paused a second time, the hominids sprang from ambush.

Vickers set his feet and dropped the fore-end of the Garand into his waiting left palm. Nilson's eyes widened, but the leveled rifle was a warning more certain than a shout. He was already swinging the Mauser to his shoulder as he spun to face his attackers. The six male hominids were strung in a line abreast, ready to cut him off whichever way he dodged. Their hands held stones. In the center of the rushing line, the blond-flashed leader was only twenty feet from Holgar.

The big Norwegian dropped his rifle and turned. "Don't shoot them!" he screamed to Vickers. "You'll wipe—"

Nilson crumpled, limp all over. The hominid standing over him raised his stone for another blow, white fur and white quartz and bright blood spattering both. Vickers fired three times, so swiftly that the last shot was still echoing before the brass of the first had spun into the bronze-red grass. He aimed for their heads because there was

no time for anything but certainty and nothing but
a head shot is instantly certain. Fresh brains are
not gray but pinkish-white, and the air was pink as
the three nearest hominids collapsed over the
body of Holgar Nilson.

The survivors were dashing away with the
gracefulness of deer, their torsos hunched slightly
forward. Vickers pounded like a fencepost running. He carried the Garand across his chest with
its safety still off. After a long moment watching,
Linda Weil picked up the medical kit and
clambered down the steps to follow the men.

At the tangle of bodies, Vickers slung aside one
hominid still arching reflexively in death. Beneath
him the leader was as rigid as the block of quartz
still locked in his right hand. Neither the entrance
nor the exit wound of the bullet had damaged the
white fur. Vickers rolled that carcass away as well.

Holgar Nilson was still breathing.

The crown and brim of Nilson's hat had been cut
by the force of the blow, and the back of the Norwegian's head was a sticky mass of blood and
short blond hair. But the skull beneath seemed
whole when Vickers probed it, and the injured
man's breathing was strong if irregular.

"Why did you kill them if you cared so much?"
Linda Weil demanded as she knelt panting in the
bloody grass. "He told you not to shoot, didn't he?
He didn't want it."

The guide shifted to give Weil more room. He
did not speak as she soaked a compress from her
canteen and held it to the gash. His index finger
crooked up to put his rifle on safe, but his eyes had
resumed their search of nearby cover.

The dark-haired woman stripped a length of
tape from the dispenser and laid it across both
scalp and compress. "Do you want to know why?"
she said. "You killed them because you hoped he

was right. You hoped that you wouldn't be a failure when we got back to the future because there wouldn't *be* a human future any more. With all your talk, you still tried to wipe man off the planet when you got an excuse." Her fingers expertly crossed the initial length of tape with two more.

"Take his feet," Vickers said. "The quicker we get him Topside, the quicker he gets to a hospital."

"I'm sure he wouldn't want to be touched any more," said the paleontologist as she stood. "Not by a slut like me." She closed the medical kit. "Besides," she added, professionally rotating the head of the hominid leader to look at it, "I have my own duties. I'm going to carry this one back."

Vickers looked at the woman without anger, without apparent emotion of any sort. Holgar Nilson outweighed him by fifty pounds; but when Vickers straightened with his partner locked in a packstrap carry, the motion was smooth and perfectly controlled. The stocky man reached down with his free hand and gripped the sling of Nilson's Mauser. He began walking the hundred yards back to the intrusion vehicle. His steps were short but regular, and his eyes kept searching the bush for danger.

There was no couch but the steel floor of the intrusion vehicle on which Nilson had slept the past two nights. Vickers laid his partner down as gently as he could, using a sleeping bag as a pillow beneath the side-turned head. Only then did the guide let himself relax, dragging great shuddering gasps of air into his lungs. His Garand leaned against him, held by the upper sling swivel. He wondered whether his arms were strong enough even to level the weapon if danger should threaten.

Linda Weil had given up her attempt to carry

the dead specimen. She was now dragging it by the arms, her back to the intrusion vehicle. Vickers started to go back to help her; then he looked down at Nilson. He eased back on his heels.

The hominid had begun sobbing.

Enough of the fatigue poisons had cleared from Vickers' muscles that he was willing to move again. He knelt beside the specimen. Her long, furry hands covered her eyes and muzzle. A tear dripped through the interstices between her fingers and splashed on the floor. Vickers' eyes followed the drop to the starburst it made in the dust. He was still heavy with fatigue. The tear had fallen beside one of the patterns the hominid had scratched in the dust with her fingertip. The guide stared dully at the marks. The abstract design suddenly shifted into a pair of stick figures. Once his mind had assimilated the pattern as a mother and child, Vickers could not believe that he had not seen it before.

"Jesus," the guide prayed.

Long fingers could reach the latch of the cage through the mesh, so Nilson had wired it shut in lieu of a padlock. Vickers leaned his rifle against a stack of labeled cartons and began to untwist the wire with both hands.

"Vickers!" cried the paleontologist. "What are you doing?"

The latch clicked open. Vickers dropped the door of the cage.

"Omigod!" the paleontologist shrieked, letting her burden fall so that she could run the last twenty yards to the vehicle.

The hominid looked from the opening to Vickers through the mesh. Her eyes were brown and shining with more than tears. She leaped instead of crawling through the opening and hit the platform running. She broke stride when she straightened

—the cage had been only a meter high—but her leap from the intrusion vehicle landed her ten feet out in the grass. Linda Weil made a despairing clutch at the little creature, but the hominid was yards away before the paleontologist's arms closed. The adolescent ran in the direction the adults had taken after the ambush, and she ran with the same loping grace.

Linda Weil stumbled forward until she caught herself on the edge of the intrusion vehicle. The sounds she was making were not words, nor were they obviously human. Vickers stepped down and touched her shoulder. "You've still got your specimens," he said quietly. "I'll help you load them."

The woman raised her head, dripping tears and mucus and despair. "You did that because you hate me, didn't you?" she asked in a choking voice.

Vickers' face was very still. "No," he said, "I did it because I don't hate anybody. Anybody human."

From the bush came the sound of joyful voices. The words themselves were not intelligible to human born five million years in the future.

Part II

TIME SAFARI

The tyrannosaur's bellow made everyone jump except Vickers, the guide. The beast's nostrils flared, sucking in the odor of the light helicopter and the humans aboard it. It stalked forward.

"The largest land predator that ever lived," whispered one of the clients.

"A lot of people think that," said Vickers in what most of the rest thought was agreement.

There was nothing in the graceful advance of the tyrannosaur to suggest its ten ton mass, until its tail side-swiped a flower-trunked cycad. The tree was six inches thick at the point of impact, and it sheared at that point without time to bend.

"Oh dear," the female photographer said. Her brother's grip on the chair arms was giving him leverage to push its cushion against the steel back-plate.

The tyrannosaur's strides shifted the weight of its deep torso, counterbalanced by the swinging of its neck and tail. At each end of the head's arcs, the

71

beast's eyes glared alternately at its prey. Except
for the size, the watchers could have been observ-
ing a grackle on the lawn; but it was a grackle seen
from a june-bug's perspective.

"Goddam, he won't hold still!" snarled Salmes,
the old-money client, the know-it-all. Vickers
smiled. The tyrannosaur chose that movement to
pause and bellow again. It was now a dozen feet
from the helicopter, a single claw-tipped stride. If
the blasting sound left one able, it was an ideal
time to admire the beauty of the beast's four-foot
head. Its teeth were irregular in length and placement, providing in sum a pair of yellowish, four-
inch deep, saws. They fit together too loosely to
shear; but with the power of the tyrannosaur's
jaw muscles driving them, they could tear the
flesh from any creature on Earth—in any age.

The beast's tongue was like a crocodile's, attached for its full length to the floor of its mouth.
Deep blue with purple veins, it had a floral appearance. The tongue was without sensory purpose
and existed only to help by rhythmic flexions to
ram chunks of meat down the predator's throat.
The beast's head scales were the size of little
fingernails, somewhat finer than those of the
torso. Their coloration was consistent—a base of
green nearing black, blurred by rosettes of a much
lighter, yellowish, hue. Against that background,
the tyrannosaur's eyes stood out like needlepoints
dripping blood.

"They don't always give you that pause,"
Vickers said aloud. "Sometimes they come—"

The tyrannosaur lunged forward. Its lower jaw,
half-opened during its bugling challenge, dropped
to full gape. Someone shouted. The action blurred
as the hologram dissolved a foot or two from the
arc of clients.

Vickers thumbed up the molding lights. He

walked to the front of the conference room, holding the remote control with which the hotel had provided him. The six clients viewed him with varied expressions. The brother and sister photographers, dentists named McPherson, whispered in obvious delight. They were best able to appreciate the quality of the hologram and to judge their own ability to duplicate it. Any fear they had felt during the presentation was buried in their technical enthusiasm afterward.

The two individual gunners were a general contractor named Mears and Brewer, a meat-packing magnate. Brewer was a short man whose full moustache and balding head made him a caricature of a Victorian industrialist. He loosened his collar and massaged his flushed throat with his thumb and index finger. Mears, built like an All-Pro linebacker after twenty years of retirement, was frowning. He still gripped the chair arms in a way that threatened the plastic. Those were normal reactions to one of Vickers' pre-hunt presentations. It meant the clients had learned the necessity of care in a way no words or still photos could have taught them. Conversely, that familiarity made them less likely to freeze when they faced the real thing.

The presentations unfortunately did not have any useful effect on people like the Salmes. Or at least on Jonathan Salmes, blond and big but with the look of a movie star, not a football player. Money and leisure could not make Salmes younger, but they made him look considerably less than his real age of forty years. His face was now set in its habitual pattern of affected boredom. As not infrequently happens, the affectation created its own reality and robbed Salmes of whatever pleasure three generations of oil money might otherwise have brought him.

Adrienne Salmes was as blond and as perfectly preserved as her husband, but she had absorbed the presentation with obvious interest. Time safaris were the property of wealth alone, and she had all the trapping of that wealth. Re-emitted light made her dress—and its wearer—the magnet of all eyes in a dim room, and her silver lame wristlet responded to voice commands with a digital display. That sort of money could buy beauty like Adrienne Salmes'; but it could not buy the inbred assurance with which she wore that beauty. She forestalled any tendency the guide might have had to think that her personality stopped with the skin by asking, "Mr. Vickers, would you have waited to see if the tyrannosaurus would stop, or would you have shot while it was still at some distance from the helicopter?"

"Umm?" said Vickers in surprise. "Oh, wait, I suppose. If he doesn't stop, there's still time for a shot; and your guide, whether that's me or Dieter, will be backing you. That's a good question." He cleared his throat. "And that brings up an important point," he went on. "We don't shoot large carnivores on foot. Mostly, the shooting platform —the helicopter—won't be dropping as low as it was for the pictures, either. For these holos I was sitting beside the photographer, sweating blood the whole time that nothing would go wrong. If the bird had stuttered or the pilot hadn't timed it just right, I'd have had just about enough time to try for a brain shot. Anywhere else and we'd have been in that fellow's gut faster'n you could swallow a sardine." He smiled. It made him look less like a bank clerk, more like a bank robber. "Three sardines," he corrected himself.

"If you used a man-sized rifle, you'd have been a damned sight better off," offered Jonathan Salmes. He had one ankle crossed on the other knee, and his chair reclined at a 45° angle.

Vickers looked at the client. They were about of an age, though the guide was several inches shorter and not as heavily built. "Yes, well," he said. "That's a thing I need to talk about. Rifles." He ran a hand through his light brown hair.

"Yeah, I couldn't figure that either," said Mears. "I mean, I read the stuff you sent, about big-bores not being important." The contractor frowned. "I don't figure that. I mean, God almighty, as big as one of those mothers is, I wouldn't feel over-gunned with a one-oh-five howitzer . . . and I sure don't think my .458 Magnum's any too big."

"Right, right," Vickers said, nodding his head. His discomfort at facing a group of humans was obvious. "A .458's fine if you can handle it—and I'm sure you can. I'm sure any of you can," he added, raising his eyes and sweeping the group again. "What I said, what I meant, was that size isn't important, penetration and bullet placement are what's important. The .458 penetrates fine—with solids—I hope to God all of you know to bring solids, not soft-nosed bullets. If you're not comfortable with that much recoil, though, you're liable to flinch. And that means you'll miss, even at the ranges we shoot dinos at. A wounded dino running around, anywhere up to a hundred tons of him, and that's when things get messy. You and everybody around is better off with you holding a gun that doesn't make you flinch."

"That's all balls, you know," Salmes remarked conversationally. He glanced around at the other clients. "If you're man enough, I'll tell you what to carry." He looked at Vickers, apparently expecting an attempt to silence him. The guide eyed him with a somewhat bemused expression. "A .500 Salmes, that's what," the big client asserted loudly. "It was designed for me specially by

Marquart and Wells, gun and bullets both. It uses shortened fifty-caliber machinegun cases, loaded to give twelve thousand foot-pounds of energy. That's enough to knock a tyrannosaurus right flat on his ass. It's the only gun that you'll be safe with on a hunt like this." He nodded toward Vickers to put a period to his statement.

"Yes, well," Vickers repeated. His expression shifted, hardening. He suddenly wore the visage that an animal might have glimpsed over the sights of his rifle. "Does anybody else feel that they need a—a *gun* like that to bring down anything they'll see on this safari?"

No one nodded to the question when it was put that way. Adrienne Salmes smiled. She was a tall woman, as tall as Vickers himself was.

"Okay, then," the guide said. "I guess I can skip the lesson to basic physics. Mr. Salmes, if you can handle your rifle, that's all that matters to me. If you can't handle it, you've still got time to get something useful instead. Now—"

"Now wait a goddamned minute!" Salmes said, his foot thumping to the floor. His face had flushed under its even tan. "Just what do you mean by that crack? You're going to teach *me* physics?"

"I don't think Mr. Vickers—" began Miss McPherson.

"I want an explanation!" Salmes demanded.

"All right, no problem," said Vickers. He rubbed his forehead and winced in concentration. "What you're talking about," he said to the floor, "is kinetic energy. That's a function of the square of the velocity. Well and good, but it won't knock anything down. What knocks things down is momentum, that's weight times velocity, not velocity squared. Anything that the bullet knocks down, the butt of the rifle would knock down by recoiling—which is why I encourage clients to carry something they can handle." He raised his eyes and pinned Salmes with them. "I've never yet had a client who weighted twelve thousand pounds, Mr. Salmes. And so I'm always tempted to tell people who talk about 'knock-down power' that they're full to the eyes."

Mrs. Salmes giggled. The other clients did not, but all the faces save Salmes' own bore more-than-hinted smiles. Vickers suspected that the handsome blond man had gotten on everyone else's nerves in the bar before the guide had opened the conference suite.

Salmes purpled to the point of an explosion. The guide glanced down again and raised his hand before saying, "Look, all other things being equal, I'd sooner hit a dino—or a man—with a big bullet than a little one. But if you put the bullet in the brain or the heart, it really doesn't matter much how big it is. And especially with a dino, if you put the bullet anywhere else, it's not going to do much good at all."

"Look," said Brewer, hunching forward and spreading his hands palms down, "I don't flinch, and I got a .378 Weatherby that's got penetration up the ass. But—" he turned his hands over and over again as he looked at them—"I'm not Annie Oakley, you know. If I have to hit a brain the size of a walnut with a four-foot skull around it— well, I may as well take a camera myself instead of the gun. I'll have *something* to show people that way."

Salmes snorted—which could have gotten him one of Brewer's big, capable fists in the face, Vickers thought. "That's another good question," the guide said. "Very good. Well. Brain shots are great if you know where to put them. I attached charts of a lot of the common dinos with the material I sent out, look them over and decide if you want to try.

"Thing is," he continued, "taking the top off a dino's heart'll drop it in a couple hundred yards. They don't charge when they're heart-shot, they just run till they fall. And we shoot from up close, as close as ten yards. They don't take any notice of you, the big ones, you could touch them if you wanted. You just need enough distance to be able to pick your shot. You see—" he gestured toward Brewer with both index fingers—"you won't have any problem hitting a heart the size of a bushel basket from thirty feet away. Brains—well, skin hunters have been killing crocs with brain shots for a century. Crocodile brains are just as small as a tyrannosaur's, and the skulls are just as big. Back where we're going, there were some that were a damn sight bigger than tyrannosaurs. But don't feel you have to. And anyway, it'd spoil your trophy if you brain-shot some of the small-headed kind."

Brewer cleared his throat. "Hey," he said, "I'd like to go back to something you said before. About using the helicopter."

"Right, the shooting platform," Vickers agreed.

"Look," said the meat-packer, "I mean . . . well, that's sort of like shooting wolves from a plane, isn't it? I mean, not, well, Christ . . . not sporting, is it?"

Vickers shrugged. "I won't argue with you," he said, "and you don't have to use the platform if you don't want to. But it's the only way you can be allowed to shoot the big carnosaurs. I'm sorry, that's just how it is." He leaned forward and spoke more intensely, popping the fingers of his left hand against his right palm. "It's as sporting as shooting tigers from elephant-back, I guess, or shooting lions over a butchered cow. The head looks just as big over your mantle. And there's no sport at all for me to tell my bosses how one of my clients was eaten. They aren't bad, the big dinos, people aren't in their scale so they'll pretty much ignore you. Wound one and it's kitty bar the door. These aren't plant eaters, primed to run if there's trouble. These are carnivores we're talking about, animals that spend most of their waking lives killing or looking for something to kill. They *will* connect the noise of a shot with the pain, and they *will* go after whoever made the noise."

The guide paused and drew back. More calmly he concluded, "So carnosaurs you'll hunt from the platform. Or not at all."

"Well, what happens if they come to us?" Salmes demanded with recovered belligerence. "Right up to the camp, say? You can't keep us from shooting then."

"I guess this is a good time to discuss arrangements for the camp," Vickers said, approaching the question indirectly. "There's four of us staff with the safari, two guides—that's me and Dieter Jost—and two pilots. One pilot, one guide, and one client—one of you—go up in the platform every day. You'll each have two chances to bag a big carnosaur. They're territorial and not too thick on the ground, but there's almost certain to be at least one tyrannosaur and a pack of gorgosaurs in practical range. The other guide takes out the rest of the clients on foot, well, on motorized wagons you could say, ponies we call them. And the pilot who isn't flying the platform doubles as camp guard. He's got a heavy machinegun—" the guide smiled—"a Russian .51 cal. Courtesy of your hosts for the tour, the Israeli government. It'll stop dinos and light tanks without a bit of bother."

Vickers' face lost its crinkling of humor. "If there's any shooting to be done from the camp,"

he continued, "that's what does it. Unless Dieter
or me specifically tell you otherwise. We're not
going to have the intrusion vehicle trampled by a
herd of dinos that somebody spooked right into it.
If something happens to the intrusion vehicle, we
don't go home." Vickers smiled again. "That might
be okay with me, but I don't think any of the rest
of you want to have to explain to the others how
you stuck them in the Cretaceous."

"That would be a paradox, wouldn't it, Mr.
Vickers?" Miss McPherson said. "That is, uh,
human beings living in the Cretaceous? So it
couldn't happen. Not that I'd want any chances
taken with the vehicle, of course."

Vickers shrugged with genuine disinterest.
"Ma'am, if you want to talk about paradox, you
need Dr. Galil and his team. So far as I understand
it, though, if there's not a change in the future,
then there's no paradox; and if there is a change,
then there's no paradox either because the change
—well, the change is reality then."

Mr. McPherson leaned forward with a frown.
"Well, surely two bodies—the same body—can't
exist simultaneously," he insisted. If he and his
sister had been bored with the discussion of fire-
arms, then they had recovered their interest with
mention of the mechanics of time transport.

"Sure they can," the guide said with the asperity
of someone who had been asked the same question
too often. He waved his hand back and forth as if
erasing the thought from a chalk board. "They do.
Every person, every gun or can of food, contains at
least some atoms that were around in the Cretaceous—or the Pre-Cambrian, for that matter. It
doesn't matter to the atoms whether they call
themselves Henry Vickers or the third redwood
from the big rock . . . ." He paused. "There's just
one rule that I've heard for true from people who

know," he continued at last. "If you travel into the future, you travel as energy. And you don't come back at all."

Mears paled and looked at the ceiling. People got squeamish about the damnedest things, thought Vickers. Being converted into energy . . . or being eaten . . . or being drowned in dark water lighted only by the dying radiance of your mind—but he broke away from that thought, a little sweat on his forehead with the strain of it. He continued aloud, "There's no danger for us, heading back into the far past. But the intrusion vehicle can't be calibrated closer than 5,000 years plus or minus so far. The, the research side—" he had almost said 'the military side,' knowing the two were synonymous; knowing also that the Israeli government disapproved intensely of statements to that effect—"was trying for the recent past—" 1948, but that was another thing you didn't admit you knew—"and they put a man into the future instead. After Dr. Galil had worked out the math, they moved the lab and cleared a quarter-mile section of Tel Aviv around the old site. They figure the poor bastard will show up sometime in the next few thousand years . . . and nobody better be sharing the area when he does."

Vickers frowned at himself. "Well, that's probably more than the, the government wants me to say about the technical side," he said. "And anyway, I'm not the one to ask. Let's get back to the business itself—which I do know something about."

"You've said that this presentation and the written material are all yours," Adrienne Salmes said with a wave of her hand. "I'd like to know why."

Vickers blinked at the unexpected question. He looked from Mrs. Salmes to the other clients, all of them but her husband staring back at him with interest. The guide laughed. "I like my job," he said. "A century ago, I'd have been hiking through Africa with a Mauser, selling ivory every year or so when I came in from the bush." He rubbed his left cheekbone where a disk of shiny skin remained from a boil of twenty years before. "That sort of life was gone before I was born," he went on. "What I have is the closest thing there is to it now."

Adrienne Salmes was nodding. Mr. McPherson put his own puzzled frown into words and said, "I don't see what that has to do with, well, you holding these sessions, though."

"It's like this," Vickers said, watching his fingers tent and flatten against each other. "They pay me, the government does, a very good salary that I personally don't have much use for." Jonathan Salmes snorted, but the guide ignored him. "I use it to make my job easier," he went on, "by sending the clients all the data *I've* found useful in the five years I've been travelling back to the Cretaceous . . . and elsewhere, but mostly the Cretaceous. Because if people go back with only what they hear in the advertising or from folks who need to make a buck or a name with their stories, they'll have problems when they see the real thing. Which means problems for me. So a month before each safari, I rent a suite in New York or Frankfurt or wherever the hell seems reasonable, and I offer to give a presentation to the clients. Nobody has to come, but most people do." He scanned the group. "All of you did, for instance. It makes life easier for me."

He cleared his throat. "Well, in another way, we're here to make life easier for you," he went on. "I've brought along holos of the standard game animals you'll be seeing." He dimmed the lights and stepped toward the back of the room. "First the sauropods, the big long-necks. The most impressive things you'll see in the Cretaceous, but a disappointing trophy because of the small heads . . . ."

"All right, ladies and gentlemen," said Dieter Jost. Vickers always left the junior guide responsible for the social chores when both of them were present. "Please line up here along the wall until the Doctor Galil directs us onto the vehicle."

The members of Cretaceous Safari 87 backed against the hangar wall, their weapons or cameras in their hands. The guides and the two pilots, Washman and Brady, watched the clients rather than the crew preparing the intrusion vehicle. You could never tell what sort of mistake a tensed-up layman would make with a loaded weapon in his or her hands.

In case the clients were not laymen at all, there were four guards seated in a balcony-height alcove in the opposite wall. They wore civilian clothes, but the submachineguns they carried were just as military as their ID cards. The Israelis were, of all people, alert to the chance that a commando raid would be aimed at an intrusion vehicle and its technical staff. For that reason, the installation was in an urban setting from which there could be no quick escape; and its corridors and rooms, including the gaping hanger itself, were better guarded than the Defense Ministry had been during the most recent shooting war.

Dr. Galil and his staff were only occasionally visible to the group on the floor of the hangar. The intrusion vehicle rested on four braced girders twenty feet high. On its underside, a cylindrical probe was repeatedly blurring and reappearing. The technicians received data from the probe on instruments plugged into various sockets on the

vehicle. Eighty million years in the past, the
cylinder was sampling its surroundings on a score
of wavelengths. When necessary, Dr. Galil himself
changed control settings. Despite that care, there
was no certainty of the surface over which the
travellers would appear—or how far or under it
they would appear. The long legs gave the intrusion vehicle a margin that might otherwise have
been achieved by a longer drop than anything
aboard would have survived.

"Well, this is it, hey?" said Jonathan Salmes,
speaking to Don Washman. To do so, Salmes had
to talk through his wife, who ignored him in turn.
"A chance to hunt the most dangerous damned
creatures ever to walk the Earth!" Salmes' hands,
evenly tanned like every other inch of exposed
skin on him, tightened still further on the beautiful bolt-action rifle he carried.

Washman's smile went no further than
Adrienne Salmes. The pilot was a big man also.
The 40 mm grenade launcher he held looked like a
sawed-off shotgun with him for scale. "Gee, Mr.
Salmes," he said in false surprise. "People our age
all had a chance to learn the most dangerous game
on Earth popped out of a spider hole with an
AK-47 in its hands. All the *men* did, at least."

Vickers scowled. "Don," he said. But Washman
was a pilot, not a PR man. Besides, Salmes had
coming anything of the sort he got.

Adrienne Salmes turned to Washman and
laughed.

A heavy-set man climbed down from the intrusion vehicle and strolled across the concrete floor
toward the waiting group. Like the guards, he
wore an ordinary business suit. He kept his hands
in his pants pockets. "Good evening, ladies and
sirs," he said in accented English. "I am Mr. Stern;
you might say, the company manager. I trust the

preparations for your tour have been satisfactory?" He eyed Dieter, then Vickers, his face wearing only a bland smile.

"All present and accounted for," said Dieter in German. At his side, Mears nodded enthusiastically.

"By God," said Jonathan Salmes with recovered vigor, "I just want this gizmo to pop out right in front of a tyrannosaurus rex. Then I'll pop *him*, and I'll double your fees for a bonus!"

Don Washman smirked, but Vickers' scowl was for better reason than that. "Ah, Mr. Salmes," the guide said, "I believe Mr. Brewer drew first shot of the insertion. Fire discipline is something we *do* have to insist on."

"Naw, that's okay," said Brewer unexpectedly. He looked sheepishly at Vickers, then looked away. "We made an agreement on that," he added. "I don't mind paying for something I want; but I don't mind selling something I don't need, either, you see?"

"In any case," said Stern, "even the genius of Dr. Galil cannot guarantee to place you in front of a suitable dinosaur. I must admit to some apprehension, in fact, that some day we will land an intrusion vehicle in mid-ocean." He gestured both elbows outward, like wings flapping. "Ah, this is a magnificent machine; but not, I fear, very precise." He smiled.

"Not precise enough to . . . put a battalion of paratroops in the courtyard of the Temple in 70 AD, you mean?" suggested Adrienne Salmes with a trace of a smile herself.

Vickers' gut sucked in. Stern's first glance was to check the position of the guards. The slightly seedy good-fellowship he had projected was gone. "Ah, you Americans," Stern said in a voice that was itself a warning. "Always making jokes about

the impossible. But you must understand that in a
small and threatened country like ours, there are
some jokes one does not make." His smile now had
no humor. Adrienne Salmes returned it with a
wintry one of her own. If anyone had believed her
question was chance rather than a deliberate
goad, the smile disabused them.

Atop the intrusion vehicle, an indicator began
buzzing in a continuous rhythm. It was not a loud
sound. The high ceiling of the hangar drank it
almost completely. The staff personnel looked up
sharply. Stern nodded again to Vickers and began
to walk toward a ground-level exit. He was whistling under his breath. After a moment, a pudgy
man stepped to the edge of the vehicle and looked
down. He had a white moustache and a fringe of
hair as crinkled as rock wool. "I believe we are
ready, gentlemen," he said.

Dieter nodded. "We're on the way, then, Dr.
Galil," he replied to the older man. Turning back
to the safari group, he went on, "Stay in line,
please. Hold the handrail with one hand as you
mount the steps, and do be very careful to keep
your weapons vertical. Accidents happen, you
know." Dieter gave a brief nod of emphasis and
lead the way. The flight of metal steps stretched in
a steep diagonal between two of the vehicle's legs.
Vickers brought up the rear of the line, unhurried
but feeling the tingle at the base of the neck which
always preceded time travel with him. It amused
Vickers to find himself trying to look past the two
men directly in front of him to watch Adrienne
Salmes as she mounted the stairs. The woman
wore a baggy suit like the rest of them, rip-stopped
Kelprin which would shed water and still breathe
with 80% efficiency. On her the mottled coveralls
had an interest which time safari clients, male or
female, could rarely bring to such garments.

The floor of the intrusion vehicle was perforated steel from which much of the anti-slip coating had been worn. Where the metal was bare, it had a delicate patina of rust. In the center of the twenty-foot square, the safari's gear was neatly piled. The largest single item was the 500-gallon bladder of kerosene, fuel both for the turbine of the shooting platform and the diesel engines of the ponies. There was some dehydrated food, though the bulk of the group's diet would be the meat they shot. Vickers had warned the clients that anyone who could not stomach the idea of eating dinosaur should bring his own alternative. It was the idea that caused some people problems—the meat itself was fine. Each client was allowed a half-cubic meter chest for personal possessions. Ultimately they would either be abandoned in the Cretaceous or count against the owners' volume for trophies.

The intrusion vehicle was surrounded by a waist-high railing, hinged to flop down out of the way during loading and unloading. The space between the rail and the gear in the center was the passenger area. This open walkway was a comfortable four feet wide at the moment. On return, with the vehicle packed with trophies, there would be only standing room. Ceratopsian skulls, easily the most impressive of the High Cretaceous trophies, could run eight feet long with a height and width in proportion.

On insertion, it was quite conceivable that the vehicle would indeed appear in the midst of a pack of gorgosaurs. That was not something the staff talked about; but the care they took positioning themselves and the other gunners before insertion was not mere form. "Mr. McPherson," Dieter said, "Mr. Mears, if you will kindly come around with me to Side Three—that's across from the stairs

here. Do not please touch the red control panel as
you pass it."

"Ah, can't Charles and I stay together?" Mary
McPherson asked. Both of the dentists carried
motion cameras with the lenses set at the 50 mm
minimum separation. A wider spread could
improve hologram quality; but it might prove
impossibly awkward under the conditions obtain-
ing just after insertion.

"For the moment," Vickers said, "I'd like you on
Side One with me, Miss McPherson. That puts two
guns on each side; and it's just during insertion."

Boots clanking on the metal stairs, the safari
group mounted the vehicle. Four members of Dr.
Galil's team had climbed down already. They
stood in a row beside the steps like a guard of
honor in lab smocks. Galil himself waited beside
the vertical control panel at the head of the stairs.
The red panel was the only portion of the vehicle
which looked more in keeping with a laboratory
than a mineshaft. Even so, its armored casing was
a far cry from the festooned breadboards that
typically marked experimental machinery.

Not that anyone suggested to the clients that the
machinery was as surely experimental as a 1940
radar set.

Dr. Galil shook hands with each member of the
group, staff and clients alike. Vickers shifted his
modified Garand rifle into the crook of his left
arm and took the scientist's hand. "Henry, I pray
you God-speed and a safe return," Galil said in
English. His grip was firm.

"God's for afterwards, Shlomo," the guide said.
"You'll bring us back, you and your boys. That's
what I have faith in."

Dr. Galil squeezed Vickers' hand again. He
walked quickly down the steps. The hangar lights
dimmed as the big room emptied of everything but

the intrusion vehicle and its cargo. Vickers took a deep breath and unlocked the T-handled switch in the center of the control panel. He glanced to either side. Miss McPherson was to his left, Mrs. Salmes to his right.

Adrienne Salmes smiled back. "Did you put me with you because you think you can't trust a woman's shooting?" she asked.

Vickers cleared his throat. "No," he lied. More loudly, he added, "We are about to make our insertion. Everyone please grip the rail with your free hand. Don't let your rifles or cameras project more than two feet beyond the railing, though." He threw the switch. A blue light on the hangar ceiling began to pulse slowly, one beat per second. Vickers' belly drew in again. At the tenth pulse, the light and the hangar disappeared together. There was an instant of sensory blurring. Some compared the sensation of time travel to falling, others to immersion in vacuum. To Vickers, it was always a blast of heat. Then the heat was real and the sun glared down through a haze thick enough to shift the orb far into the red. The intrusion vehicle lurched in a walloping spray. Ooze and reeds sloshed sideways to replace those scalloped out of the slough and transported to the hangar in Tel Aviv. The vehicle settled almost to the full depth of its legs.

"Christ on a crutch!" snarled Don Washman, hidden from Vickers by the piled gear. "Tell us its a grassy clearing and drop us in a pissing swamp! Next time it'll be a kelp bed!" In a different voice he added, "Target."

All of Vickers' muscles had frozen when he thought they were about to drown. They were safe after all, though, and he turned to see the first dinosaur of the safari.

It was a duckbill—though the head looked more

like that of a sheep than a duck. Jaw muscles and
nasal passages filled the hollows of the snout
which early restorations had left bare. The dinosaur had been dashing through the low pines
fringing the slough when the crash and slap of the
insertion caused it to rear up and attempt to stop.
Reeds and water sprayed in a miniature echo of
the commotion the vehicle itself had made.

The firm soil of the shore was only ten feet from
the vehicle, roughly parallel to Side Four. The
duckbill halted, almost in front of Washman and
Jonathan Salmes. Scrabbling for traction in muck
covered by two feet of water, the beast tried to
reverse direction. The pilot leveled his grenade
launcher but did not fire. Vickers stepped to the
corner where he could see the target. It lacked the
crests that made many similar species excellent
trophies, but it was still two tons at point-blank
range and the first dino the clients had seen in the
flesh. "Go ahead," he said to Salmes. "It's yours."

The duckbill lunged back toward the shore,
swinging the splayed toes of its right foot onto
solid ground. Salmes' rifle slammed. It had an
integral muzzle brake to help reduce recoil by re-
directing muzzle gases sideways. The muzzle blast
was redirected as well, a palpable shock in the
thick air. The duckbill lurched, skidding nose-first
through a tree. Its long hind legs bunched under it
while the stubby forelegs braced to help the beast
rise. If it could get to the well-beaten trail by
which it had approached the slough, it would disappear.

"Good, good," said Vickers. His voice was tinny
in his own ears because of the muzzle blast. "Now
finish it with another one at the base of the tail."
Fired from such short range, Salmes' bullet could
be expected to range through the duckbill's body.

It was certain to rip enough blood vessels to let the beast's life out quickly, and it might also break the spine.

The second shot did not come. The duckbill regained its feet. There was a rusty splotch of blood against the brown-patterned hide of its left shoulder. Vickers risked a look away from the shore to see what was the matter with Salmes. The client had a glazed expression on his face. His big rifle was raised, but its butt did not appear to be solidly resting on his shoulder. Don Washman wore a disgusted look. Beyond both gunners, Mr. McPherson knelt and shot holo tape of the beast leaping back toward the trees.

"Shoot, for Chrissake!" Vickers shouted.

Salmes' rifle boomed again. A triple jet of smoke flashed from the bore and muzzle brake. Salmes cried out as the stock hit him. The bullet missed even the fringe of ten-foot pine trees. The duckbill disappeared into them.

Vickers carefully did not look at Salmes—or Adrienne Salmes, standing immediately behind the guide with her rifle ready to shoot if directed. She had snickered after her husband's second shot. "First we'll find a dry campsite and move the gear," Vickers started to say.

The forest edge exploded at the duckbill burst back through it in the midst of a pack of dromaeosaurs.

In the first flaring confusion, there seemed to be a score of the smaller carnivores. In fact, there were only five—but that was quite enough. One had the duckbill by the throat and was wrapping forelegs around the herbivore's torso to keep from being shaken loose. The rest of the pack circled the central pair with the avidity of participants in a gang rape. Though the carnivores were bipedal,

they bore a talon on each hind foot that was a
sickle in size and lethality. Kicking from one leg,
the hooting dromaeosaurs slashed through the
duckbill's belly hide. Soft, pink coils of intestine
spilled out into the water.

One of the half-ton carnivores cocked its head at
the group on the intrusion vehicle. The men on
Side Four were already spattered with the duckbill's blood. "Take 'em," Vickers said. He punched
a steel-cored bullet through the nearest dromaeosaur's skull, just behind its eyes.

Washman and Adrienne Salmes fired while
Vickers' cartridge case was still in the air. The
pilot's grenade launcher chugged rather than
banging, but the explosion of its projectile against
the chest of a carnivore was loud even to ears
numbed by the muzzle blasts of Salmes' rifle. The
grenade was a caseless shaped charge which could
be used point-blank without endangering the firer
with fragments. Even so, the concussion from less
than twenty feet rocked everyone on the near side
of the vehicle. There was a red flash and a mist of
pureed dinosaur. A foreleg, torn off at the shoulder, sailed straight into the air. Two of the dromaeosaurs bolted away from the blast, disappearing
among the trees in flat arcs and sprays of dirt and
pine straw.

Vickers' target had fallen where it stood. All
four limbs jerked like those of a pithed frog. The
dromaeosaur Adrienne Salmes had shot dropped
momentarily, then sprang to its feet again. The tall
woman worked the bolt of her rifle smoothly without taking the butt from her shoulder. The
grenade explosion did not appear to have disconcerted her. The guide, poised to finish the beast,
hesitated. Adrienne shot again and the dino's
limbs splayed. Its dark green hide showed clearly
the red and white rosette between the shoulders

where the second bullet had broken its spine.

Dieter Jost leaned past Mr. McPherson and put a uranium penetrator through the brain of the duck-bill, ending its pain. All four of the downed dinosaurs continued to twitch.

"Jesus," said Don Washman quietly as he closed the breech on a grenade cartridge.

Although he had only fired once, Henry Vickers replaced the 20-round magazine of his Garand with a fresh one from his belt pouch. "Mr. McPherson," he said, "I hope you got good pictures, because I swear that's the most excitement I've had in a long time in this business."

Dieter had moved back to watch the slough with Steve Brady. Most of the clients crowded to Side Four to get a better view of the Cretaceous and its denizens. Adrienne Salmes had not moved from where she stood beside Vickers. She thumbed a second cartridge into the magazine of her rifle and closed the breech. "Still doubt I can shoot?" she asked with a smile.

"Heart and spine," the guide said. "No, I guess you can back me up any day of the week. I tell you, dromaeosaurs aren't as impressive as some of the larger carnivores, but they're just as dangerous." He looked more carefully at her rifle, a Schultz and Larsen with no ornamentation but the superb craftsmanship that had gone into its production. "Say, nice," Vickers said. "In .358 Norma?"

The blonde woman smiled with pleasure. "It's the same rifle I've used for everything from whitetails to elephant," she said. "I'd planned to bring something bigger, but after what you said, I had five hundred bullets cast from bronze and loaded at the factory for me. Johnnie—" she glanced at her husband, now loudly describing how he had shot the duckbill to the other clients. "Well," Adrienne continued quietly, "I'm the hunter in the household, not him. I told him he was crazy to have a cannon like that built, but he listens to me as badly as he listens to everyone else."

"That may be a problem," Vickers muttered. More loudly, he said, "All right, I think it's time to start setting up camp on top of this ridge. Around now, it's asking for trouble to be any closer than a hundred yards to the water, especially with this much meat nearby. After Steve and I get the ponies assembled, we'll need everybody's help to load them. Until then, just try not to get in the way."

Sometimes working with his hands helped Vickers solve problems caused by the human side of his safaris. It did not seem to do so on this occasion. Of course, a client who was both arrogant and gun-shy was a particularly nasty problem.

But Vickers was irritated to realize that it also bothered him that Don Washman and Mrs. Salmes seemed to be getting along very well together.

The campfire that evening provided an aura of human existence more important than the light of its banked coals. The clients had gone to sleep— or at least to their tents. That the Salmes at least were not asleep was evident from the sound of an argument. The double walls of the tents cut sound penetration considerably, but there were limits. Steve Brady shoved another log on the fire and said, "Damn, but I swear that chainsaw gets heavier every time I use it. Do you suppose the Israelis designed them to be air-dropped without parachutes?"

"You want a high horsepower-to-weight ratio, you don't use a diesel," agreed Dieter Jost with a shrug. "If you want a common fuel supply for everything and need diesel efficiency for the ponies, though—well, you get a heavy chainsaw."

"Can't imagine why she ever married him," Don Washman said. "Beef like that's a dime a dozen. Why, you know he didn't even have balls enough to chamber a third round? He's scared to death of that gun, scared almost to touch it now."

"Yeah," agreed Vickers, working a patch into the slot of his cleaning rod, "but the question's what to do about it. I don't have any good answers, God knows."

"Do?" Washman repeated. "Well, hell, leave him, of course. She's got money of her own—"

Brady broke into snorting laughter. Dieter grimaced and said, "Don, I do not think it is any business of ours how our clients live. The Salmes are adults and can no doubt solve their own problems." He pursed his lips. The fire threw the shadow of his bushy moustache misshapenly against his cheeks. "As for our problem, Henry, why don't we offer him the use of the camp gun? The .375? I think Mr. Salmes' difficulty is in precisely the same category as the more usual forms of mechanical breakdown or guns falling into the river."

"Fine with me if you can talk him into it," Vickers said dubiously, "but I wouldn't say Salmes is the sort to take a well-meant suggestion." He nodded toward the tent. The couple within seemed to be shouting simultaneously. "Or any other kind of suggestion," he added.

"Things would sure be simpler if they didn't allow booze on safaris," Brady said.

"Things would be simpler for us if our employers paid us to sleep all day and drink schnapps," said Dieter Jost. He tugged a lock of hair absently. "That does not comport well with economic realities, however. And so long as each of our clients has paid fifty thousand American dollars for the privilege of spending two weeks in the Cretaceous, it is unrealistic to assume that the staff will be treated as anything but the hired help. If drunken clients make the job more difficult, then that is simply one of the discomforts of the job. Like loading gear in the heat, or tracking down an animal that a client has wounded. It is easier for our employers, Mr. Stern and those above him, to hire new staff members than it would be to impose their underlings' view on persons of the sort who take time safaris."

"Moshe Cohn was head guide when I made my first insertion," said Vickers aloud. His cleaning rod rested on his lap beside the Garand, but he had not run it through the bore yet. "He told a client —a Texan, it was a US safari that time too— that he'd be better off to slack up a little on his drinking while he was in the field. The client was generally too stiff to see a dino, much less shoot one." The guide's forefinger tapped the breech of his rifle as he recalled the scene. "He said to Moshe, 'Jew-boy, you sound just like my third wife. One more word and I'll whip you with my belt, just like I did her.' Moshe broke his hand on the Texan's jaw. When we got back, the government—the Israeli but very pragmatic government—fired Moshe and denied him compensation for his hand. Ten days in the field with broken bones, remember." Vickers paused, then went on, "That taught me the rules. So far, I've been willing to live by them."

Don Washman laughed. "Right, when you hit a client, use your gunstock," he said and opened another beer.

Technically Steve Brady had the first watch, even though all four staff members were up. The alarm panel was facing Steve when it beeped, therefore. "Jesus!" the stubby, long-haired pilot blurted when he saw the magnitude of the signal fluorescing on the display. "Down the trail—must be a herd of something!"

Don Washman upset his fresh beer as he ran to the spade grips of the heavy machine-gun. It was in the center of the camp, on ground slightly higher than its immediate surroundings but by no means high enough to give the weapon an unbroken field of fire. The staff had sawed clear a campsite along the game trail leading down to the intrusion vehicle two hundred yards away. Assuming that animals were most likely to enter the area by the trail, Dieter had sited the tents on the other side of the gun. The next day they could assemble the six-foot high tower for the gun, but time had been too short to finish that the first night.

While the other staff members crouched over weapons, Vickers darted to the three occupied tents. The sensor loop that encircled the camp 100 yards out could pick up very delicate impacts and relay them to the display screen. This signal, however, was already shaking the ground. Miss McPherson poked her head out of the tent she shared with her brother. "What—" the dentist began.

The file of huge ceratopsians rumbled into sight on their way to the water to drink. They were torosaurs or a species equally large. In the dim glow of the fire, they looked more like machines than anything alive. Their beaks and the tips of their triple horns had a black glint like raku ware, and they averaged twice the size of elephants.

The tent that Mears and Brewer shared shuddered as both clients tried to force their way through the opening simultaneously. Vickers lifted the muzzles of their rifles skyward as he had been waiting to do. "No shooting now," he cried over the thunder of the dinosaurs. "In the morning we'll follow them up."

Adrienne Salmes slipped out of her tent before Vickers could reach over and take her rifle. It was pointed safely upward anyway. Despite the hour-long argument she had been engaged in, the blonde woman looked calm and alert. She looked breath-takingly beautiful as well—and wore only her rifle. "If you can wait a moment for my fire-power," she said to Vickers without embarrassment, "I'll throw some clothes on." The guide nodded.

The bony frills at the back of the ceratopsians' skulls extended their heads to well over the height of a man. Less for protection than for muscle attachment, the frills locked the beasts' heads firmly to their shoulders. The bulging jaw muscles that they anchored enabled the ceratopsians to literally shear hardwood the thickness of a man's thigh. The last thing a safari needed was a herd of such monsters being stampeded through the camp. A beast wounded by a shot ill-aimed in the darkness could lead to just that result.

Mears and Brewer were staring at the rapid procession in wonder. The left eye of each torosaur glinted in the firelight. "Mother o' God, what a trophy!" Brewer said.

"Best in the world," Vickers agreed. "You'll go back with one, never fear." He looked at the McPhersons to his other side. The dentists were clutching their holo cameras, which were almost useless under the light conditions. "And you'll get your fill too," Vickers said. "The trip isn't cheap, but I've never yet guided a client who didn't think he'd gotten more than he bargained for." Though a drunken SOB like Jonathan Salmes might spoil that record, he added silently.

Adrienne Salmes re-emerged from her tent, wearing her coveralls and boots. Mears and

Brewer had been so focused on the herd of torosaurs that the guide doubted the men had noticed her previous display. She was carrying a sleeping bag in addition to her rifle. Vickers raised an eyebrow. Adrienne nodded back at the tent. "Screaming beauty seems to have passed out," she said, "but I'm damned if I'll stay in the tent with him. Going on about his shoulder, for God's sake, and expecting sympathy from *me*. Is it all right if I doss down in the open?"

The ceratopsians were sporting in the water, making as much noise as the Waikiki surf. Vickers smiled. "They could eat tree trunks and drink mud," he said, as if he had not heard the client's question. "And I still meet people who think mammals are better adapted for survival than dinos were." He turned to Adrienne Salmes. "It's all right, so long as you stay out of the gun's way," he said, "but you'll wash away if it rains. And we're bound to get at least one real gully-washer while we're here."

"Hell, there's an easy answer to that," said Don Washman. He had strolled over to the tents when it became clear no predators had followed the torosaurs. "One of us is on watch all night, right? So there's always a slot open in the staff tents. Let noble hunter there sleep by himself, Hank. And she shoots well enough to be a pro, so let her stay dry with us too." He gave his engaging smile.

The other clients were listening with interest. "Maybe if Mr. McPherson wants to trade—" Vickers began in a neutral voice.

Adrienne Salmes hushed him with a grimace. "I'm a big girl now, Mr. Vickers," she snapped, "and I think I'm paying enough to make my own decisions. Don, if you'll show me the tent, I'll resume getting the sleep I've been assured I'll need in the morning."

Washman beamed. "Let's see," he said, "Steve's got watch at the moment, so I suppose you're my tentmate till I go on at four in the morning . . . ."

They walked toward the tent. Dieter, standing near the fire with his rifle cradled, looked from them to Vickers. Vickers shrugged. He was thinking about Moshe Cohn again.

"Platform to Mobile One," crackled the speaker of the unit clipped to Vickers' epaulet. Vickers threw the last of the clamps that locked the two ponies into a single, articulated vehicle. "Go ahead, Dieter," he said.

"Henry, the torosaurs must have run all night after they left the water," the other guide announced through the heavy static. "They're a good fifteen klicks west of camp. But there's a sauropod burn just three klicks south and close to the river. Do you want me to drop a marker?"

Vickers frowned. "Yeah, go ahead," he decided. He glanced at but did not really see the four clients, festooned with gear, who awaited his order to board the ponies. "Any sign of carnosaurs?"

"Negative," Dieter replied, "but we're still looking. I spotted what looked like a fresh kill when we were tracking the torosaurs. If we don't get any action here, I'll carry Miss McPherson back to that and see what we can stir up."

"Good hunting, Dieter," Vickers said. "We'll go take a look at your sauropods. Mobile One out." Again his eyes touched the clients. He appeared startled to see them intent on him. "All right," he said, "if you'll all board the lead pony. The other's along for trophies—sauropods this time, we'll get you the ceratopsians another day. Just pull down the jump seats."

The guide seated himself behind the tiller bar and clipped his rifle into its brackets. His clients stepped over the pony's low sides. The vehicle was the shape of an aluminum casket, scaled up by a half. A small diesel engine rode over the rear axle. Though the engine was heavily muffled, the valves sang trills which blended with the natural sounds of the landscape. Awnings were pleated into trays at either end of the vehicle, but for today the trees would be sun-screen enough.

Don Washman waved. He had strung a tarp from four trees at the edge of the clearing. In that shade he was pinning together the steel framework of the gun tower. The alarm and his grenade launcher sat beside him.

"Take care," Vickers called.

"You take care," the pilot responded with a broad grin. "Maybe I can lose the yo-yo and then we're all better off." He jerked his head toward the tent which still held Jonathan Salmes. Dieter had tried to arouse Salmes for breakfast. Because Vickers was sawing at the time, no one but Dieter himself heard what the client shouted. Dieter, who had served in at least three armies and was used to being cursed, had backed out of the tent with a white face. Vickers had shut down the saw, but the other guide had shaken his head. "Best to let him sleep, I think," he said.

Remembering the night before, Vickers wished that it was Brady and not Washman who had the guard that day. Oh, well. "Hold on," he said aloud. He put the pony into gear.

Just west of the crest on which they had set up camp, the height and separation of the trees increased markedly. Small pines and cycads were replaced by conifers that shot over one hundred feet in the air. Everything east of the ridgeline was in the floodplain, where the river drowned tree roots with a regularity that limited survival to the smaller, faster-growing varieties. The thick-barked monsters through which Vickers now guided the ponies were centuries old already. Barring lightning or tornado, they would not change appreciably over further centuries. They were the food of the great sauropods.

The forest was open enough to permit the pony to run at over 15 mph, close to its top speed with the load. The saplings and pale, broad-leafed ferns which competed for the dim light were easily brushed aside. Animal life was sparse, but as the pony skirted a fallen log, a turkey-sized coelurosaur sprang up with a large beetle in its jaws. Mears' .458 boomed. There was an echo-chamber effect from the log which boosted the muzzle blast to a near equal for that of the Salmes' .500. Everyone on the pony jumped—Vickers more than the rest because he had not seen the client level his rifle. The dinosaur darted away, giving a flick of its gray-feathered tail as it disappeared around a trunk.

"Ah, don't shoot without warning," the guide said, loudly but without looking around. "It's too easy to wound something that you should have had backup for. Besides, we should be pretty close to the sauropods—and they make much better targets."

Even as Vickers spoke, the forest ahead of them brightened. The upper branches still remained, but all the limbs had been stripped below the level of sixty feet. One tree had been pushed over. It had fallen to a 45° angle before being caught and supported by the branches of neighboring giants. The matted needles were strewn with fresh blankets of sauropod droppings. They had a green, faintly Christmasy scent. Vickers stopped the vehicle and turned to his clients. "We're getting very close," he said, "and there'll be plenty of shooting for everybody in just a moment. But there's also a chance of a pack of carnosaurs nearby for the same reason that we are. Keep your eyes open as we approach—and for *God's* sake don't shoot until I've said to." His eyes scanned the forest again and returned to Adrienne Salmes. A momentary remembrance of her the night before, a nude Artemis with rifle instead of bow, made him smile. "Mrs. Salmes," he said, "would you watch behind us, please? Carnivores are likely to strike up a burn as we did . . . and I can't watch behind us myself."

Adrienne grinned. "Why Mr. Vickers, I think you've just apologized for doubting I could shoot," she said. She turned and faced back over the towed pony, left arm through the sling of her rifle in order to brace the weapon firmly when she shot.

Vickers eased forward the hand throttle. They were past the marker beacon Dieter had dropped from the shooting platform. The responder tab on the guide's wrist had pulsed from green to red and was now lapsing back into fire-orange; he cut it off absently. The sounds of the dinosaurs were audible to him now: the rumble of their huge intestines; the slow crackle of branches being stripped of their needles, cones, and bark by the sauropods' teeth; and occasional cooing calls which the clients, if they heard them over the ringing of the diesel, probably mistook for those of unseen forest birds.

The others did not see the sauropods even when Vickers cut the motor off. They were titanosaurs or a similar species, only middling huge for their sub-order. Vickers pointed. Mears, Brewer, and McPherson followed the line of the guide's arm, frowning. "It's all right now, Mrs. Salmes," Vickers said softly. "The dinos will warn us if predators get near." Adrienne Salmes faced around as well.

"Oh, Jesus Christ," someone whispered as he realized what Vickers was pointing out. It was incredible, even to the guide, how completely a score or more of thirty-ton animals could blend into an open forest. In part, it may have been that human minds were not used to interpreting as animals objects which weighed as much as loaded semis. Once recognized, the vast expanses of russet and black hide were as obvious as inkblot pictures which someone else has described.

Silently and without direction, McPherson stepped from the pony and spread the lenses of his camera. Vickers nodded to the others. "They won't pay attention to a normal voice," he said—in a quieter than normal voice. "Try to avoid sudden movements, though. They may think it's a warning signal of some kind." He cleared his throat. "I want each of you to mark a target—"

"That one!" whispered Mears urgently, a boy in the toystore, afraid his aunt will reneg on her promise of a gift unless he acts at once. The big contractor was pointing at the nearest of the sauropods, a moderate-sized female only thirty feet away.

"Fine, but wait," the guide said firmly. "I'll position each of you. When I call 'fire', go ahead—but only then. They won't attack anything our size, but they might step on one of us if they were startled at the wrong time. That big, they don't have to be hostile to be dangerous."

The nearby female, which had been browsing on limbs twenty feet high, suddenly stepped closer to a tree and reared up on her hind legs. She anchored herself to the trunk with her forefeet, each armed with a single long claw. It shredded bark as it gripped. With the grace and power of a derrick, the titanosaur's head swung to a high branch, closed, and dragged along it for several yards. It left only bare wood behind.

With his left hand, Vickers aimed a pen-sized laser pointer. A red dot sprang out on the chest of the oblivious titanosaur. "There's your aiming point," the guide said. "If she settles back down before I give the signal, just hit her at the top of the shoulder."

Mears nodded, his eyes intent on the dinosaur.

Vickers moved Brewer five yards away, with a broadside shot at a large male. McPherson stood beside him, using a pan-head still camera on the six sauropods visible within a stone's throw. The dentist's hands were trembling with excitement.

Vickers took Adrienne Salmes slightly to the side, to within twenty yards of another male. He chose the location with an eye on the rest of the herd. Sauropods had a tendency to bolt straight ahead if aroused.

"Why does this one have bright red markings behind its eyes?" Adrienne asked.

"First time I ever saw it," the guide said with a shrug. "Maybe some professor can tell you when you get back with the head." He did not bother to gesture with the laser. "Ready?" he asked.

She nodded and aimed.

"Fire!"

The three gunners volleyed raggedly. The thick tree trunks acted as baffles, blurring the sharpness of the reports. The gunfire had the same feeling of muffled desecration as farts echoing in a cathedral. The red-flashed titanosaur began striding forward. Adrienne Salmes worked her bolt and fired again. A wounded animal gave a warning call, so loud and low-pitched that the humans' bowels trembled. Mrs. Salmes fired again. The titanosaur was a flickering picture in a magic lantern formed by open patches between six-foot tree boles. The huntress began to run after her disappearing prey.

Vickers grabbed her shoulder, halting her with an ease that belied his slender build. She turned on him in fury. "I won't let a wounded animal go!" she screamed.

"It won't go far," Vickers said. He released her. "We'll follow as soon as it's safe." He gestured, taking in the bellowing, mountainous forms padding in all directions among the even larger trees. "They'll circle in a moment. Then it'll be safe for things our size to move," he said.

Russet motion ceased, though the tidal bellowing of over a dozen sauropods continued. Mears was still firing in the near distance. Brewer had lowered his rifle and was rubbing his shoulder with his left hand. "Let's get everybody together," the guide suggested, "and go finish off some trophies."

Brewer's expression was awed as they approached. "It really did fall," he said. "It was so big, I couldn't believe . . . . But I shot it where you said and it just ran into the tree." He waved. "And I kept shooting and it fell."

The haunches of the titanosaur were twice the height of a man, even with the beast belly-down in the loam. McPherson pointed at the great scars in the earth beneath the sauropod's tail. "It kept trying to move," he said in amazement. "Even though there was a tree in the way. It was kicking away, trying to get a purchase, and I thought the *tree* was going to go over. But it did. The, the dinosaur. And I have a tape of all of it!"

Mears, closest to the bellowing giants, was just as enthusiastic. "Like a shooting gallery!" he said, "but the tin ducks're the size of houses. God Almighty! I only brought one box of ammo with me. I shot off every last slug! God Almighty!"

The titanosaurs had quieted somewhat, but they were still making an odd series of sounds. The noises ranged from bird calls as before, to something like the venting of high-pressure steam. Vickers nodded and began walking toward the sounds. He had caught Adrienne Salmes' scowl of distaste at the contractor's recital. If the guide agreed, it was still not his business to say so.

The herd was larger than Vickers had estimated. Forty of the sauropods were in a circle facing outwards around a forest giant, which was so much bigger than its neighbors that it had cleared a considerable area. Several of the beasts were rearing up. They flailed the air with clawed forefeet and emitted the penetrating steam-jet hiss that seemed so incongruous from a living being. Mears raised his rifle with a convulsed look on his face before he remembered that he had no ammunition left.

McPherson was already rolling tape. "Have you reloaded?" the guide asked, looking from Salmes to Brewer. The blonde woman nodded curtly while the meat packer fumbled in the side pocket of his coveralls.

"I don't see the one I hit," Adrienne Salmes said. Her face was tight.

"Don't worry," the guide said quietly. "It's down, it couldn't have made it this far the way you hit it. It's the ones that weren't heart-shot that we're dealing with now."

"That's not my responsibility," she snapped.

"It's no duty you owe to me," Vickers agreed, "or to anything human."

Brewer snicked his bolt home. Vickers' laser touched the center of the chest of a roaring titanosaur. Orange pulmonary blood splashed its tiny head like a shroud. "On the word, Mr. Brewer," he said, "if you would."

Adrienne said, "All right." She did not look at

Vickers.

Across the circle, eighty yards away, a large male was trying to lick its belly. Its long neck strained, but it was not flexible enough to reach the wound. The laser pointer touched below the left eye. "There?" the guide asked.

Adrienne nodded and braced herself, legs splayed. Her arms, sling, and upper body made a web of interlocking triangles.

The guide swung his own weapon onto the third of the wounded animals. "All right," he said.

Adrienne's Schultz and Larsen cracked. The light went out of the gut-shot sauropod's eye. Undirected, the rest of the great living machine began slowly to collapse where it stood. Brewer was firing, oblivious of his bruised shoulder in the excitement. Vickers put three rounds into the base of his own target's throat. Its head and neck were weaving too randomly to trust a shot at them.

Either the muzzle blasts or the sight of three more of their number sagging to the ground routed the herd. Their necks swung around like compass needles to iron. With near simultaneity, all the surviving titanosaurs drifted away from the guns. Their tails were held high off the ground.

Adrienne Salmes lowered her rifle. "God Almighty, let me use that!" Mears begged, reaching out for the weapon. "I'll pay you—"

"Touch me and I'll shove this up your bum, you bloody butcher!" the blonde woman snarled.

The contractor's fist balled. He caught himself, however, even before he realized that the muzzle of the .358 had tilted in line with his throat.

"The river isn't that far away," said Vickers, pointing in the direction the sauropods had run. "We'll follow in the pony—it's a sight worth seeing. And taping," he added.

The undergrowth slowed the hunters after they

recrossed the ridgeline, but the titanosaurs were still clearly evident. Their heads and even hips rocked above the lower vegetation that sloped toward the river. The herd, despite its size and numbers, had done surprisingly little damage to its rush to the water. The pony repeatedly had to swing aside from three-inch saplings which had sprung back when the last of the titanosaurs had passed.

But the beasts themselves were slowed by the very mechanics of their size. Their twelve-foot strides were ponderously slow even under the goad of panic. The tensile strength of the sauropods' thigh bones simply was not equal to the acceleration of the beasts' mass to more than what would be a fast walk in a man. The hunters reached a rocky spur over the mudflats fringing the water just as the leading titanosaurs splashed into the stream 150 yards away. The far bank of the river was lost in haze. The sauropods continued to advance without reference to the change in medium. Where a moment before they had been belly-deep in reeds, now they were belly-deep in brown water that was calm except for the wakes of their passage. When the water grew deeper, the procession sank slowly. The beasts farthest away, in mid-stream over a quarter mile out, were floating necks and tails while the forefeet propelled them by kicking down into the bottom muck.

"Don't they hide underwater and snorkel through their necks?" Brewer asked. Then he yipped in surprise as his hand touched the barrel of his Weatherby. The metal was hot enough to burn from strings of rapid fire and the Cretaceous sunlight.

Vickers nodded. He had heard the question often before. "Submarines breathe through tubes because the tubes are steel and the water pressure doesn't crush them," he explained. "Sauropods don't have armored gullets, and their lungs aren't diesel engines inside a steel pressure hull. Physics again. Besides, they float—the only way they could sink would be to grab a rock."

As Vickers spoke, the last titanosaur in the line sank.

"Well, I'll be damned!" the guide blurted.

The sauropod surfaced again a moment later. It blew water from its lungs as it gave the distress cry that had followed the shooting earlier.

The mild current of the river had bent the line of titanosaurs into a slight curve. The leaders were already disappearing into the haze. None of the other beasts even bothered to look back to see the cause of the bellowing. No doubt they already knew.

The stricken titanosaur sank again. It rolled partly onto its left side as it went under the surface this time. It was still bellowing, wreathing its head in a golden spray as it disappeared.

"I think," said Adrienne Salmes dryly, "that this time the rock grabbed the dinosaur."

Vickers grunted in reply. He was focusing his binoculars on the struggle.

Instead of rising vertically, the sauropod rolled completely over sideways. Clinging to the herbivore's left foreleg as it broke surface was something black and huge and as foul as a tumor. The linked beasts submerged again in an explosion of spray. Vickers lowered the binoculars, shivering. They were not common, even less commonly seen. Great and terrible as they were, they were also widely hated. For them to sun themselves on mudbanks as their descendants did would have been to court death by the horns and claws of land animals equally large. But in their own element, in the still, murky waters, they were lords without peer.

"Christ Almighty," Mears said, "was that a whale?"

"A crocodile," the guide replied, staring at the roiling water. "Enough like what you'd find in the Nile or the Congo that you couldn't tell the difference by a picture. Except for the size." He paused, then continued, "The science staff will be glad to hear about this. They always wondered if they preyed on the big sauropods too. It seems that they preyed on *any* goddam thing in the water."

"I'd swear it was bigger than the tyrannosaurus you showed us," Adrienne Salmes observed, lowering her own binoculars.

Vickers shrugged. "As long, at least. Probably heavier. I looked at a skull, a fossil in London . . . I don't know how I'd get one back as a trophy . . . . It was six feet long, which was impressive; and three feet wide, which was incredible, a carnivore with jaws three feet *wide*. Tyrannosaurs don't compare, no. Maybe whales do, Mr. Mears. But nothing else I know of."

There were no longer any titanosaurs visible. The herd had curved off down-stream, past the intrusion vehicle and the hunting camp. They were lost against the haze and the distant shoreline by now. The water still stirred where the last of them had gone down, but by now the struggles must have been the thrashings of the sauropod's autonomic nervous system. The teeth of the crocodile were six inches long; but they were meant only to hold, not to kill. The water killed, drowning a thirty-ton sauropod as implacably as it would any lesser creature anchored to the bottom by the crocodile's weight.

"We'd best take our trophies," Vickers said at last. No one in the world knew his fear of drowning, no one but himself. "The smell'll bring a pack of gorgosaurs soon, maybe even a tyrannosaur. I don't want that now, not with us on the ground."

The guide rubbed his forehead with the back of his left hand, setting his bush hat back in place carefully. "The ponies convert to boats," he said, patting the aluminum side. "The tread blocks can be rotated so they work like little paddle wheels." He paused as he swung the tiller bar into a tight circle. "I guess you see why we don't use them for boats in the Cretaceous," he added at last. "And why we didn't keep our camp down on the intrusion vehicle."

Vickers was even quieter than his wont for the rest of the morning.

The shooting platform had returned before the ponies did, the second of them dripping with blood from the titanosaur heads. Two heads had Mears' tags on them, though the contractor had finished none of the beasts he had wounded. The best head among those he had sprayed would have been the one the guide had directed Adrienne Salmes to kill—with a bullet through the skull that destroyed all trophy value.

There were no game laws in the Cretaceous, but the line between hunters and butchers was the same as in every other age.

The McPhersons greeted each other with mutual enthusiasm. Their conversation was technical and as unintelligible to non-photographers as the conversation of any other specialists. Jonathan Salmes was sitting on a camp stool, surly but alert. He did not greet the returning party, but he watched the unloading of the trophies with undisguised interest. The right side of his face was puffy.

"We've found a tyrannosaur," Dieter called as he and the pilots joined Vickers. That was good news, but there was obvious tension among the

other members of the staff. Brady carried a spray
gun loaded with antiseptic sealer. A thorough
coating would prevent decay for almost a month,
ample time to get the heads to proper taxi-
dermists.

When Dieter was sure that all the clients were
out of earshot, he said in a low voice, "Don has
something to tell you, Henry."

"Eh?" prompted Vickers. He set one of the
sauropod heads on the spraying frame instead of
looking at the pilot.

"I had to clobber Salmes," Washman said, lifting out the red-flashed trophy. "He was off his
head—I'm not sure he even remembers. There was
a mixed herd of duckbills came down the trail. He
came haring out of his tent with that gun of his. He
didn't shoot, though, he started chasing them
down the trail." The pilot straightened and
shrugged. Steve Brady began pumping the spray
gun. The pungent mist drifted down wind beyond
the gaping heads. "I grabbed him. I mean, who
knows what might be following a duckbill? When
he swung that rifle at me, I had to knock him out
for his own good. Like a drowning man." Washman shrugged again. "His gun wasn't even loaded,
you know?"

"Don, run the ponies down to the water and mop
them out, will you?" Vickers said. The pilot
jumped onto the leading vehicle and spun them off
down the trail. The two guides walked a little to
the side, their rifles slung, while Brady finished
sealing the trophies. "It's going to have to be reported, you know," Vickers said. "Whether
Salmes does or not."

"You or I might have done the same thing,"
Dieter replied.

"I'm not denying that," the senior guide
snapped. "But it has to be reported."

The two men stood in silence, looking out at a

forest filled with sounds that were subtly wrong. At last Dieter said, "Salmes goes up in the platform with you and Don tomorrow, doesn't he?"

Vickers agreed noncommittally.

"Maybe you ought to go with Steve instead," Dieter suggested. He looked at Vickers. "Just for the day, you know."

"Washman just flies us," Vickers said with a shake of his head. "I'm the one that's in contact with the client. And Don's as good as pilots come."

"That he is," the other guide agreed, "that he is. But he is not a piece of furniture. You are treating him as a piece of furniture."

Vickers clapped his companion on the shoulder. "Come on," he said, "Salmes'll be fine when he gets his tyrannosaur. What we ought to be worrying about is three more for the others. If Salmes goes home with a big boy and the rest have to settle for less—well, it says no guarantees in the contracts, but you know the kind of complaints the company gets. That's the kind of problem we're paid to deal with. If they wanted shrinks instead of guides, they'd have hired somebody else."

Dieter laughed half-heartedly. "Let us see what we can arrange for lunch," he said. "At the moment, I am more interested in sauropod steak than I am in the carnivores that we compete with."

"Damn, the beacon cut out again!" Washman snarled. There was no need of an intercom system; the shooting platform operated with only an intake whine which was no impediment to normal speech. The silence was both a boon to coordination and a help in not alarming the prey. It did, however, mean that the client was necessarily aware of any technical glitches. When the client was Jonathan Salmes—

"God damn, you're not going to put *me* on that way!" the big man blazed. He had his color back and with it all his previous temper. Not that the bruise over his right cheekbone would have helped. "One of the others paid you to save the big one for them, didn't they?" he demanded. "By God, I'll bet it was my wife! And I'll bet it wasn't money either, the—"

"Take us up to a thousand feet," Vickers said sharply. "We'll locate the kill visually if the marker isn't working. Eighty tons of sauropod shouldn't be hard to spot."

"Hang on, there it's on again," said the pilot. The shooting platform veered slightly as he corrected their course. Vickers and Salmes stood clutching the rail of the suspended lower deck which served as landing gear as well. Don Washman was seated above them at the controls, with the fuel tank balancing his mass behind. The air intake and exhaust extended far beyond the turbine itself to permit the baffling required for silent running. The shooting platform was as fragile as a dragonfly; and it was, in its way, just as efficient a predator.

By good luck, the tyrannosaur had made its kill on the edge of a large area of brush rather than high forest. The platform's concentric-shaft rotors kept blade length short. Still, though it was possible to maneuver beneath the forest canopy, it was a dangerous and nerve-wracking business to do so. Washman circled the kill at 200 feet, high enough that he did not need to allow for trees beneath him. Though the primary airflow from the rotors was downward, the odor of tens of tons of meat dead in the sun still reached the men above. The guide tried to ignore it with his usual partial success. Salmes only wrinkled his nose and said, "Whew, what a pong." Then, "Where is it? The tyrannosaurus?"

That the big killer was still nearby was obvious from the types of scavengers on the sauropod. Several varieties of the smaller coelurosaurs scrambled over the corpse like harbor rats on a drowned man. None of the species weighed more than a few hundred pounds. A considerable flock of pterosaurs joined and squabbled with the coelurosaurs, wings tented and toothless beaks stabbing out like shears. There were none of the large carnivores around the kill—and that implied that something was keeping them away.

"Want me to go down close to wake him up?" Washman asked.

The guide licked his lips. "I guess you'll have to," he said. There was always a chance that a pterodactyl would be sucked into the turbine when you hovered over a kill. The thought of dropping into a big carnosaur's lap that way kept some guides awake at night. Vickers looked at his client and added, "Mr. Salmes, we're just going to bring the tyrannosaur out of wherever it's lying up in the forest. After we get it into the open, we'll maneuver to give you the best shot. All right?"

Salmes grunted. His hands were tight on his beautifully-finished rifle. He had refused Dieter's offer of the less-bruising camp gun with a scorn that was no less grating for being what all the staff had expected.

Washman dropped them vertically instead of falling in a less wrenching spiral. He flared the blades with a gentle hand, however, feathering the platform's descent into a hover without jarring the gunners. They were less than thirty feet in the air. Pterosaurs, more sensitive to moving air than the earth-bound scavengers, squealed and hunched their wings. The ones on the ground could not take off because the down-draft anchored them. The pilot watched carefully the few still circling above them.

"He's—" Vickers began, and with his word the tyrannosaur strode into the sunlight. Its bellow was intended to chase away the shooting platform. The machine trembled as the sound induced sympathetic vibrations in its rotor blades. Coelurosaurs scattered. The cries of the pterosaurs turned to blind panic as the downdraft continued to frustrate their attempts to rise. The huge predator took another step forward. Salmes raised his rifle. The guide cursed under his breath but did not attempt to stop him.

At that, it should have been an easy shot. The tyrannosaur was within thirty feet of the platform and less than ten feet below them. All it required was that Salmes aim past the large head as it swung to counterweight a stride and rake down through the thorax. Perhaps the angle caused him to shoot high, perhaps he flinched. Vickers, watching the carnosaur over his own sights, heard the big rifle crash. The tyrannosaur strode forward untouched, halving the distance between it and the platform.

"Take us up!" the guide shouted. If it had not been a rare trophy, he might have fired himself and announced that he had 'put in a bullet to finish the beast'. There were three other gunners who wanted a tyrannosaur, though; if Salmes took this one back, it would be after he had shot it or everyone else had an equal prize.

Salmes was livid. He gripped the bolt handle, but he had not extracted the empty case. "God damn you!" he screamed. "You made it wobble to throw me off! You son of a bitch, you robbed me!"

"Mr. Salmes—" Vickers said. The tyrannosaur was now astride the body of its prey, cocking its head to see the shooting platform fifty feet above it.

"By God, you want another chance?" Washman
demanded in a loud voice. The platform plunged
down at a steep angle. The floor grating blurred
the sight of the carnosaur's mottled hide. Its up-
turned eye gleamed like a strobe-lit ruby.

"Jesus *Christ!*" Vickers shouted. "Take us the
hell up, Washman!"

The platform steadied, pillow soft, with its floor
fifteen feet from the ground and less than twenty
from the tyrannosaur. Standing on the sauropod's
corpse, the great predator was eye to eye with
Vickers and his client. The beast bellowed again as
it lunged. The impulse of its clawed left leg rolled
the sauropod's torso.

Salmes screamed and threw his rifle to the grating. The guide leveled his Garand. He was no
longer cursing Washman. All of his being was focused on what would be his last shot if he missed
it. Before he could fire, however, the shooting platform slewed sideways. Then they were out of the
path of the charging dinosaur and beginning to
circle with a safe thirty feet of altitude. Below
them, the tyrannosaur clawed dirt as it tried to
follow.

Salmes was crying uncontrollably.

"Ah, want me to hold it here for a shot?" Washman asked nervously.

"We'll go on back to the camp, Don," the guide
said. "We'll talk there, all right?"

"Whatever you say."

Halfway back, Vickers remembered he had not
dropped another marker to replace the one that
was malfunctioning. God knew, that was the least
of his problems.

"You know," Brewer said as he forked torosaur
steaks onto the platter, "it tastes more like buffalo
than beef; but if we could get some breeding stock
back, I'd by God find a market for it!"

Everyone seemed to be concentrating on their meat—good, if pale and lean in comparison with feed-lot steer. "Ah," Vickers said, keeping his voice nonchalant. He looked down at the table instead of the people sitting around it. "Ah, Dieter and I were talking . . . . We'll bunk outside tonight. The, ah, the rest of that pack of dromaeosaurs chased some duckbills through the camp this morning, Steve thinks. So just for safety's sake, we'll both be out of the tent . . . . So, ah, Mrs. Salmes—"

Everyone froze. Jonathan Salmes was turning red. His wife had a forkful of steak poised halfway to her mouth and her eyebrows were rising. The guide swallowed, his eyes still fixed on his plate, and plowed on. "That is, you can have your own tent. Ah, to sleep in."

"Thank you," Adrienne Salmes said cooly, "but I'm quite satisfied with the present arrangements."

Dieter had refused to become involved in this, saying that interfering in the domestic affairs of the Salmes was useless at best. Vickers was sweating now, wishing that there was something to shoot instead of nine pairs of human eyes fixed on him. "Ah," he repeated, "Mrs. Salmes—"

"Mr. Vickers," she overrode him, "who I choose to sleep with—in any sense of the term—is none of your business. Anyone's business," she added with a sharp glance across the table at her husband.

Jonathan Salmes stood up, spilling his coffee cup. His hand closed on his fork; each of the four staff members made unobtrusive preparations. Cursing, Salmes flung the fork down and stalked back to his tent.

The others eased. Vickers muttered, "Christ." Then, "Sorry, Dieter, I . . . ." The thing that bothered him most about the whole incident was that he was unsure whether he would have said anything at all had it been Miss McPherson in Don's bed instead of someone he himself found attractive. Christ . . . .

"Mr. Vickers?" Adrienne Salmes said in a mild voice.

"Umm?" His steak had gotten cold. With Brewer cutting and broiling the meat, the insertion group was eating better than Vickers could ever remember.

"I believe Mr. Brady is scheduled to take me up in the platform tomorrow?"

"Yeah, that's right," Vickers agreed, chewing very slowly.

"I doubt my—husband—will be going out again tomorrow," the blonde woman continued with a nod toward his tent. "Under the circumstances, I think it might be better if Mr. Brady were left behind here at the camp. Instead of Don."

"Steve?" Dieter asked.

Brady shrugged. "Sure, I don't need the flying time. But say—I'm not going to finish ditching around the tents by myself. I've got blisters from today."

"All right," said Dieter. "Henry, you and Don—" no one was looking directly at Washman, who was blushing in embarrassment he had damned well brought on himself—"will take Mrs. Salmes up after the tyrannosaur tomorrow." Vickers and Brady both nodded. "The rest of us will wait here to see if the duckbills come through again as they have become accustomed. Steve, I will help you dig. And if the duckbills have become coy, we will ride down the river margin a little later in the morning and find them. Perhaps Mr. Salmes will feel like going with us by then."

Thank God for Dieter, Vickers thought as he munched another bite of his steak. He could always be counted on to turn an impossible social situation into a smoothly functioning one. There would be no trouble tomorrow after all.

The bulging heads of three torosaurs lay between the gun tower and the fire. There the flames and the guard's presence would keep away the small mammals that foraged in the night. As Miss McPherson followed her brother to their tent, she paused and fingered one of the brow horns of the largest trophy. The tip of the horn was on a level with the dentist's eyes, even though the skull lay on the ground. "They're so huge, so . . . powerful," she said. "And for them to fall when you shoot at them, so many of them falling and running . . . . I could never understand men who, well, who shot animals. But with so many of them everywhere—it's as if you were throwing rocks at the windows of an abandoned house, isn't it? It doesn't seem to hurt anything, and it's . . . an attractive feeling."

"Mary!" objected her brother, shadowed by the great heads.

"Oh, I don't mean I'm sorry that I didn't bring a gun," continued Mary McPherson calmly, her fingers continuing to stroke the smooth black horn. "No, I'm glad I didn't. Because if I had had a gun available this morning, I'm quite sure I would have used it. And after we return, I suppose I would regret that. I suppose." She walked off toward the tent. The rhythms of her low-voiced argument with her brother could be heard until the flaps were zipped.

"Dieter tells me they bagged sixteen torosaurs today," Vickers said. "Even though the intrusion vehicle hasn't room for more than one per client." Only Washman, who had the watch, and Adrienne Salmes were still at the campfire with him.

"*I* bagged one," the woman said with an emphatic flick of her cigar. "Jack Brewer shot five:

and I sincerely hope that idiot Mears hit no more than ten, because that's all Dieter and I managed to finish off for him." She had unpinned her hair as soon as she came in from the field. In the fire-light it rolled across her shoulders like molten amber.

"Dieter said that too," Vickers agreed. He stood, feeling older than usual. "That's why I said 'they'." He turned and began to walk back to the tent where Dieter was already asleep. There had been no point in going through with the charade of sleeping under the stars—overcast, actually—since the dromaeosaurs were daylight predators. They were as unlikely to appear in the camp after dark as the Pope was to speak at a KKK rally.

To the guide's surprise—and to Don Washman's—Adrienne rustled to her feet and followed. "Mr. Vickers," she said, "might I speak to you for a moment, please?"

Vickers looked at her. As the staff members did, and unlike the other clients, the blonde woman carried her weapon with her at all times. "All right," he said. They walked by instinct to the shooting platform, standing thirty feet away at the end of the arc of tents. The torosaur heads were monstrous silhouettes against the fire's orange glow. "Would it bother you as much if I were a man?" she asked bluntly.

"Anything that makes my job harder bothers me," Vickers said in half-truth. "You and Don are making my job harder. That's all."

Adrienne stubbed out her small cigar on the platform's rail. She scattered the remnants of the tobacco on the rocky soil. "Balls," she said distinctly. "Mr. Vickers—Henry, for Christ's sake—my husband was going to be impossible no matter what. He's here because I was going on a time safari and he was afraid to look less of a man than his wife was. Which he is. But he was going to be terrified of his rifle, he was going to pack his trunk with Scotch, and he was going to be a complete prick because that's the way he is."

"Mrs. Salmes—"

"Adrienne, and let me finish. I didn't marry Jonathan for his money—my family has just as much as his does. I won't claim it was a love match, but we . . . we seemed to make a good pair. A matched set, if you will. He won't divorce me—" her dimly-glimpsed index finger forestalled another attempt by the guide to break in—"because he correctly believes I'd tell the judge and the world that he couldn't get it up on our wedding night. Among other things. I haven't divorced him because I've never felt a need to. There are times that it's been marvelously useful to point out that 'I *do* after all have a husband, dearest . . . .'"

"This is none of my business, Mrs. Salmes—"

"Adrienne!"

"Adrienne, dammit!" Vickers burst out. "It's none of my business, but I'm going to say it anyway. You don't have anything to prove. That's fine, we all should be that way. But most of my clients have a lot to prove, to themselves and to the world. Or they wouldn't be down here in the Cretaceous. It makes them dangerous, because they're out of normal society and they may not be the men they hoped they were after all. And your husband is very God damned dangerous, Adrienne. Take my word for it."

"Well, it's not *my* fault," the woman said.

"Fault?" the guide snapped. "Fault? Is it a pusher's fault that kids OD on skag? You're god-damn right it's your fault! It's the fault of everybody involved who doesn't make it better, and you're sure not making it better. Look, you wouldn't treat a gun that way—and your husband is a human being!"

Adrienne frowned in surprise. There was none

of the anger Vickers had expected in her voice when she said, "So are you, Henry. You shouldn't try so hard to hide the fact."

Abruptly, the guide strode toward his tent. Adrienne Salmes watched him go. She took out another cigar, paused, and walked carefully back to the fire where Washman waited with the alarm panel. The pilot looked up with concern. Adrienne sat beside him and shook her hair loose. "Here you go, Don sweetest," she said, extending her cigar. "Why don't you light it for me? It's one of the things you do so well."

Washman kissed her. She returned it, tonguing his lips; but when his hand moved to the zipper of her coveralls, she forced it away. "That's enough until you go off guard duty, dearest," she said. She giggled. "Well—almost enough."

Jonathan Salmes hunched in the shadow of the nearest torosaur head. He listened, pressing his fists to his temples. After several more minutes, he moved in a half-crouch to the shooting platform. In his pocket was a six-inch wooden peg, smooth and close-grained. It was whittled from a root he had worried from the ground with his fingers. Stepping carefully so that his boots did not scrunch on the metal rungs, Salmes mounted the ladder to the pilot's seat. He paused there, his khaki coveralls strained, white face reflecting the flames. The couple near the fire did not look up. The pilot was murmuring something, but his voice was pitched too low to hear . . . and the words might have been unintelligible anyway, given the circumstances.

Jonathan Salmes shuddered also. He moved with a slick grace that belied the terror and disgust frozen on his face. He slipped the dense peg from his pocket. Stretching his right arm out full length while he gripped the rotor shaft left-handed, Salmes forced the peg down between two of the angled blades of the stator. When he was finished, he scrambled back down the ladder. He did not look at his wife and the pilot again, but his ears could not escape Adrienne's contented giggle.

"Hank, she just isn't handling right this morning," Don Washman said. "I'm going to have to blow the fuel lines out when we get back. Must've gotten some trash in the fuel transferring from the bladder to the cans to the tank. Wish to hell we could fuel the bird directly, but I'm damned if I'm going to set down on the intrusion vehicle where it's sitting now."

Vickers glanced down at the treetops and scowled. "Do you think we ought to abort?" he asked. He had not noticed any difference in the flight to that point. Now he imagined they were moving slower and nearer the ground than was usual, and both the rush of air and the muted turbine whine took on sinister notes.

"Oh . . . ," the pilot said. "Well, she's a lot more likely to clear herself than get worse—the crud sinks to the bottom of the tank and gets sucked up first. It'll be okay. I mean, she's just a little sluggish, is all."

The guide nodded. "M—" he began. After his outburst of the night before, he was as embarrassed around Adrienne Salmes as a boy at his first dance. "Ah, Adrienne, what do you think?"

The blonde woman smiled brightly, both for the question and the way it was framed. "Oh, if Don's willing to go on, there's no question," she said. "You know I'd gladly walk if it were the only way to get a tyrannosaurus, Henry—if you'd let me, I mean. We both know that when we go back in today, I've had my last chance at a big carnosaur until you've rotated through all your clients again.

Including my husband."

"We'll get you a tyrannosaur," Vickers said.

Adrienne edged slightly closer to the guide. She said softly, "Henry, I want you to know that when we get back I'm going to give Johnnie a divorce."

Vickers turned away as if slapped. "That's none of my business," he said. "I—I'm sorry for what I said last night."

"Sorry?" the woman repeated in a voice that barely carried over the wind noise. "For making me see that I shouldn't make a doormat of ... someone who used to be important to me? Don't be sorry." After a pause, she continued, "When I ran for Congress ... God I was young! I offended it must have been everybody in the world, much less the district. But Johnnie was fantastic. I owe what votes I got to hands he shook for me."

"I had no right to talk," Vickers said. By forcing himself, he managed to look the blonde woman in the eyes.

Adrienne smiled and touched his hand where it lay on the forestock of his rifle. "Henry," she said, "I'm not perfect, and the world's not going to be perfect either. But I can stop trying to make it actively worse."

Vickers looked at the woman's hand. After a moment, he rotated his own to hold it. "You've spent your life being the best man around," he said, as calm as he would be in the instant of shooting. "I think you've got it in you to be the best person around instead. I'm not the one to talk ... but I think I'd be more comfortable around people if more of them were the way you could be."

With a final squeeze, Vickers released Adrienne's hand. During the remainder of the fifteen-minute flight, he concentrated on the ground below. He almost forgot Washman's concern about the engine.

Dieter Jost flicked a last spadeful of gritty soil from the drainage ditch and paused. Steve Brady gave him a thumbs-up signal from the gun tower where he sat. "Another six inches, peon," he called to the guide. "You need to sweat some."

"Fah," said Dieter, laughing. "If it needs to be deeper, the rain will wash it deeper—not so?" He dug the spade into the ground and began walking over to the table. They had found a cache of sauropod eggs the day before. With the aid of toro-saur loin and freeze-dried spices from his kit, Brewer had turned one of them into a delicious omelet. Brewer, Mears, and the McPhersons were just finishing. Dieter, who had risen early to finish ditching the tents, had worked up quite an appe-tite.

"Hey!" Brady called. Then, louder, "Hey! Mr. Salmes, that's not safe! Come back here, please!"

The guide's automatic rifle leaned against the gun tower. He picked it up. Jonathan Salmes was carrying his own rifle and walking at a deliberate pace down the trail to the water. He did not look around when the guard shouted. The other clients were staring in various stages of concern. Cradling his weapon, Dieter trotted after Salmes. Brady, standing on the six-foot tower, began to ro-tate the heavy machinegun. He stopped when he realized what he was doing.

The guide reached Salmes only fifty yards from the center of the camp, still in sight of the others. He put a hand on the blond man's shoulder and said, "Now, Mr. Salmes—"

Salmes spun like a mousetrap snapping. His face was white. He rang his heavy rifle off Dieter's skull with enough force to tear the stock out of his hands. The guide dropped as if brainshot. Salmes backed away from the fallen man. Then he turned and shambled out of sight among the trees.

"God damn!" Steve Brady said, blinking in surprise. Then he thought of something even more frightening. He unslung his grenade launcher and jumped to the ground without bothering to use the ladder. "If that bastard gets to the intrusion vehicle—" he said aloud, and there was no need for him to finish the statement.

Brady vaulted the guide's body without bothering to look at the injury. The best thing he could do for Dieter now was to keep him from being stranded in the Cretaceous. Brady's hobnails skidded where pine needles overlay rock, but he kept his footing. As the trail twisted around an exceptionally large tree, Brady caught sight of the client again. Salmes was not really running; or rather, he was moving like a man who had run almost to the point of death.

"Salmes, God damn you!" Brady called. He raised the grenade launcher. Two dromaeosaurs burst from opposite sides of the trail where they lay ambushed. Their attention had been on Salmes; but when the guard shouted, they converged on him.

The leftward dromaeosaur launched itself toward its prey in a flat, twenty-foot leap. Only the fact that Brady had his weapon aimed permitted him to disintegrate the beast's head with a point-blank shot. Death did nothing to prevent the beast from disemboweling Brady reflexively. The two mutilated bodies were thrashing in a tangle of blood and intestines as the remaining clients hurtled around the tree. They skidded to a halt. Mr. McPherson, who held Salmes' rifle—his sister had snatched up Dieter's FN a step ahead of him—began to vomit. Neither Salmes nor the other dromaeosaur were visible.

Jonathan Salmes had in fact squelched across the mud and up the ramp of the intrusion vehicle. He had unscrewed the safety cage from the return switch and had his hand poised on the lever. Something clanged on the ramp behind him.

Salmes turned. The dromaeosaur, panicked by the grenade blast that pulped its companion's head, was already in the air. Salmes screamed and threw the switch. The dromaeosaur flung him back against the fuel bladder. As everything around it blurred, the predator picked Salmes up with its forelegs and began methodically to kick him to pieces with its right hind foot. The dinosaur was still in the process of doing so when the submachineguns of the startled guards raked it to death with equal thoroughness.

The broad ribs of the sauropod thrust up from a body cavity that had been cleared of most of its flesh. There was probably another meal on the haunches, even for a beast of the tyrannosaur's voracity. If Adrienne missed the trophy this morning, however, Vickers would have to shoot another herbivore in the vicinity in order to anchor the prize for the next client.

Not that there was much chance that the blonde woman was going to miss.

Adrienne held her rifle with both hands, slanted across her chest. Her hip was braced against the guardrail as she scanned the forest edge. If she had any concern for her balance, it was not evident.

"Okay, down to sixty," Don Washman said, barely enough height to clear the scrub oaks that humped over lower brush in the clearing. The lack of grasses gave the unforested areas of the Cretaceous an open aspect from high altitude. Lower down, the spikes and wooden fingers reached out like a hedge of spears.

The tyrannosaur strode from the pines with a hacking challenge.

"Christ, he's looking for us," the pilot said. The carnosaur slammed aside the ribs of its kill like bowling pins. Its nostrils were flared, and the sound it made was strikingly different from the familiar bellow of earlier occasions.

"Yeah, that's its territorial call," Vickers agreed. "It seems to have decided that we're another tyrannosaur. It's not just talking, it wants our blood."

"S'pose Salmes really hit it yesterday?" Washman asked.

Vickers shook his head absently. "No," he said, "but the way you put the platform in its face after it'd warned us off . . . . Only a tyrannosaur would challenge another tyrannosaur that way. They don't have much brain, but they've got lots of instinctive responses; and the response we've triggered is, well . . . a good one to give us a shot. You ready, Adrienne?"

"Tell me when," the blonde woman said curtly. Washman was swinging the platform in loose figure-8s about 150 yards distant from the carnosaur. They could not circle at their present altitude because they were too low to clear the conifer backdrop. Adrienne aimed the Schultz and Larsen when the beast was on her side of the platform, raising the muzzle again each time the pilot swung onto the rear loop of the figure.

"Don, see if you can draw him out from the woods a little farther," the guide said, squinting past the barrel of his Garand. "I'd like us to have plenty of time to nail him before he can go to ground in the trees."

"Ah, Hank . . . ," the pilot began. Then he went on, "Oh, hell, just don't blow your shots. That's all I ask." He put the controls over and wicked up.

There was a noticeable lag before the turbine responded to the demand for increased power. The section of root slapped as it vibrated from the stator and shot into the rotors spinning at near-maximum velocity.

"If you'll stand over here, Mis—Adrienne," Vickers said, stepping to the back rail of the platform. The client followed with brittle quickness. "When I say shoot," Vickers continued, "aim at the middle of the chest."

Washman had put the platform in an arc toward the tyrannosaur. The big carnivore lunged forward with a series of choppy grunts like an automatic cannon. The pilot rotated the platform on its axis, a maneuver he had carried out a thousand times before. This time the vehicle dipped. It was a sickening, falling-elevator feeling to the two gunners and a heart-stopping terror to the man at the controls who realized it was not caused by clumsiness. The platform began to stagger away from the dinosaur, following the planned hyperbola but lower and slower than intended.

"Nail him," Vickers said calmly, sighting his rifle on the green-mottled sternum for the backup shot.

Partial disintegration of the turbine preceded the shot by so little that the two seemed a single event. Both gunners were thrown back from the rail. Something whizzed through the side of the turbine and left a jagged rent in the housing. Adrienne Salmes' bullet struck the tyrannosaur in the lower belly.

"Hang on!" Don Washman shouted needlessly. "I'm going to try—"

He pulled the platform into another arc, clawing for altitude. To get back to camp they had to climb over the pine forest that lay between. No one knew

better than the pilot how hopeless that chance
was. Several of the turbine blades had separated
from the hub. Most of the rest were brushes of
boron fiber now, their casing matrices destroyed
by the peg or harmonics induced by the imbal-
ance. But Washman had to try, and in any case
they were curving around the wounded tyrannosaur while it was still—.

The whole drive unit tore itself free of the rest of
the shooting platform. Part of it spun for a
moment with the rotor shafts before sailing off in
a direction of its own. Had it not been for the oak
tree in their path, the vehicle might have smashed
into the ground from fifty feet and killed everyone
aboard. On the other hand, Don Washman just
might have been able to get enough lift from the
auto-rotating blades to set them down on an even
keel. Branches snagged the mesh floor of the platform and the vehicle nosed over into the treetop.

They were all shouting, but the din of bursting
metal and branches overwhelmed mere human
noise. Vickers held the railing with one hand and
the collar of his client's garment with the other.
Both of the rifles were gone. The platform continued to tilt until the floor would have been vertical had it not been so crumpled. Adrienne Salmes
was supported entirely by the guide. "For God's
sake!" she screamed. "Let go or we'll go over *with*
it!"

Vickers' face was red with the impossible strain.
He forced his eyes down, feeling as if even that
minuscule added effort would cause his body to
tear. Adrienne was right. They were better off
dropping onto a lower branch—or even to the
ground forty feet below—than they would be
somersaulting down in the midst of jagged metal.
The platform was continuing to settle as branches
popped. Vickers let go of the blonde woman.

Screaming at the sudden release of half the load, he loosed his other hand from the rail.

The guide's eyes were shut in a pain reflex. His chest hit a branch at an angle that saved his ribs but took off a plate-sized swatch of skin without harming his tunic's tough fabric. He snatched convulsively at the limb. Adrienne, further out on the same branch, seized him by the collar and armpit. Both her feet were locked around the branch. She took the strain until the guide's overstressed muscles allowed him to get a leg up. The branch swayed, but the tough oak held.

Don Washman was strapped into his seat. Now he was staring straight down and struggling with the jammed release catch. Vickers reached for the folding knife he carried in a belt pouch. He could not reach the pilot, though. "Don, cut the strap!" he shouted.

A large branch split. The platform tumbled outward and down, striking on the top of the rotor shafts. The impact smashed the lightly-built aircraft into a tangle reeking of kerosene. Don Washman was still caught in the middle of it.

The limb on which Vickers and Adrienne Salmes balanced was swaying in harmony with the whole tree. When the thrashing stopped, the guide sat up and eyed the trunk. He held his arms crossed tightly over his chest, each hand squeezing the opposite shoulder as if to reknit muscles which felt as if they had been pulled apart. Nothing was moving in the wreckage below. Vickers crawled to the crotch. He held on firmly while he stepped to a branch three feet lower down.

"Henry," Adrienne Salmes said.

"Just wait, I've got to get him out," Vickers said. He swung down to a limb directly beneath him, trying not to wince when his shoulders fell below the level of his supporting hands.

"Henry!" the blonde woman repeated more urgently. "The tyrannosaur!"

Vickers jerked his head around. He could see nothing but patterns of light and the leaves that surrounded him. He realized that the woman had been speaking from fear, not because she actually saw anything. There was no likelihood that the carnosaur would wander away from its kill, even to pursue a rival. Adrienne, who did not understand the beast's instincts, in her fear imagined it charging toward them. The guide let himself down from the branch on which he sat, falling the last five feet to the ground.

Adrienne thought Vickers must have struck his head during the crash. From her vantage point, thirty feet in the air and well outboard on the limb that supported her, she had an excellent view of the tyrannosaur. Only low brush separated it from the tree in which they had crashed. The beast had stood for a moment at the point Washman lifted the platform in his effort to escape. Now it was ramping like a creature from heraldry, balanced on one leg with its torso high and the other hind leg kicking out at nothing. At first she did not understand; then she saw that each time the foot drew back, it caressed the wounded belly.

Suddenly the big carnivore stopped rubbing itself. It had been facing away from the tree at a 30° angle. Now it turned toward the woman, awesome even at three hundred yards. It began to stalk forward. Its head swung low as usual, but after each few strides the beast paused. The back raised, the neck stretched upward, and now Adrienne could see that the nostrils were spreading. A leaf, dislodged when Vickers scrambled to the ground, was drifting down. The light breeze angled it toward the oncoming dinosaur.

Vickers cut through one of the lower cross-straps holding Washman five feet in the air with his seat above him. The pilot was alive but unconscious. The guide reached up for the remaining strap, his free hand and forearm braced against the pilot's chest to keep him from dropping on his face.

"Henry, for God's sake!" the woman above him shouted. "It's only a hundred yards away!"

Vickers stared at the wall of brush, his lips drawn back in a snarl. "Where are the guns? Can you see the guns?"

"I can't see them! Get back, for God's sake!"

The guide cursed and slashed through the strap. To take Washman's weight, he dropped his knife and bent. Grunting, Vickers manhandled the pilot into position for a fireman's carry.

The tyrannosaur had lowered its head again. Adrienne Salmes stared at the predator, then down at Vickers staggering under the pilot's weight. She fumbled out one of her small cigars, lit it, and dropped the gold-chased lighter back into her pocket. Then she scrambled to the bole and began to descend. The bark tore the skin beneath her coveralls and from the palms of both hands.

From the lowest branch, head-height for the stooping Vickers, Adrienne cried, "Here!" and tried to snatch Washman from the guide's back. The pilot was too heavy. Vickers thrust his shoulders upward. Between them, they slung Washman onto the branch. His arms and legs hung down to either side and his face was pressed cruelly into the bark.

The tyrannosaur crashed through the woody undergrowth twenty feet away. It stank of death, even against the mild breeze. The dead sauropod, of course, rotting between the four-inch teeth and smeared greasily over the killer's head and breast

. . . but beyond the carrion odor was a tangible sharpness filling the mouths of guide and client as the brush parted.

Vickers had no chance of getting higher into the oak than the jaws could pick him off. Instead he turned, wishing that he had been able to keep at least his knife for this moment. Adrienne Salmes dragged on her cigar, stood, and flung the glowing cylinder into the wreckage of the platform: "Henry!" she cried, and she bent back down with her hand out to Vickers.

One stride put the tyrannosaur into the midst of the up-ended platform. As flimsy as the metal was, its edges were sharp and they clung instead of springing back the way splintered branches would. The beast's powerful legs had pistoned it through dense brush without slowing. It could still have dragged the wreckage forward through the one remaining step that would have ended the three humans. Instead, it drew back with a startled snort and tried to nuzzle its feet clear.

The kerosene bloomed into a sluggish red blaze. The tyrannosaur's distended nostrils *whuffed* in a double lungful of the soot-laden smoke that rolled from the peaks of the flames. The beast squealed and kicked in berserk fury, scattering fire-wrapped metal. Its rigid tail slashed the brush, fanning the flames toward the oak. Deeply-indented leaves shrivelled like hands closing. Vickers forgot about trying to climb. He rolled Don Washman off the branch again, holding him by the armpits. The pilot's feet fell as they would. "While we've got a chance!" the guide cried, knowing that the brush fire would suffocate them in the treetop even if the flames themselves did not climb so high.

Adrienne Salmes jumped down. Each of them wrapped one of the pilot's arms around their shoulders. They began to stumble through the brush, the backs of their necks prickling with the heat of the fire.

The tyrannosaur was snarling in unexampled rage. Fire was familiar to a creature which had lived a century among forests and lightning. Being caught in the midst of a blaze was something else again. The beast would not run while the platform still tangled its feet, and the powerful kicks that shredded the binding metal also scattered the flames. When at last the great killer broke free, it did so from the heart of an amoeba a hundred yards in diameter crackling in the brush. Adrienne and the guide were struggling into the forest when they heard the tyrannosaur give its challenge again. It sounded far away.

"I don't suppose there's any way we could retrieve the rifles," Adrienne said as Vickers put another stick on their fire. It was a human touch in the Cretaceous night. Besides, the guide was chilly. They had used his coveralls to improvise a stretcher for Washman, thrusting a pruned sapling up each leg and out the corresponding sleeve. They had not used the pilot's own garment for fear that being stripped would accelerate the effects of shock. Washman was breathing stertorously and had not regained consciousness since the crash.

"Well, I couldn't tell about yours," Vickers said with a wry smile, "but even with the brush popping I'm pretty sure I heard the magazine of mine go off. I'd feel happier if we had it along, that's for sure."

"I'm going to miss that Schultz and Larsen," the woman said. She took out a cigar, looked at it, and slipped it back into her pocket. "Slickest action they ever put on a rifle. Well, I suppose I can find another when we get back."

They had found the saplings growing in a sauropod burn. Fortunately, Adrienne had retained her sheath knife, a monster with a saw-backed, eight-inch blade that Vickers had thought a joke—until it became their only tool. The knife and the cigaret lighter, he reminded himself. Resiny wood cracked, pitching sparks beyond the circle they had cleared in the fallen needles. The woman immediately stood and kicked the spreading flames back in toward the center.

"You saved my life," Vickers said, looking into the fire. "With that cigar. You were thinking a lot better than I was, and that's the only reason I'm not in a carnosaur's belly."

Adrienne sat down beside the guide. After a moment, he met her eyes. She said, "You could have left Don and gotten back safely yourself."

"I could have been a goddam politician!" Vickers snapped, "but that wasn't a way I wanted to live my life." He relaxed and shook his head. "Sorry," he said. She laughed and squeezed his bare knee above the abrasion. "Besides," Vickers went on, "I'm not sure it would have worked. The damned tyrannosaur was obviously tracking us by scent. Most of what we know about the big carnivores started a minute or two before they were killed. They . . . I don't mean dinos're smart. But their instincts are a lot more efficient than you'd think if you hadn't watched them."

Adrienne Salmes nodded. "A computer isn't smart either, but that doesn't keep it from solving problems."

"Exactly," Vickers said, "exactly. And if the problem that tyrannosaur was trying to solve was us—well, I'm just as glad the fire wiped out our scent. We've got a long hike tomorrow lugging Don."

"What bothers me," the blonde woman said carefully, "is the fact it could find us easily enough if it tried. Look, we can't be very far from the camp, not at the platform's speed. Why don't we push on now instead of waiting for daylight?"

Vickers glanced down at the responder on his wrist, tuned to the beacon in the center of the camp. "Five or six miles," he said. "Not too bad, even with Don. But I think we're better off here than stumbling into camp in the dark. The smell of the trophies is going to keep packs of the smaller predators around it. They're active in the dark, and they've got damned sharp teeth."

Adrienne chuckled, startling away some of the red eyes ringing their fire. Vickers had whittled a branch into a whippy cudgel with an eye toward bagging a mammal or two for dinner, but both he and his client were too thirsty to feel much hunger as yet. "Well," she said, "we have to find something else to do till daybreak, then—and I'm too keyed up to sleep." She touched Vickers' thigh again.

All the surrounding eyes vanished when a dinosaur grunted.

It could have been a smaller creature, even an herbivore; but that would not have made it harmless. In the event, it was precisely what they feared it was when the savage noise filled the forest: the tyrannosaur hunting them and very close.

The fire was of branches and four-foot lengths of sapling they had broken after notching with the knife. Vickers' face lost all expression. He grabbed the unburned end of a billet and turned toward the sound. "No!" Adrienne cried. "Spread the fire in a line—it won't follow us through a fire again!"

It was the difference between no good chance and no chance at all. Vickers scuffed a bootload of coals out into the heaped pine needles and ran into the night with his brand. The lowest branches of the pines were dead and dry, light-starved by the

foliage nearer the sky. The resin-sizzling torch
caught them and they flared up behind the guide.
Half-burned twigs that fell to the forest floor
flickered among the matted needles. Vickers already was twenty yards from their original campfire when he remembered that Don Washman still
lay helpless beside it.

The dozen little fires Vickers had set, and the
similar line Adrienne Salmes had ignited on the
other side of the campfire, were already beginning
to grow and merge. The guide turned and saw the
flames nearing Washman's feet, though not—
thank God—his head. That was when the tyrannosaur stepped into view. In the firelight it was hard
to tell the mottled camouflage natural to its hide
from the cracked and blistered areas left by the
earlier blaze. Vickers cursed and hurled his torch.
It spun end over end, falling short of its intended
target.

The tyrannosaur had been advancing with its
head hung low. It was still fifteen feet high at the
hips. In the flickering light, it bulked even larger
than the ten tons it objectively weighed. Adrienne
looked absurd and tiny as she leaped forward to
meet the creature with a pine torch. Behind her
the flames were spreading, but they were unlikely
to form a barrier to the beast until they formed a
continuous line. That was seconds or a minute
away, despite the fact that the fuel was either dry
or soaking with pitch.

Adrienne slashed her brand in a figure-8 like a
child with a sparkler. Confused by the glare and
stench of the resinous flames, the carnosaur
reared back and took only a half step forward—
onto the torch Vickers had thrown.

The guide grabbed up the poles at Washman's
head. He dragged the pilot away from the fire like
a pony hauling a travois. When the tyrannosaur
screeched, Vickers dropped the stretcher again

and turned, certain he would see the beast striding easily through the curtain of fire. Instead it was backing away, its great head slashing out to either side as if expecting to find a tangible opponent there. The blonde woman threw her torch at the dinosaur. Then, with her arms shielding her face, she leaped across the fire. She would have run into the bole of a tree had Vickers not caught her as she blundered past. "It's all right!" he shouted. "It's turned! Get the other end of the stretcher."

Spattering pitch had pocked but not fully ignited Adrienne's garments. The tears furrowing the soot on her cheeks were partly the result of irritants in the flames. "It'll be back," she said. "You know it will."

"I'll have a rifle in my hands the next time I see it," the guide said. "This is one dino that won't be a matter of business to shoot."

The alarm awakened the camp. Then muzzle flashes lit the white faces of the clients when the first dinosaur trotted down the trail. Even the grenade launcher could not divert the monsters. After a long time, the gunfire slackened. Then Miss McPherson returned with additional ammunition.

Somewhat later, the shooting stopped for good.

If he had not been moving in a stupor, the noise of the scavengers would have warned Vickers. As it was, he pushed out of the trees and into a slaughteryard teeming with vermin on a scale with the carcasses they gorged on. Only when Mears cried out did the guide realize they were back in the camp. The four clients were squeezed together on top of the machinegun tower.

Vickers was too shocked to curse. He set down his end of the stretcher abruptly. The other end was already on the ground. "Henry, do you want

the knife?" Adrienne asked. He shook his head
without turning around.

There were at least a dozen torosaurs sprawled
on the northern quadrant of the camp, along the
trail. They were more like hills than anything that
had been alive, but explosive bullets from the 12.7
mm machinegun had opened them up like chain-
saws. The clients were shouting and waving rifles
in the air from the low tower. Vickers, only fifty
feet away, could not hear them because of the
clatter of the scavengers. There were well over one
hundred tons of carrion in the clearing. Literally
thousands of lesser creatures had swarmed out of
the skies and the forest to take advantage.

'Lesser' did not mean 'little' in the Cretaceous.

Vickers swallowed. "Can you carry Don alone if
I lead the way?" he asked. "We've got to get to the
others to find out what happened."

"I'll manage," the woman said. Then, "You
know, they must have fired off all their ammunition. That's why they're huddled there beside—"

"I know what they goddam did!" the guide
snarled. "I also know that if there's one goddam
round left, we've got a chance to sort things out!"
Neither of them voiced the corollary. They had
heard the tyrannosaur challenge the dawn an hour
earlier. Just before they burst into the clearing,
they had heard a second call; and it was much
closer.

Adrienne knelt, locking one of the pilot's arms
over her shoulders. She straightened at the knees,
lifting her burden with her. Washman's muscles
were slack. "That's something I owe my husband
for," Adrienne gasped. "Practice moving drunks.
When I was young and a fool."

Vickers held one of the stretcher poles like a
quarterstaff. He knew how he must look in his

underwear. That bothered him obscurely almost as much as the coming gauntlet of carrion-eaters did.

A white-furred pterosaur with folded, twenty-foot wings struck at the humans as they maneuvered between two looming carcasses. Vickers slapped away the red, chisel-like beak with his staff. Then he prodded the great carrion-eater again for good measure as Adrienne staggered around it. The guide began to laugh.

"What the hell's so funny?" she demanded.

"If there's an intrusion vehicle back there," Vickers said, "which there probably isn't or these sheep wouldn't be here now, maybe I'll send everybody home without me. That way I don't have to explain to Stern what went wrong."

"That's a hell of a joke!" Adrienne snapped.

"Who's joking?"

Because of the huge quantity of food, the scavengers were feeding without much squabbling. The three humans slipped through the mass, challenged only by the long-necked pterosaur. Fragile despite its size, the great gliding creature defended its personal space with an intensity that was its only road to survival. Met with equal force, it backed away of necessity.

Dieter Jost lay under the gun tower, slightly protected by the legs and crossbraces. He was mumbling in German and his eyes did not focus. Vickers took the pilot's weight to set him by the ladder. Mears hopped down and began shrieking at Adrienne Salmes, "God damn you, your crazy husband took the time machine back without us, you bitch!"

Vickers straightened and slapped the contractor with a blow that released all the frustrations that had been building. Mears stumbled against the tower, turned back with his fists bunched, and stopped. The blonde woman's knife was almost touching his ribs.

"Where's Steve?" the guide asked loudly. He was massaging his right palm with his left as if working a piece of clay between them.

Miss McPherson jumped to the ground. In the darkness the tower had drawn them. Since both boxes of 12.7 mm ammunition had been sluiced out into the night, it was obviously irrational to stay on a platform that would not reach a tyrannosaur's knee . . . but human reason is in short supply in a darkened forest. "One of the dinosaurs killed him," the older woman blurted. "We, we tried to keep Mr. Jost safe with us, but we ran out of bullets and, and, the last hour has been—"

Brewer had a cut above his right eyebrow. He looked shell-shocked but not on the edge of hysteria as his three companions were. "When it was light enough to search," he said, "I got your ammo out. I thought it might work in his—" he gestured toward Dieter beneath him—"rifle. Close but no cigar." The meat packer's fingers traced the line which a piece of bursting cartridge case had drawn across his scalp.

"Well, we put the fear of God into 'em," Mears asserted sullenly. "They've been afraid to come close even though we're out of ammo now. But how d'we get *out* of here, I want to know!"

"We don't," Vickers said flatly. "If the intrusion vehicle's gone, we are well and truly screwed. Because there's never yet been an insertion within a hundred years of another insertion. But we've got a closer problem than that, because—"

The tyrannosaur drowned all other sounds with its roar.

Vickers stepped into the nearer of the ponies without changing expression. The engine caught when he pushed the starter. "Adrienne," he said, "get the rest of them down to the slough—Don and Dieter in the pony. Fast. If I don't come back, you're on your own."

Adrienne jumped in front of the vehicle. "We'll both go."

"God damn it, *move!*" the guide shouted. "We don't have time!"

"We don't know which of us it's tracking!" the woman shouted back. "I've got to come along!"

Vickers nodded curtly. "Brewer," he called over his shoulder, "get everybody else out of here before a pack of carnosaurs arrives and you're in the middle of it." He engaged the pony's torque converter while the blonde woman was barely over the side. As they spun out southward from the camp, the guide shouted, "Don't leave Don and Dieter behind, or so help me—"

"How fast can it charge?" Adrienne asked as they bounced over a root to avoid a tangle of berry bushes.

"Fast," Vickers said bluntly. "I figure if we can reach the sauropods we killed the other day, we've got a chance, though."

They were jouncing too badly for Adrienne to stay in a seat. She squatted behind Vickers and hung onto the sides. "If you think the meat's going to draw it off, won't it stop in the camp?" she asked.

"Not that," said the guide, slamming over the tiller to skirt a ravine jeweled with flecks of quartz. "I'm betting there'll be gorgosaurs there by now, feeding. That's how we'd have gotten carnosaur heads for the other gunners, you see. The best chance I can see is half a dozen gorgosaurs'll take care of even *our* problem."

"They'll take care of us too, won't they?" the woman objected.

"Got a better idea?"

The smell of the rotting corpses would have guided them the last quarter mile even without the marker. The tyrannosaur's own kill had been several days riper, but the sheer mass of the five titanosaurs together more than equalled the effect. The nearest of the bodies lay with its spine toward the approaching pony in a shaft of sunlight through the browsed-away top cover. Vickers throttled back with a curse. "If there's nothing here," he said, "then we may as well bend over and kiss our asses goo—"

A carnosaur raised its gory head over the carrion. It had been buried to its withers in the sauropod's chest, bolting bucket-loads of lung tissue. Its original color would have been in doubt had not a second killer stalked into sight. The gorgosaurs wore black stripes over fields of dirty sand color, and their tongues were as red as their bloody teeth. Each of the pair was as heavy as a large automobile, and they were as viciously lethal as leopards, pound for pound.

"All right," Vickers said quietly. He steered to the side of the waiting pair, giving the diesel a little more fuel. Three more gorgosaurs strode watchfully out of the forest. They were in an arc facing the pony. The nearest of them was only thirty feet away. Their breath rasped like leather pistons. The guide slowed again, almost to a stop. He swung the tiller away.

One of the gorgosaurs snarled and charged. Both humans shouted, but the killer's target was the tyrannosaur that burst out of the forest behind the pony. Vickers rolled the throttle wide open, sending the vehicle between two of the lesser carnivores. Instead of snapping or bluffing, the tyrannosaur strode through the gorgosaur that had tried to meet it. The striped carnosaur spun to the ground with its legs flailing. Pine straw sprayed as it hit.

"It's still coming!" Adrienne warned. Vickers hunched as if that could coax more speed out of the little engine. The four gorgosaurs still able to run had scattered to either side. The fifth threshed on the ground, its back broken by an impact the tyrannosaur had scarcely noted. At another time the pack might have faced down their single opponent. Now the wounded tyrannosaur was infuriated beyond questions of challenge and territory.

"Henry, the river," the woman said. Vickers did not change direction, running parallel to the unseen bank. "Henry," she said again, trying to steady herself close to his ear because she did not want to shout, not for this, "we've done everything else we could. We have to try this."

A branch lashed Vickers across the face. His tears streamed across the red brand it left on his cheek. He turned as abruptly as the pony's narrow axles allowed. They plunged to the right, over the ridgeline and into the thick-set younger trees that bordered the water. Then they were through that belt, both of them bleeding from the whipping branches. Reeds and mud were roostering up from all four wheels. The pony's aluminum belly began to lift. Their speed dropped as the treads started to act as paddles automatically.

"Oh dear God, he's stopping, he's stopping," Adrienne whimpered. Vickers looked over his shoulder. There was nothing to dodge now that they were afloat, only the mile of haze and water that they would never manage to cross. The tyrannosaur had paused where the pines gave way to reeds, laterite soil to mud. It stood splay-legged, turning first one eye, then the other, to the escaping humans. The bloody sun jeweled its pupils.

"If he doesn't follow—" Vickers said.

The tyrannosaur stepped forward inexorably. The muddy water slapped as the feet slashed through it. Then the narrow keel of the breastbone cut the water as well. The tyrannosaur's back sank to a line of knobs on the surface, kinking horizontally as the hind legs thrust the beast toward its prey. The carnosaur moved much more quickly in the water than did the vehicle it pursued. The beast was fifty yards away, now, and there was no way to evade it.

They were far enough out into the stream that Vickers could see the other pony winking on the bank a half mile distant. Brewer had managed to get them out of the charnel house they had made of the camp, at least. "Give me your knife," Vickers said. Twenty feet away, the ruby eye of the carnosaur glazed and cleared as its nicitating membrane wiped away the spray.

"Get your own damned knife!" Adrienne said. She half-rose, estimating that if she jumped straight over the stern she would not overset the pony.

Vickers saw the water beneath them darken, blacken. The pony quivered. There was no wake, but the tons of death slanting up from beneath raised a slick on the surface. They were still above the crocodile's vast haunches when its teeth closed on the tyrannosaur.

The suction of the tyrannosaur going under halted the pony as if it had struck a wall. Then the water rose and slapped them forward. Vickers' hand kept Adrienne from pitching out an instant after she had lost the need to do so. They drew away from the battle in the silt-golden water, fifty yards, one hundred. Vickers cut off the engine. "The current'll take us to the others," he explained. "And without the paddles we won't attract as much attention."

Adrienne was trying to resheathe her knife. Finally she held the leather with one hand and slipped the knife in with her fingers on the blade as if threading a needle. She looked at Vickers. "I didn't think that would work," she said. "Or it would work a minute after we were . . . gone."

The guide managed to laugh. "Might still happen," he said, nodding at the disturbed water. "Off-hand, though, I'd say the 'largest land predator of all time' just met something bigger." He sobered. "God, I hope we don't meet its mate. I don't want to drown. I really don't."

Water spewed skyward near the other pony. At first Vickers thought one of the clients had managed to detonate a grenade and blow them all to hell. "My God," Adrienne whispered. "You said they couldn't . . . ."

At the distance they were from it, only the gross lines of the intrusion vehicle could be identified. A pair of machineguns had been welded onto the frame, and there appeared to be a considerable party of uniformed men aboard. "I don't understand it either," Vickers said, "but I know where to ask." He reached for the starter.

Adrienne caught his arm. He looked back in surprise. "If it was safer to drift with the current before, it's still safer," she said. She pointed at the subsiding froth from which the tyrannosaur had never re-emerged. "We're halfway already. And besides, it gives us some time—" she put her hand on Vickers' shoulder—"for what I had in mind last night at the campfire."

"They're watching us with binoculars!" the guide sputtered, trying to break away from the kiss.

"They can all sit in a circle and play with themselves," the blonde woman said. "We've earned this."

Vickers held himself rigid for a moment. Then he reached out and began to spread the pony's front awning with one hand.

The secretary wore a uniform and a pistol. When he nodded, Vickers opened the door. Stern sat at the metal desk. Dr. Galil was to his right and the only other occupant of the room. Vickers sat gingerly on one of the two empty chairs.

"I'm not going to debrief you," Stern said. "Others have done that. Rather, I am going to tell you certain things. They are confidential. Utterly confidential. You understand that."

"Yes," Vickers said. Stern's office was not in the Ministry of Culture and Tourism; but then, Vickers had never expected that it would be.

"Dr. Galil," Stern continued, and the cherubic scientist beamed like a Christmas ornament, "located the insertion party by homing on the alpha waves of one of the members of it. You, to be precise. Frankly, we were all amazed at this breakthrough; it is not a technique we would have tested if there had been any alternative available."

Vickers licked his lips. "I thought you were going to fire me," he said flatly.

"Would it bother you if we did?" Stern riposted.

"Yes." The guide paused. The fear was greater now that he had voiced it. He had slept very little during the week since the curtailed safari had returned. "It—the job ... suits me. Even dealing with the clients, I can do it. For having the rest."

Stern nodded. Galil whispered to him, then looked back at Vickers. "We wish to experiment with this effect," Stern continued aloud. "Future rescues—or resupplies—may depend on it. There are other reasons as well." He cleared his throat.

"There is the danger that we will not be able to consistently repeat the operation," Dr. Galil broke in. "That the person will be marooned, you see. For there must of course be a brain so that we will have a brain wave to locate. Thus we need a volunteer."

"You want a base line," Vickers said in response to what he had not been told. "You want to refine your calibration so that you can drop a man—or men—or tanks—at a precise time. And if your base line is in the Cretaceous instead of the present, you don't have the problem of closing off another block each time somebody is inserted into the future before you get the technique down pat."

Stern grew very still. "Do you volunteer?" he asked.

Vickers nodded. "Sure. Even if I thought you'd let me leave here alive if I didn't, I'd volunteer. For that. I should have thought of the—the research potential—myself. I'd have blackmailed you into sending me."

The entryway door opened unexpectedly. "I already did that, Henry," said Adrienne Salmes. "Though I wouldn't say their arms had to be twisted very hard." She stepped past Vickers and laid the small receiver on Stern's desk beside the sending unit. "I decided it was time to come in."

"You arranged this for me?" Vickers asked in amazement.

"I arranged it for us," Adrienne replied, seating herself on the empty chair. "I'm not entirely sure that I want to retire to the Cretaceous. But—" she looked sharply at Stern—"I'm quite sure that I don't want to live in the world our friends here will shape if they do gain complete ability to manipulate the past. At least in the Cretaceous, we know what the rules are."

Vickers stood. "Shlomo," he said shaking Dr. Galil's hand, "you haven't failed before, and I don't see you failing now. We won't be marooned.

Though it might be better if we were." He turned to the man behind the desk. "Mr. Stern," he said, "you've got your volunteers. I—we—we'll get you a list of the supplies we'll need."

Adrienne touched his arm. "This will work, you know," she said. She took no notice of the others in the room. "Like the crocodile."

"Tell me in a year's time that it *has* worked," Vickers said.

And she did.

Part III

BOUNDARY LAYER

The great carnivore's jaws slammed like a tomb door. "Henry," said Adrienne Vickers, "the drug's wearing off. We're going to have a very angry tyrannosaurus in a moment." The blonde woman's voice was slightly louder than was necessary to be heard over the unmuffled blatting of the crawler's diesel. She lowered the muzzle of her rifle, well aware that if she stretched the weapon out at arm's length, it would rap the dinosaur's jagged yellow teeth.

Henry Vickers risked a brief look over his shoulder. Although the crawler moved at little more than a fast walk, it was twelve feet wide and the forest had not been cleared for its passage. The last thing the hunter wanted was to have to back the articulated vehicle, especially if the tyrannosaur shackled to the bed was really awakening. "Umm," he said to his wife, "it's probably just reflex. Anyway, we don't have much farther to go. Give it another jolt from the capture gun if you

have to—" he ran a finger down the barrel of the
smoothbore clipped to the crawler's splash board
—"but we don't want it to overdose and die on us."

"We don't want it to wake up and eat us, either,"
the blonde woman said tartly. She was standing,
facing backward in the open cab of the vehicle.
Her buttocks rested on the rim of the splashboard.
"Besides, it'll die a few days after they get it back
Topside anyway. From the fungus or whatever.
You know that."

Thus far, the dinosaur's yawn did seem to have
been an isolated incident, Vickers thought. He
counter-steered to square off his approach to the
gap between two huge pine trees. "They may have
cured that problem by now," he said, keeping his
voice more reasonable than he felt. The tyrannosaur's teeth *were* very close to his back, and he too
was far from certain that the shackles would hold
if the creature lunged with all its strength. "Anyway, Adrienne, even if it dies, we'll have brought
back a live tyrannosaur. That . . . that's worth
having done, I think. I don't need to apologize for
the things I've brought in dead, but . . . I think this
is worth doing." After a pause he added, "Besides
—I trust you to handle our friend if he gets ram-
bunctious."

Adrienne snorted, but she smiled as well. The
flattery showed affection; and in addition, it was
true. Vickers' back was turned toward an eight-
ton predator, with nothing but his wife's cool accuracy to save him if the creature broke free.
"Well," the tall blonde said, "if it were me, they'd
make do Topside with something a lot easier to
handle than this boy, at least until I was sure they
could keep it alive themselves. But I suppose I can
humor you this once."

The crawler bulled into, then mounted, the de-
caying mass of a fallen tree. Vickers had climbed

the obstacle on the way out, racing from camp toward the drug-numbed tyrannosaur. Until he had returned with the crawler, his wife had to guard the creature alone and fend off lesser predators. The vehicle's bed, a twelve by fifty-foot trough on six axles, had been empty the first time it encountered the tree bole. Now . . . the crawler had carried heavier loads: adult torosaurs with horns like flint spears, and once an immature sauropod which weighed at least twelve tons. Never before, however, had the cargo been so potentially dangerous if it awakened before being unloaded into the holding cage at the permanent camp.

The diesel bellowed as the tracks of the cab unit bit, spewing fibers of russet, rotting wood over the bed and its burden. Then the log gave way and the multiple wheels lurched over its remains, squealing and creaking like sows at the trough.

There were no other problems before the crawler snorted out of the forest into the large clearing of the base camp. "Home is the hunter," Adrienne murmured ironically as she glanced over her own shoulder. But it *was* home to the pair of them, though it had few enough amenities. They had never even bothered to name it. For safety from the things that rushed to water and the things that preyed on them there, the camp had been built five hundred feet from the river. The current drove rams that lifted water into a settling tank. Purification had proven unnecessary: repeated testing had failed to turn up any microbes which would be harmful to humans who had evolved some seventy million years in the future.

The house itself was on posts three feet high to discourage some of the nastier vermin. For a hundred yards in every direction stretched a belt of broad-leafed ground cover akin to ivy. Adrienne had wanted grass, but the Israeli officials Topside had vetoed the notion. True grasses had appeared in the Eocene, ten or so million years further up the line. It was no secret—to the pair of them in the Cretaceous base camp—that the intentions of the scientists working on time intrusion, and the orders of the government officials above them, were to modify the present by selectively changing the past. The potential for change from the early introduction of grass was considerable and of utterly unguessable direction. It was not a chance that those in charge were willing to risk for aesthetics.

There was a twenty-meter patch of raw earth and sand, well to the west of the house: the impact point for the intrusion vehicles which served as the only communication between the station and Topside. Topside was what had been the present when Vickers and Adrienne had volunteered to run a permanent base in the Cretaceous. When an intrusion vehicle impacted, everything within the sphere of its field was exchanged with an identical sphere at the impact point. On one-shot hunting intrusions, that was of no significance. Here, where repeated transfers would otherwise have dug a deepening pit in the Cretaceous soil, it had been necessary to stack the return point in the hangar Topside with sandbags. Vickers sometimes wondered what effect the synthetic fabric of the bags would have had if it had been discovered in Cretaceous strata during the historical past. But it hadn't, of course; and if the non-degradable plastic *had* been dug up in 1920, say, then that fact would simply have become part of the present in which Dr. Shlomo Galil of Cambridge University developed a technique of time intrusion.

At least, that was one theory.

Vicker's declutched the left track to swing the

crawler wide around the impact point. The next
intrusion was not due for forty hours, but there
was no reason to take chances with an effect that
could lop you into pieces separated by seventy
million years. Adrienne looked from the holding
cage they were approaching back to the slack-
muscled tyrannosaur. "Well," she said, "you were
right, Henry. Though I'd as soon you were as careful with your own safety as you used to be with
your clients'."

If Vickers intended a reply, it was lost in the
hissing of a corona discharge. An intrusion vehicle
was appearing almost two days early.

Vickers halted the crawler in surprise, just
short of the gate of the great steel holding cage.
Adrienne touched her husband's shoulder. Her
eyes were back on their drugged captive. "Run it
in, Henry," she said. "They won't be ready to load
for a while anyway—" though the sides of the intrusion vehicle were down and the platform
looked empty save for six passengers—"and I
don't want our friend to lie here with just the
chains to hold him. Not any longer than he has to."

The hunter nodded and drove on into the cage.
He left the tyrannosaur shackled and the crawler
in the cage instead of driving it out the far end
empty. The two humans exited through the
narrow escape hatch in time to meet their visitors
in front of the house.

Five of the newcomers were young men in
fatigue uniforms, glancing about nervously at the
lowering forest as if they expected a pack of
carnosaurs to burst upon them. The sixth man's
name was Avraham Stern, and he was head of the
Time Intrusion Project. Only in its advertising was
that project primarily concerned with safaris of
rich civilians entering the past to hunt the biggest
of game. Stern was a dumpy, bulky man who

looked as uncomfortable in fatigues as he usually did in a business suit. "Mrs. Salmes," he said, "Mr. Vickers, good day. I regret to surprise you this way."

The captive dinosaur was beginning to gurgle with increasing power. Stern and the Vickers ignored it, but the five young soldiers edged together instinctively. "Events," Stern continued, "require that we borrow you from the, ah, habitat phase for a time. Since that means closing down this station, I thought it best to inform you in person. I have brought these gentlemen—" he nodded toward the clustered soldiers—"to aid in carrying materials to the intrusion vehicle."

"What do you mean, 'close down the station'?" Vickers asked very softly. Both Stern and the blonde woman showed they recognized the emotions underlying the words. The official ostentatiously moved his hand away from his sagging trousers' pocket. Adrienne ran her finger along the noses of the bullets in her cartridge belt, counting the rounds.

"Nothing like that, I assure you," Stern said in careful reassurance. "There will be another station soon, and you two will be manning it. Only . . . for the moment, we have need of the best Cretaceous hunting guide available. And that is you, Mr. Vickers."

The hunter relaxed a trifle, but Adrienne asked sharply, "Getting one particular guide is that important? More important than the project?"

Stern frowned. "Mrs. Salmes—" he began.

"'Mrs. Vickers' now, as you damned well know," Adrienne snapped.

"Mrs. Vickers," the official continued, nodding again toward the soldiers, "you understand that while these gentlemen are discrete, they are young. And there is no reason for them to be con-

cerned with the research aspects of our program."
No reason for them to learn, that was, that the
permanent station was a hinge in experiments to
calibrate the intrusion vehicles more accurately.
When that governmentally-desired end was
achieved, it would be possible to insert a body of
men into the historical past. With the Israeli
government choosing the place and purpose of
such an intrusion, the world could be expected to
change very abruptly.

The blonde woman shook her head with the perfect arrogance of one born to wealth and beauty.
"Give me a reason to believe you, Stern," she said.
"Sure, Henry's the best—" she squeezed her husband's arm without breaking eye contact with the
Israeli official—"but you have other guides. I
know how important this . . . habitat phase is to
you. I don't believe you're closing it down, even
temporarily, just because somebody wants to go
hunting for dinos."

Stern sighed. For a moment he looked less like a
bear than like a great, sad ape who faced a world
too complex to be understood and too dangerous
to be ignored. "Mrs. Vickers," he said, "a party of
important persons will be hunting the Cretaceous.
It is necessary that one of them . . . the US Secretary of State . . . have a good hunt in order that he
become—receptive to proposals of the host
government. Our government. Otherwise—" Stern
tongued his lips but continued—"otherwise, it is
believed in some quarters that there will be no
time to pursue the habitat experiments to their
conclusion. Madame, that is as open as I can
possibly be."

"All right," said Vickers, touching his wife's
hand to end the discussion. He too had a weary
look, that of a workman who had ended his shift
and been unexpectedly recalled to deal with an

emergency. Behind him, the tyrannosaur grunted savagely. "It'll take two loads," the hunter said. "I'll put another dart in the dino and we'll send him Topside alone. Then they can return the vehicle for the rest of us and the gear."

Stern shook his head impatiently. "I regret, Mr. Vickers," he said, "that I have not made myself clear. Duration in the past is concurrent with duration—Topside, as you know, unless the point of intrusion or of return is changed. There will be no second trip. Time, ah, Topside, is of . . . considerable importance. We cannot now afford the delay of staging a second intrusion into this time horizon. Further, there have been excellent results achieved by homing insertions in on your alpha pattern, Mr. Vickers . . . but it is by no means a certain technique. Even if *I* were willing to risk being stranded in the Cretaceous myself—" he ventured a smile that had as much humor in it as Stern's smiles ever did—"I assure you that my superiors would be quite displeased at the realization that I had risked stranding *you* at this juncture. No, the animal stays."

"Henry," said Adrienne, "go ahead and give him another dart before he tears the crawler apart." She looked at Stern. "The animal goes, I think," she added calmly. "We'll leave everything else except the guns and go back with the tyrannosaur ourselves."

One of the soldiers blurted something in startled Hebrew. All five of the young men looked aghast. Even Stern seemed to have lost some of his aplomb. "Do you live to infuriate me, woman?" he demanded, his hands at his sides and clenched. "Is this your only joy? There are millions, *billions* of every sort of beast to be captured at your leisure. I have said *this* is an emergency. The creature will die within days anyway, surely you know that?

Why do you persist in goading me?"

"Because," Adrienne said in a voice as gray and frigid as her eyes, "we've taken a live tyrannosaur, Henry and I, and we're going to bring it back no matter what happens to it then. Because we've come this far with it . . . and because it's worth doing, I think."

Henry Vickers chuckled companionably and turned. The great carnivore had lifted its head off the bed of the crawler and was making metallic noises as it strained against its shackles. The capture gun thumped. Its long, white-feathered hypodermic arched through the bars of the cage to bury itself in the tyrannosaur's throat. Vickers broke the action of the gun and drew another dart cartridge from his pouch.

Stern blinked as if the previous conversation had not taken place. "You have only that with you, Mr. Vickers?" he asked. "Not a real rifle, that is?"

Vickers smiled, no longer weary. "I have Adrienne," he replied. "I don't have anything to worry about with her around, Mr. Stern. You of all people should appreciate that." He began to laugh aloud as the drug took hold and the dinosaur shuddered back into restive somnolence.

Their boots clashed on the concrete floor as they inspected the equipment. The heels sent a babble of echoes whispering from one end of the warehouse to the other. Stern carried a briefcase, Vickers only the stapled flimsies listing the equipment and personnel of the safari. Both men were accustomed by their professions to speak in a voice that carried only to the intended listener; and even that murmur was masked by their ricochetting footsteps.

"The public relations team with its cameras, the cook, and supplies for such supernumeraries will be inserted on the other vehicle," Stern said.

The guide shook his head in disgust. "Christ," he said, "I wish somebody'd talked to me while this was still being planned. It's going to be a mare's nest on site with all these untrained people running around, you know." He ran his finger over the fresh rubber of the track beside him. The half-tracked vehicles themselves were at least forty years old, but Stern assured him that they had been rebuilt and re-engined for the intrusion. "I want Martinus Duisberg for the other guide," Vickers said. "You must have a line on where he is, even though you've retired him."

The official nodded. "Mr. Duisberg is on his farm outside Bloemfontein," he said. "Unfortunately, he is not suitable for guiding safaris—and especially this safari—since his accident."

The guide spun, popping the papers in his hand. "You want them safe?" he demanded. "Fine! I want them safe too. Cooch Duisberg is a crack shot and as steady a hand as you've ever had on your payroll. This accident you're talking about—"

"There is more required, Mr. Vickers, than—"

"—this *accident* occurred when a client panicked and wrapped his arms around Cooch from behind! And he *still* dropped the megalosaur, even though it caught his face in its foreclaws before it died."

Stern nodded in agreement. "Mr. Duisberg was not held responsible for the accident," he said. "As you know, he was retired on full pension. But a guide whose face—shall we say, bears the stigmata of catastrophe?—is not a suitable advertisement for a sports activity. There is more required than skill in hunting. The, the client in this case *must* return satisfied. The other guide will be Mr. Thomas Warren, whose skill in the . . . client relations aspects is perhaps equalled only by your skills in the hunt itself, Mr. Vickers. You, of course, will be in charge."

Vickers snorted. "Except," he said, "that with the US Secretary of State and the Prime Minister of Israel present, we're none of us in charge, are we? If Secretary Cardway has to be kept happy at all costs, then do I have the authority to say 'No' if he wants the helicopter to set down right in front of a carnosaur?"

"We have considered that point," the official said, looking up at the lighted ceiling instead of meeting Vickers' eyes. "The risk of a shooting platform failing while in the air is unacceptable on this hunt."

"That was sabotage before. You know that."

"Turbines can fail under field conditions in the Cretaceous," Stern continued inexorably. "As you imply, we could not realistically deny the Secretary use of a shooting platform, a helicopter, if one were available. Therefore, the equipment for this safari does not include a shooting platform. These half-tracks—" he patted the steel side—"will carry the hunters. Each has a swivel for a heavy machine gun on the bulkhead behind the cab. That way there will be a pair of machine guns protecting the Secretary at all times. And the Prime Minister, of course."

"Christ," the guide muttered, "Christ." He looked again at the long personnel list in his hand. "All right, this one—Craig, John C. Attendant. What the hell does that mean? And why is he starred as a 'must include' on the first intrusion with the brass?"

"Mr. Craig is a Secret Service employee, as I understand," Stern said. He still would not look at his companion.

"A bodyguard," Vickers said. "Marvelous, absolutely necessary on a safari—a body-guard." His voice was growing harsh in timbre without becoming louder. "Bloody tanks that'll raise a racket and a dust-cloud for miles around, no helicopter to locate game, and now I'm squiring around a bodyguard to keep me from assassinating somebody besides! Is everybody Topside gone crazy?"

Stern looked at him. With his right hand, the official rubbed his forehead and the edge of his gray, short-cropped hair. "Sometimes I wonder, Mr. Vickers," he said at last. "But I soldier on despite that. I think you can appreciate the . . . attitude. As to the reason we did not protest at Mr. Craig's presence . . . . Well. Our understanding is that the request comes from the permanent officials—the civil service officials, that is to say—rather than from Secretary Cardway himself, who likes to perceive himself as being able to cope with anything. He is from Texas, I believe. But since the Secretary cleared the request, we thought it—impolite —to object to what others considered to be a necessary precaution. The Americans, you Americans, are understandably concerned about, yes, the possibility of assassination. And since the . . . unexpected can occur, we agreed."

"'We   Americans',"   Vickers   repeated disgustedly. "I voted for somebody or other when I turned eighteen, and that's as much contact with politics as I needed to have in this life, Stern. I could do without what this hunt's turning into." The guide sighed and looked at the half-track again. The armor had been stripped off and replaced with sheetmetal panelling on a tubular steel frame. "All right," Vickers said. "Get a twelve-foot step ladder and weld it, open, to the bed of one of these trucks. No, that won't take the stress when we run cross-country. Weld a series of brackets front and back and clamp the ladder into them. It's got to hold when we're going hell for twenty through the brush."

The official blinked. "If you wish," he said. "But God in heaven, why?"

"Because if we're in brush ten or a dozen feet high," the guide said, "we won't be able to spot game without a shooting platform. With the ladder here, we'll be able at least to see over anything but a proper forest . . . and that'll be open lower down anyway. If your main job is to make Secretary Cardway happy, you're not making it any easier on yourselves by leaving the bird Topside."

"As you wish, of course," Stern said. He looked around. "Are there any other changes besides the ladder you feel necessary?"

"Adrienne's going."

"No."

Guide and official stared at each other, measuring, judging. "Mrs.—your wife," Stern said at last, "is an estimable but self-willed person. This safari will not be a place for a—for another person who is self-willed."

"I want a back-up gun I can trust on this one," Vickers said flatly. "Adrienne's quite attractive, she won't scare anybody away. If you won't send Cooch Duisberg, you'll send her. Or I don't go. I'm sorry, Stern, that's the way it is."

Stern frowned, but in perplexity rather than anger. The furrows cleared slowly. "You know, Mr. Vickers," he said, "I believe you are concerned about your own safety."

Vickers face was very still. His index finger probed an old boil scar on his left elbow. "That's against the law?" he asked.

Stern shook his head abruptly. "No, on the contrary," he said. "A man must be willing to take what risks are necessary—but I have never felt comfortable around those who would as soon be dead as alive. I sometimes have thought that you were in that category, Mr. Vickers."

The guide did not smile. "Maybe I was. I'm not now. Does Adrienne go, or do I stay?"

"She goes, Mr. Vickers, she goes," the official said with a sigh. "I will assume that you know what you are doing, unlike the remainder of us. Is there anything further?"

Vickers turned and turned back, his pale eyes flicking around the warehouse, empty except for the two of them and the piled stores. "This is very important, isn't it?" he said, his words little more than movements of his lips. "Why, Mr. Stern? What is Israel about to do that absolutely requires the support of the United States?"

Stern's lip quirked. He said, "Do you make that a condition of your cooperation, Mr. Vickers?" he asked with a sneer. "Is that what you are telling me?"

The guide shook his head. "No," he said, "I'm sure I'm not supposed to know that. And God willing, Adrienne and I will be back in the Cretaceous before whatever happens happens. The thing is, it's just possible that if I knew what you were trying to accomplish, I could help. But that's your decision."

"No, you are not to know that," the official agreed. He smiled, an expression without humor but one with which Vickers could readily identify. "I thought you were going to try to force me to tell you. That would not have happened, of course."

Vickers thumbed a track idler. He was not looking at Stern.

"Some three years ago," Stern whispered, "an atomic weapon was shipped from Pakistan's nuclear research facility outside Islamabad. Its intended delivery point was Tripoli, Libya. But there was an accident."

"Israeli aircraft sank the freighter carrying the bomb in the Persian Gulf," Vickers remembered aloud.

"That is correct," Stern said, without expression, almost without sound. Vickers was watching his lips now. "It is our understanding that another Arab-developed weapon is about to be shipped. There will be another incident. But this time the weapon is to be carried by a Russian frigate."

"Jesus Christ," the guide said, and the words were not a curse. "And you think the Russians'll roll over and play dead if the US is willing to back you—back you without reservation. With its collective finger on the button." He paused again. "And I hear it said that Secretary Luther Cardway might as well be President, so far as foreign affairs go."

The Israeli official shrugged minusculy. "The Secretary is known to view matters in a very—masculine—fashion. This hunt appeared to be an ideal way to broach the question to him. Because without American support . . . we cannot fight all Russia alone. And what chance is there for the State of Israel with nuclear weapons in Libyan hands?"

It was Vickers turn to sigh. "What chance is there for the rest of the world if nobody backs down this time?" he asked, but it wasn't a question that anyone could answer yet. He kicked the track again. "All right," he said, "I'll do my best. But—" he looked down at the floor—"I've learned in my work not to ask questions that are too narrow." Vickers caught the official's eyes again. His voice took on the crisp certainty of a rifle chambering the next round. "You ask, 'How can my client get that particular dino . . .?' and you wind up taking a chance. If you ask instead, 'How can my client have a good safari and take home trophies that'll knock their eyes out in Dubuque?' —that's a different question. And it's the right question. You're asking, 'How can we get away with sinking a Russian ship?' and—"Vickers broke off abruptly, shaking his head. "But that's your affair."

During the rest of the afternoon, the two men spoke to each other only in monosyllables.

The exhaust boomed and paused, boomed and paused, then grunted in one final burst before the driver cut the engine. He had maneuvered the half-track atop the intrusion vehicle and parked it next to its twin. The ground guide who had directed him lowered his arms. The echoes were lost in the roar of the fans in the hangar ceiling. Intrusion Vehicle Beth and its hangar were both larger and far slicker than the prototypes which Vickers' previous safaris had used. Instead of being completely open like its predecessor, the central area of Vehicle Beth could be closed behind hinged steel walls as a protection against all but the largest life forms that might encounter it. The fifty-caliber machine guns, mounted during the intrusion on all four corners, could handle anything that ever lived on Earth. Vickers felt uncomfortable around the stucco and sleek armor not because it was less functional than what it replaced but because it differed. Vickers knew he would have been happier a block away on cramped, rusty Vehicle Aleph—but of course, he needed to accompany the clients on the primary vehicle.

He wondered where Adrienne was.

A pair of men wearing field gear, one of them carrying a rifle, came through an access door across the hangar from Vickers. The older man was Stern, but Vickers recognized also the tall, sandy-haired fellow to the official's left. The new-comer tilted back his snakeskin-banded bush hat, then waved and called, "Ah, Vickers, there you are! We'd been expecting you in the office, you know."

Now that the two half-tracks were loaded on the intrusion vehicle, lines of workmen with fork-lifts were running up and down the ramp like columns of driver ants. Vickers kept a careful eye on the equipment as he walked toward Stern and his companion around the edge of the hangar. It would have been easier to stride under the pillar-like legs of the intrusion vehicle—but that was as bad a habit here as it had been in the Cretaceous. "Good morning, Mr. Stern," Vickers said, shaking hands with the official. "And you're Thomas Warren, I believe. I think we met a few years ago. A pleasure to work with you." The guides shook hands. "But I don't know," Vickers continued, "why anyone expected me in the office. I've been here watching the loading, like always."

"We thought perhaps a brief assembly away from the machinery," said Stern over the back-ground noise, "and the, ah, crowd, was desirable Just yourselves and the main participants."

"Umm, well," Vickers said, agreeing not in words but by the fact he was following the other two men as they drifted back toward the door through which they had entered. "I hope," he added to Warren, "that you've had a chance to check them out with their weapons. I just dropped in the day before yesterday, so to speak." The other guide's rifle was a heavy bolt-action, old but well-cared for. The cartridges in loops in Warren's vest were larger than a man's middle fingers. Judging from them, the rifle was chambered for .416 Rigby, a round no less adequate for being over eighty years old.

"I say, that would be a help, wouldn't it?"
Warren was remarking cheerfully. They were out
of the hangar now. Most of the racket was
absorbed by the door and the acoustic tile of the
hallway. At that, they almost collided with a pair
of harrassed technicians pushing a laden utility
cart toward the intrusion vehicle. "No chance of
that, though," the British guide continued as the
cart squealed away from them around a corner,
"what with the schedule fellows like that are on.
Stern got me an interview with Cardway, thank
goodness, and he told me that he had the very rifle
his father had taken a big tusker with in 1927.
That's something, at least."

"But can he use it?" Vickers demanded, scowl-
ing unconsciously at the floor as he strode along
between the two bigger men.

Warren laughed. "Well, I doubt that, old boy,"
he said with a sudden twang in his voice. "But
then, he'll scarcely be the first of my clients who
didn't know his arse from a hole in the ground,
will he?"

Stern grunted a warning before he opened the
door marked, 'Coordinator' in English and
Hebrew. At a desk within sat a female secretary,
looking acutely uncomfortable in the midst of the
dozen armed men who otherwise filled the room.
A firecracker in the hall would set off World War
III, Vickers thought. He caught himself before he
said the same thing aloud. Uniforms alternated
with clothes so plain as to be uniforms themselves. "They're waiting in the inner office," said
Stern with a scowl that cleared a path as abruptly
as his big shoulders could have. He reached for
the doorknob.

"Just a minute," Vickers muttered. To the secretary he said, "Would you have gotten any calls for

me to the facility?" He was looking at the type-
writer, not the girl's dark face.

"Ah—"

"Yes, she would have done so," said Stern impatiently. "Mr. Henry Vickers, child."

"Ah—" the girl repeated.

"Nothing from my wife?" pressed Vickers.
"Adrienne, ah, Vickers?"

"N-no, sir," the girl said, terrified by the
situation and the guide's expression. Actually, the
expression derived from embarrassment as great
as the secretary's own.

Vickers swallowed. He pushed past Stern and
entered the inner office before his companions.

There were three men dressed in coveralls in the
inner room. The older pair rose with the false
smiles as habitual to a politician as dung-eating is
to some dogs. The youngest of the three, a clean-
shaven man of thirty with black hair and a face as
blank as the nose of a bullet, also reacted to the
surprise. His hand dropped reflexively within the
attache case open on his lap. It gripped but did not
raise the Uzi submachine gun in the case. When he
recognized Stern and Warren, his fingers relaxed
but his expression did not. "Mr. Secretary, Mr.
Prime Minister," Stern said quickly, "this is
Henry Vickers, our chief guide for the operation.
That is, the hunting expedition."

"Good to meet you, Vickers," rumbled Luther
Cardway. He gripped the hunter's hand, firmly
enough to feel the muscles beneath the calluses
respond. He did not squeeze quite so firmly that
even Vickers could have sworn it had been a contest. "They tell me you're an American. That's
good. Guess it's you, me, and Craig here against
the rest." He nodded down at the bodyguard.
Craig was trying with embarrassment to aim his

weapon away from the principal who had stepped into his line of fire.

"Ah," said Vickers, looking at Cardway's chin instead of raising his eyes to meet the other's, "it won't be a contest, Mr.—sir. There's enough game in the Cretaceous for anybody. And big enough for anybody."

"Yes, indeed," said Thomas Warren, in a jovial voice as well-modulated as the Secretary's. "At my suggestion, we're making quite a High Cretaceous insertion—just before the extinctions, when the most impressive species were present. We may get you a world's record triceratops, Mr. Secretary."

Cardway gave a quick negative jerk of his head, the amicable mask slipping. "A tyrannosaurus," he said. "Screw the rest. I want to go back with a tyrannosaurus rex that could've eaten my father's elephant for lunch. You'd have thought the old man was the bravest son of a bitch in the world to see him act out the kill back in Brownsville with the stuffed head over the mantle and the gun he got it with . . . . Say—" the good humor returned— "let's see what you think of this, Vickers."

Luther Cardway was big without being soft, as handsome in person as he was on television with his make-up on—and far more forceful. Only the relative thickness of individual hairs betrayed them as the result of a scalp transplant. It was not until Cardway turned to fumble with the walnut gun case beside his chair that Prime Minister Greenbaum came out of the shade. The Israeli was smaller than his American colleague and looked frail. Vickers remembered that Greenbaum was supposed to be a landscape painter of more than hobbyist reputation; that fitted well enough with the man's appearance. Only Greenbaum's eyes belied the general look of benign forgetfulness. The eyes might have suited General Patton. Catching Vickers' glance, the Prime Minister said, "I'm glad to see you turned up, Mr. Vickers. Though Avraham assured us that you must be nearby, that there was no one in the world more dependable than you." His accent was as British as Warren's.

"Ah, crossed wires," Vickers said, certain he was flushing. "I, ah, assumed we'd meet in the hangar."

"Assume makes an ass of 'U' and me," Cardway said, dominating the gathering again. He held a double-barrelled rifle, an elephant gun in the classic sense, and was presenting it to Vickers. The guide took the weapon in his right hand and broke the action by habit. He was edgy at being in a room full of people carrying loaded guns. The muzzle of his own cradled M14 pointed at the ceiling, and even that made him uncomfortable.

Though not as uncomfortable as the live cartridges winking from the twin chambers of the rifle he had just been handed. Cardway had indeed been carrying the weapon loaded. Safety or no, it would not have been the first rifle to go off when it was dropped. "Ah," Vickers said. "Might be best to carry it open till we're ready to insert. Ah, not many tyrannosaurs in Tel Aviv."

"Fine weapon, there, fine," Warren put in, watching Cardway's expression carefully out of the corners of his eyes. "A Gibbs, yes. You bloody well can whistle for this sort of quality today."

Actually, as Vickers knew and Warren surely knew, the rifle was by no means an exceptional example of its type. The only engraving was a scroll on either lockplate, and the wood-to-metal fit of the parts was adequate rather than ideal. Whatever the elder Cardway had told his son, he had spent less on his elephant gun than others had been known to do. Still, finish and engraving never killed a game animal, and this .470 Nitro Express

was quite capable of smashing through the heart
or skull of a dinosaur. 'Serviceability' had always
been Vickers' watchword. No one was likely to
point to the guide's own fiberglas-stocked military
rifle as a triumph of the gunmaker's art either.
"Looks a very fine gun," Vickers said, handing it
back. "Ah, I hope you've had a chance to practice
with it to, to get the feel of it?"

"I've shot it, sure," the Secretary said in a hardening voice. He snapped the breech closed.
Vickers winced but held back a comment. The
bodyguard, Craig, was noticeably disturbed also.
"I'm not afraid of the kick, if that's what you
mean," Cardway continued. "And I'm not afraid to
get close to my work, either. My father shot his
elephant when it came out of the bamboo right on
top of him. Mordecai told me—" the Prime
Minister winced in turn, knowing what was coming and knowing now that he should not have said
it—"that the dinos'll let you get about as close as
you've got the nerve for. Well, I've got the nerve to
poke this right in their guts." He brandished his
rifle. "Believe me."

Vickers believed him. So did Stern, judging
from the official's stiff expression. The guide remembered Stern's explanation of why there would
be no helicopter on this safari. That decision made
increasingly good sense.

"Well then, gentlemen," Stern said. "I think it
has become time to report to the hangar. The
support personnel have—"

Rising voices in the outer office focused Stern's
whole attention as well as that of the men around
him. Over the deeper rumble of the males, Vickers
heard Adrienne saying, " . . . and I'll be God
damned if you do any such thing!"

"Ah, my wife," the guide explained hurriedly.
"She spent yesterday on business affairs, the trust

she set up when we—" Was Secretary Cardway supposed to know about the Habitat Phase—ah, "two years ago. She's just arrived." As much as anything to forestall questions, Vickers opened the door.

Adrienne stood in the outer office, looking like a Doberman in the midst of wolves. A burly man wearing the eagles of an American colonel had poised his hand an inch away from the receiver of Adrienne's Schultz and Larsen rifle. The colonel turned when the inner door opened. "Hello, darling," Adrienne said, striding past the colonel to kiss her husband's cheek. "Paunchy here—" the officer's gut sucked in reflexively—"thinks I'm going to trust him with my rifle ten minutes before we insert!"

"Sir," said the colonel stiffly to the Secretary of State, visible through the doorway, "she isn't on my list, and I had no intention of letting somebody with a gun—"

"Colonel Platt," said Stern, overriding the American's voice as he stepped toward the man, "the error is mine entirely. Mrs. Vickers is indeed a part of the expedition, and she could properly have been admitted." He cleared his throat heavily. "Now, as I was saying. I believe the support personnel have gathered at their respective stations. If we proceed to Hangar Beth, our insertion can go forward as scheduled. The pressure of time on our, our principals, is of course very great." He motioned toward the hall door.

Vickers' tongue touched his lips. He followed Stern's gesture without comment. His wife wore coveralls, faded like his own by months of sun and use. The fabric slid easily over the skin by which it had been worn smooth. Her rifle was the one she had bought after her first time safari, also worn to perfect functioning by two years of service around their Cretaceous base. But Adrienne Vickers herself wore her hair in a coif as rigid and golden as a Cellini casting, and her face was still in tiger-striped make-up which Vickers presumed had become fashionable while he had been living in the Cretaceous. While Adrienne and he had been isolated in the Cretaceous.

"Alex took me out after we finished with the records," Adrienne was prattling. "I swear I never thought Tel Aviv had a night life, and I suppose it really doesn't, but my God, I'm not about to complain. But we wound up in Jaffa and I looked at the time, well—I had to *buy* a taxi to get me back to the suite in time to change. Literally buy one! I left Alex trying to decide whether the check should be charged to entertainment or as a business expense. After all, that's the sort of thing I *pay* an accountant for, isn't it?"

They pushed through the swinging doors. The bustle within the hangar had given way to a sullen hush. The exhaust fans were shut down, leaving the air still. Eight men wearing fatigues and holding grenade launchers came to attention along the far wall. On the intrusion vehicle, laden already with the paraphernalia of a time safari, were the technicians making their last-minute adjustments to the machinery.

"Glad you had a good time," Vickers said. "Ah, I've been thinking. You . . . I'm sure you can't have cleared up all your affairs in one, one day. Why don't you stay for now." He was examining the receiver of his rifle, his index finger digging into the pock mark left by the old boil. "I'll be back in two weeks, I suppose. Then we'll, we'll . . . ."

"My God, Henry, you think I'm going to leave you alone with this rat-pack?" the tall blonde said in a clear voice. "Not likely. Not likely at all!"

The chime which replaced the buzzer at the old

facility sounded. Aboard the intrusion vehicle was an older man with an air of authority. He waved. He was not Dr. Galil, who was probably superintending the more difficult follow-up insertion in Hangar Aleph. Stern called a command and the uniformed men began to trudge up the ramp onto the vehicle's open veranda. Refinements in technique had permitted the new platform to stand on six-foot pillars instead of the braced twenty-foot I-beams which had supported the original vehicle. There was no longer any possibility that the vehicle would be inserted with its base platform more than a few feet above the terrain of the intrusion site. Still, though Vickers trusted Dr. Galil and his team completely, the change made his subconscious uneasy.

At least it was better than wondering if the Secretary of State was going to stumble and put a 500-grain bullet through your back.

The uniformed men had stationed themselves on the intrustion vehicle. One stood on each of the sides, while the remaining four were manning the heavy machine guns.

"Mr. Vickers," Stern said formally, "you will please take charge."

Like hell, the guide thought, but he glanced over the line of men following him. Craig had discarded his attache case and carried the sub-machine gun openly. Prime Minister Greenbaum was armed with a half-stocked Mannlicher, heavy and glisteningly new. So far as Vickers knew, the Israeli was no hunter. He had apparently been given—and accepted—some excellent advice regarding equipment. Thomas Warren was last, cradling his Rigby comfortably. "Who's manning the old vehicle?" Vickers asked Stern abruptly.

The official raised his eyebrows. "The photographic team," he said, "and the cook. The follow-up insertion carries none of the truly necessary supplies and personnel, of course."

"Wait a minute," the guide insisted, trying to pitch his voice low. Adrienne stirred at his side. "You mean there's nobody aboard who's made an insertion before? Good God, man, if the timing's only three seconds out, they'll insert five klicks away from the initial group! They need somebody experienced along."

Stern shrugged impatiently. "They have weapons," he said. "They have been instructed."

"Instructed my ass," Vickers said. "Warren! Ah, Thomas. Get on over to the old hangar ASAP and nursemaid the back-up crew, will you?"

"Mr. Warren!" Stern snapped. In a lower voice he said, "Mr. Vickers, you are both of you essential to the initial intrusion. The follow-up vehicle is not to be your first concern."

"Henry, I'll go," Adrienne said quietly. Vickers turned, the anger meant for others in his eyes. "No," she said, "it'll be all right. Somebody has to be with the vehicle, but you know Dr. Galil will bring it in on time. You needed someone you could trust along for just this sort of job. Well, that's why I'm along."

"Adrienne—"

"You *do* trust me, don't you?"

Vickers sighed. He checked his watch, a mechanical chronometer because the intrusion field interfered with quartz-synchronized watches. "Right," he said. "We—I'll see you in thirty-seven minutes."

His wife flashed him a smile and strode back out of the hangar. Her hips were as sleekly functional as they had been the day he first noticed them, climbing the steps of an intrusion vehicle ahead of him. Adrienne was pulling a handkerchief from her pocket. As she swung through the doors, she appeared to be rubbing the skin-tone from her face.

"Mr. Warren," Vickers said to the other guide, "if you'll lead the Prime Minister to Side 3, we'll begin boarding. Mr. Secretary, you and I will stand on Side 1, that's the one with the ramp. Mr. Stern, Side 4; Mr. Craig—"

"Side 1," the bodyguard said flatly. "With Secretary Cardway."

"I hope you never get a chance to see what a charging carnosaur would think of that toy you carry," Vickers said.

"Look," Craig retorted, "I've got orders, I've got a job to do, and I'm going to do it."

The guide shrugged. "All right," he said, "since you're unarmed, it won't affect the vehicle's safety no matter where you stand. Shall we go?"

It was going to be a great hunt, Vickers thought as he waited for the others to board. But he had known that from the beginning.

The insertion was flawless, a textbook job. The indirect lighting on the sandfinished ceiling of the hangar suddenly flared into a blue-white sky with the sun directly overhead. Simultaneously, a volume of landscape and Cretaceous atmosphere replaced the intrusion vehicle in what had been the present but now was the future 65,000,000 years removed.

Secretary Cardway grunted. Vickers glanced at him after a quick scan indicated there was no danger immediate to the vehicle. The Secretary looked as if his elevator had dropped the last ten feet. Time intrusion always involved sensory scrambling, but that was momentary. Already the big politician had regained his composure and was staring out at his new surroundings with his rifle near his shoulder.

The vehicle had been inserted onto a plain ex-

tending across the arc of Vickers' eyesight. It was
covered by a brushy mixture of evergreen and
spiny succulents. The foliage was made duller and
paler by a coating of dust. From the slight vantage
of the intrusion vehicle's height, it was possible to
see that game trails webbed the brush, meandering as dark shadows against the blurred reflec-
tance of the shrubs they separated. And all across
the plain, sunlight flashed on scales as dinosaurs
lifted up to see what had caused the sudden noise.

Eighty yards from Secretary Cardway one of the
misnamed duckbills, a saurolophus, raised its
head. It sniffed the air while its teeth continued
grinding what looked like fronds of Spanish
Bayonet. The dinosaur's lower jaw was ratcheting
back and forth, pulling in more of the fibrous
mass at each stroke. The motion was bizarrely
alien to men subconsciously expecting the creature to slide its jaw sideways as a cow does when
chewing. The saurolophus' beak was bright red,
and the beast's head bore a hollow, bony crest
faired to the back of its neck by a flap of azure
skin. It was an adult male, a large one, and an excellent trophy.

But Vickers did not expect to hear the Secretary
say, *"Goddam a tyrannosaur!"* the instant before
he loosed off his right barrel at the herbivore.

Dust leaped from nearby foliage stricken by the
muzzle blast of the rifle, but the windless plain
drank all echoes of the shot. The dinosaur lowered
its head, untouched by the bullet. Neither the
sound nor the human scent caught by its keen nostrils were labeled as threats by the creature's
brain. It had simply returned to its meal.

Secretary Cardway broke his rifle open. The
automatic ejector spat out the empty case, leaving
the live round in the left breech to gleam like
Odin's eye. Fumblingly, Cardway reloaded. "God-

dam, first shot and I got a tyrannosaur!" he was saying. "Goddam it was easy. Goddam I wish the old bastard was alive now to see what I'll have looking down at his goddam elephant!"

"Of course, they're devilish brutes to kill," said Thomas Warren from nearby. Vickers' breath caught. The other guide had left his station, walking around the platform to attend what was going on. It was only a slight mitigation of his offense —what if a *real* carnivore had sprung onto the side of the platform Warren was supposed to be covering?—to note that he had brought Prime Minister Greenbaum with him. "I think Henry or myself need to go down and crack the blighter again, just to be on the safe side," the Englishman continued, winking at Vickers past the Secretary's turned head.

"It was a saurolophus," Vickers said, his left hand as tight on the forestock of his rifle as he wished it could be on Warren's throat. "And what the—"

"Nobody finishes my kills without me!" Cardway said, snapping closed the breech of his Gibbs. "Come on, then."

"Wait!" cried three voices simultaneously, Vickers joined by Stern and Greenbaum. The Secretary of State had already taken a step forward while Vickers cursed himself mentally for positioning the damned fool on the side with the ramp. "Ah," the guide said, "we'll crank up one of the trucks and go down in it when we get the machine gun remounted. I don't like to enter this brush on foot." Behind Warren, Stern's head was nodding vigorously, like a donkey engine.

"Like hell we will!" Cardway retorted. He gestured with his rifle at the walled center of the intrusion vehicle. "It'll take a goddam hour to unpack one of them—" and that was, Vickers

knew, a conservative estimate. Cardway's heavy
rifle slashed back like a saber, tracing a line
across the guide's chest with its double muzzles.
"Come on, Mordecai. You and I can show 'em
what men are like if they're too pussy to walk fifty
feet!"

Vickers' mind clicked over possibilities like
beads of an abacus. All anger, all emotion was
gone. If there had been carnivores in the
immediate vicinity, the plant-eaters would not
have returned to feeding so soon after being
aroused. The worst danger, therefore, was the
chance that one of the herbivores would bolt out
of the brush and trample the hunters. That was
not a risk the guide cared to take, but the alternative appeared to be clubbing the Secretary of
State and carrying him back Topside unconscious.
"All right," Vickers said. "Mr. Secretary, you and I
will—"

"And Mordecai!"

The Prime Minister nodded without enthusiasm. Vickers swallowed and continued, "The
three of us will go down after that saurolophus.
Warren, you'll stay up here where there's enough
height to warn us if necessary. And for God's sake,
stay where you belong this time!"

"Mr. Vickers," said Stern, "I am under your
orders if you desire another gun."

The guide's mouth opened, but he bit off the
response frustration had intended when he
realized that Stern was armed after all. The official had obviously had his rifle waiting on the
intrusion vehicle instead of carrying it around the
Tel Aviv facility like the rest of them. It was a
Browning FAL, for many years the Israeli service
issue. Seeing it reminded Vickers in a rush of
Dieter Jost, who had carried a similar weapon . . .
and who, had he survived his last safari, might

have been present now in the place of Warren.

Stern caught the stare and misinterpreted it. His heavy face darkened in something like a blush. "I am not boasting that I am a crack shot like you and need only the small bullets, Mr. Vickers," the official said. "This I carried in the Sinai—better than a weapon I do not have time to learn, though it was many years ago." He raised his chin. "My nerve will not fail."

Vickers quirked a smile that was half embarrassment. "Neither would your good judgment, Avraham," he said. "Stay up here with Warren and the troops, and yell if you see trouble coming." To the pair of officials he continued, "We'll follow the trail we've landed in the middle of, cut through the brush if we have to when we get close. You'll have the shot, Mr. Secretary, so you'll lead if it gets tight. I'll be right behind you, and—"

"I'll be right behind him," said the bodyguard, "and look, I don't like the idea of anybody firing past the Secretary. You can—"

"Craig, shut the hell up!" Cardway snarled impatiently before Vickers could form a response. "Come on, let's go!" The bodyguard, blank-faced and clutching his Uzi like a reliquary, brought up the end of the short column.

Secretary Cardway reached the bottom of the ramp, took two steps further along the game trail, and paused. He had realized for the first time what a difference the intrusion vehicle's height had made. The brush on which dinosaurs could be heard browsing was only about eight feet tall. The trails, worn through it by the hips of the great beasts, were broad but often not cleared to the sky. To either side the brush grew gnarled and spiky, as inhospitable as a barbed-wire entanglement. The effect was less that of standing in a

grape arbor than it was walking down the center
of a subway tunnel, listening to the tracks hum.

Vickers started to move forward. The trail was
wide enough for two to walk abreast. The Secretary began to move again, with more determination at each step. "Sir," the guide whispered, "not
so fast. We don't want to—we want to have time
for a good shot."

Cardway looked puzzled. Vickers had forgotten
that their quarry was supposed to be wounded.
The Secretary slowed from the rear run toward
which he had been building, however. The guide
glanced back to check Greenbaum and Craig. They
were all right, though Craig seemed to be crowd-
ing the Prime Minister somewhat. Vickers could
no longer see the men on the intrusion vehicle
through the dappled tanglings of brush. He should
have thought to bring along a wand with a pennon
for this sort of situation. Of course, if he had expected the situation, he might have refused to take
out the safari after all. The millstone-crunching of
a dinosaur's teeth was becoming very loud.
Hadrosaurs like the beast they were after were
not carnivorous, of course, but neither was a
threshing machine carnivorous; and threshing machines had killed their share of the unwary over
the years.

The bush to their right was a multi-stemmed
clump with leaves like green glass teardrops. It
shuddered as something pulled a huge mouthful
out of the other side. Cardway raised his rifle.
Vickers touched the politician's shoulder for
attention and shook his head. Then he knelt and
used the fore-end of his own weapon to gently
press a line of sight between the bush and its
neighbor. A male saurolophus, possibly even the
one Cardway had fired at, was facing them within
spitting distance.

The dinosaur was chewing with its short forelegs lowered but not quite touching the ground. Its
neck was raised at right angles to the straight,
horizontal line of its back and counter-balancing
tail. If it saw Vickers, it ignored him. The guide
leaned his head back out of the way. With his free
hand he motioned Cardway forward into the gap
he was holding open. Then Vickers tapped himself
on the breastbone with index and middle fingers
to indicate the proper aiming point. Secretary
Cardway knelt with a set expression, advancing
his rifle.

Vickers knew the shot would be deafening, but
the reality was stunningly worse than he had
expected. Cardway spun over on his back like a
sacked passer, losing his grip on the rifle. The
meat-axe *smack!* of the bullet was lost in the
muzzle blast, but the ground shook as the stricken
hadrosaur fell.

Vickers backed a step. He leveled his own rifle
one-handed toward the brush in case the saurolophus burst through. Then he picked up the Secretary's weapon as well. Vickers' head rang. His
first thought had been that the old Gibbs had exploded, either because metal had crystallized or
because of trash in the bore. The big weapon was
apparently undamaged, however, except for the
dirt that now clung to its exterior. Vickers
thumbed the locking key. The breeches clicked
open and the ejectors kicked out both the cartridges, empty. The rifle had doubled, shock of the
first discharge firing the second barrel almost
simultaneously.

The Secretary was rising groggily to his knees.
Vickers thrust the empty Gibbs at him. His hearing was beginning to return. The wounded hadrosaur was kicking on the ground close by. "Load
one barrel," the guide shouted. "It's firing both to-

gether."

"Goddam if I do!" Cardway replied. His mouth was shouting, but his words rang through a long tunnel. "Give me yours!"

Vickers twisted his M14 away from the hands spread to grasp it. "No," he said, "just load one round."

"You worthless sonofabitch!" snarled the white-faced politician, "you give me that gun now or you'll regret the day you were born!"

The guide's knuckles tightened on the Gibbs, held now in bar rather than in offering. The surface of his mind was slick as glass. The instant before Vickers might have acted, Prime Minister Greenbaum stepped between the two men. He held out his Mannlicher, saying, "Here, Luther; I'm sure this will finish the job."

Cardway's rage evaporated. He snatched the bolt-action rifle from his colleague without a word. Instead of kneeling again to fire beneath the spreading foliage, the big Texan began thrusting himself between the bushes. He seemed oblivious to the thorns that ripped at his coveralls.

Vickers paused momentarily, but he could neither restrain his client nor allow him to go alone. Throwing himself on his belly, the guide squirmed on knees and elbows around the other side of the bush past which they had fired. He cleared the obstacle an instant before Cardway could. The hadrosaur lay on its side, its spine toward the hunters. Its tail was flailing sideways, cracking against the earth on every downward stroke. The brush was splashed with bright arterial blood, further evidence that at least one of Cardway's bullets had been a solid hit.

The dinosaur was only six feet away. Vickers aimed at the beast's spine but did not fire. He prayed that if it became necessary to shoot, the grit on the bolt of his M14 would not·jam it. The magazine was loaded with modern armor-piercing rounds, penetrators of depleted uranium which could drill through an inch of steel. Anyone can miss a shot, however, no matter how short the range; and the nineteen rounds remaining in the magazine might as well be on the Moon for all the good they would be to a jammed rifle.

Secretary Cardway forced through the brush with thorns hanging from his sleeves and the backs of his hands bleeding. He aimed the Mannlicher and emptied it with five point-blank shots as quickly as he could work the spoon-handle bolt. The recoil of the big rifle—it was chambered for .458 Magnum—did not appear to bother him, despite the bruising his shoulder must have taken when the Gibbs doubled. Vickers watched his client carefully. The look on the Secretary's face as he fired was chilling.

The crashing shots ended when Cardway ran out of ammunition. The struggles of the hadrosaur had disintegrated into a quivering as lifeless as the collapse of a house of cards. Splotches of blood gummed the dust that obscured the patterning of the beast's back-scales.

Vickers stood up slowly, porting his rifle. "Splendid trophy, sir," he said.

The Secretary was lowering the muzzle of the Mannlicher. "Yes," he said in a thick voice. "Goddam it, yes." Behind him, the brush quaked to pass his wild-eyed bodyguard.

Time safaris always held an element of danger, Vickers thought. Usually, however, the greatest danger was from the local wildlife.

"Right," said Thomas Warren, as if he were an amateur magician demonstrating card tricks. "Here's the culprit."

The lock-work of the Gibbs double was strewn on the linen tablecloth in front of the British guide. Around him sat Vickers and his wife, Stern, Greenbaum, and Cardway. The audience wore expressions of interest and, in the last case, considerable impatience. Craig, the bodyguard, stood stiffly a pace behind the Secretary. He continually moved his head in nervous jerks to check behind him. "The sear, you see," Warren continued, prodding the little piece again with his index finger. "Not worn, really, just polished down a little too closely in the final assembly. These big express chamberings give quite a jolt—as you know, old chap, as you know. In this case, it's enough to jolt the left hammer spang off its sear when the right barrel fires. Sometimes, at any rate. More common a problem than you might think with these old darlings—" the guide rapped the joined barrels with his fingernail. "One reason I've always kept to a magazine rifle."

"Well, fix the goddam thing, then!" Secretary Cardway snapped. "You're not on the payroll to run your mouth."

Adrienne's hand, resting companionably on her husband's shoulder, tightened. Warren's smile, however, appeared to be quite genuine as he replied, "Well you see, old boy, that's the problem. Short of fitting another sear, there's not a great deal to be done. Not a bloody thing, really. Use it as a single shot, that is. Or I dare say, there's a spare gun or two about the camp—isn't that so, Vickers?"

Henry Vickers had a good idea of how the Secretary would react if he were offered the camp gun —a functional but very battered Ruger in .375 H&H. Fortunately, Prime Minister Greenbaum forestalled him by saying, "Luther, when I held your gun I found that it suits me far better than the one I purchased for myself. I would appreciate it no end if you would agree to exchange with me."

Adrienne got up, muttering something under her breath. The support crew was sprawled around the campfire, a discreet ten meters from their betters at the table. A pair of startled soldiers made room for the blonde woman when she tapped them on the shoulders.

"All right, that's settled," the Secretary was saying as if he had just made a concession. "Now," the Texan continued, poking an index finger across the table at Vickers, "I've got another bone to pick. *You* told me that I was going after a tyrannosaurus this morning."

The guide's fist clenched in his lap. "Ah," he temporized, "your saurolophus is really an exceptional trophy."

"I'm not wasting my time here to bring back a goddam duckbill!" Cardway said, jabbing with his finger as if it were a pistol. "You lied to me once and you won't do it again, hear? I want a tyrannosaurus rex." He stood abruptly and strode toward his private tent. His back was straight, his carriage in every way that of a leader. Craig followed him at a respectful distance.

Vickers was pale. Stern said softly, "He has a very—selective—memory. I suppose we can hope that if matters in the long run turn out to his liking, his memory will select the positive aspects of the hunt as well."

In an equally low voice, looking at Vickers, the Prime Minister said, "I am not a hunter, you understand. It does not matter what gun I carry or indeed if I carry one. But if I *did* hunt, if I were as keen on the chase as, as you are, as anyone could be—I would still have done the same thing I just did." The little Israeli took a deep breath and continued, his whispered words freighted with genuine concern. "I am here to be the dutiful child, you see, the child who does whatever his papa pleases and is therefore rewarded with a treat. Only this time, the treat is his . . . his right to exist, his life. You see? I regret what I must bear, and what I must ask able gentlemen like yourselves to bear; but there is no choice."

Vickers shook himself. "It's all right," he said, looking at his hands. "Only . . . only, I don't see how anybody that—abrasive—expects to get elected *anything*. But they say he was almost President in the last election and he probably *will* make it the next time."

The Prime Minister's smile was tired. "Oh, you must not think Mr. Cardway is this way at all times. Only with people who must accept the behavior, underlings, dependents. If the United States needed a concession from Israel, he would be in a very different temper with me, with us, I assure you. Though he would still treat his own aide like dirt." Greenbaum paused, shaking his head ruefully. "I sometimes find myself giving speeches even in the shower," he said. "Well, gentlemen, good night."

Stern watched the smaller man walking to the tent the two of them shared. "Best I go as well," the official said. "Otherwise I will disturb him when I enter. A man of great courage, that one. Great courage." He stood.

"But not great enough courage to refuse to start World War III," Vickers said.

Stern looked down at the guide for a long moment; but in the end he walked off without responding.

The whole compound area was covered with a tent of mosquito netting, suspended from high poles. The covering must have been manufactured for the hunt. Reflected light brightened the inner face of the net to opacity, except where insects clung and fluttered on the exterior. There appeared to be a breed of hawk moth with wings the size of a man's hands. Vickers had seen no flowers impressive enough to justify such a monster, but perhaps they were night-blooming. He hadn't trained himself to observe flowers, anyway. He'd never guided a client who wanted to kill a rose.

There was laughter from the group around the fire, half-stilled at a sergeant's gruff order. Adrienne's liquid trill choked off a moment later. "Quite a lady, your wife," said Thomas Warren. He was fitting a screw into a sideplate. "Must prove quite a—" his eyes flicked sideways, toward Vickers—"handful for you."

"Instead of worrying about that," Vickers said, "you might give some thought to how we'll keep Cardway from running into the brush after his first carnosaur, the same as he did with the duckbill this morning." Then, "I'm going to bed."

Warren whistled between his teeth as he finished reassembling the rifle. His face bore the smile of a death-camp guard.

The ten-inch lizard racing down the center of the game trail actually gained on the half-track momentarily. Then the little creature's burst of energy gave out. It faltered, an olive shadow against the gray soil. From Vickers' vantage point, clinging to the front rail of the truck box beside the gun, it looked as if the front wheels would inevitably crush the lizard. At the last instant, however, the reptile spurted sideways into the shade and safety of the brush. Vickers found he was unexpectedly pleased at that.

"Hold it up here," he said on his cordless throat mike. There was no point in trying to speak directly to the driver while they were in motion. Even though the cab was open-topped, the treads and the racket of brush clanging constantly on

both sides of the vehicle provided a background of
deafening white noise.

Obediently, the soldier driving slowed the half-
track to a stop. He shared the cab with one of the
propaganda staffers who looked a little green. Not
only was the ride a rough one for anyone not accustomed to it, quite a few of the higher branches
were slapping the wind-screen. Its plexiglas held
despite deep scarring, but masses of six-inch
thorns at eye height were bound to be disconcerting. The ponies, the little diesel carts which time
safaris ordinarily used, would have slipped down
the trails with less noise and infinitely greater
comfort; but you couldn't mount a fifty-caliber
machine gun on one of them.

Well, it had yet to be proven that you could hunt
dinos from these monsters.

"Give me those binoculars," Secretary Cardway
said. He pushed past Vickers as the guide started
to mount the ladder. The cargo area of the half-
track was cramped. Besides the gear and the
braced ladder, there were six people: Vickers and
his wife; Cardway and his bodyguard; the soldier
manning the machine gun; and a holograph
cameraman like the one in the cab. Only the fact
that too many people were in the way kept Adrienne from jerking the Secretary back by his collar.

"Adrienne," the guide cautioned in an under-
tone, hoping the cold-eyed Craig had not inter-
preted her brief tension correctly. "Here you are,
sir," he continued, handing up his binoculars.
With luck, Cardway would not drop them.
"There's sign of ceratopsians—ah, that's triceratops and the like, the horns—and, ah, duckbills,
hadrosaurs, all around. With the ladder, it should
be possible to pick out a number of nice trophies.
We'll ring them with the other track, then, and
move in."

Secretary Cardway had climbed a few steps and begun to scan their surroundings in a cursory fashion. The air was almost dead still. The plume of dust raised by their passage lay behind them like a still picture. A kilometer to the right hung a frozen ridge of gray, the track of the other vehicle more or less parallelling their own progress on another trail. That half-track stopped as well. Though it was not fitted with a ladder, Vickers could see Warren standing on the hood to eye the plain.

"Look, I'm tired of this dicking around," Cardway said as he dropped to the bed again. He allowed Vickers to retrieve the binoculars and scramble up the ladder, but he did not seem interested in what the guide was doing. "I didn't come to get duckbills and what-have-you," the Secretary continued, "and I didn't come to get my kidneys pounded out on some goddam antique. If this is the best you Jews can manage, maybe the Arabs ought to get a crack at it."

"Not only will a ceratopsian head make an elephant's look like something the cat caught," Vickers said, glad for their sakes that Stern and the Prime Minister were in the other vehicle, "but the meat is a first-rate way to lure the big carnosaurs—like tyrannosaurus—in. We didn't dare use the saurolophus carcass that way—I'm not about to toll a tyrannosaur to within fifty yards of where I'm sleeping. But when we drop a triceratops a reasonable distance away, it'll bring meat-eaters from horseflies to as big as they come on land." He waved skyward. "The big ones follow those," he added, waggling his index finger cryptically without taking the glasses from his eyes.

Adrienne stepped onto the side bulkhead, using the ladder to steady her. She caught the look of bafflement on Cardway's face as he stared upward. He was uncertain whether Vickers had been pointing or merely gesturing. "What look like little dots up there," explained the tall woman, "see them? Those're pterodactyls the size of airplanes—heavier than a man is, at least. They have eyesight to shame a condor, and a ten-ton carcass draws them from a hundred miles. The carnosaurs follow, unless they're on a fresh kill of their own." As an afterthought Adrienne said, "That's how we captured a tyrannosaur alive, you know—followed them to a kill. Just Henry and I."

"I don't care what you've—" the Secretary began.

"Hush!" snapped Adrienne, her body suddenly rigid. She leaned into her own binoculars as if bracing against their recoil. "Henry," she said in a tense, quiet voice. "Between us and the others, just ahead. Doesn't that look like . . .?"

Vickers looked down to be sure of the bearing, then found the target with his naked eyes. Targets, three of them—he raised and refocused the glasses—sure enough, dryptosaurs or a carnivore damned similar, and the leading one had to be ten yards long.

"Mobile One to Two," Vickers said urgently into his lapel mike.

"Go ahead," crackled Warren's voice from both the unit on Vickers' shoulder and the console in the cab. The words were slightly out of phase, echoes of themselves.

"We've got three carnosaurs between us, just three hundred meters ahead and quartering across our front. See them?" The dryptosaurs' heads were flexed back on serpentine necks. From the withers rearward, the beasts' spines were straight and parallel to the ground save for the slight hump over the hip joint. The long bodies flexed from side to side but not vertically as they cut through the brush. The vegetation was sparser here than it was near the camp, but it still should have been more of a hindrance to the beasts' progress than it seemed to be. The dryptosaurs trotted through the brush like cruisers on a calm sea, only their heads and backs visible to the watching hunters. Their hides were dun, splotched with maroon as dark as dried blood.

"Give me those!" Cardway said.

"Go buy your own binoculars," Adrienne retorted. "*I* did."

"Yes, by God," the radio said. "I'd say we were in a bit of luck, wouldn't you? Shall we—"

The rest of Warren's words were lost in the unexpected crash of a rifle. Vickers looked down, open-mouthed. The PR man in the cab had bent over as if clubbed. His hands were covering his ears—too late. Secretary Cardway was still ajar from the recoil of the Mannlicher. He ejected the spent case and raised the weapon for a second shot.

Three-hundred yard accuracy with an elephant gun was a task beyond most experts; it was assuredly beyond the Secretary of State, shooting off-hand with a weapon he had not sighted in himself. The carnosaurs paused in their lazy striding, cocking their heads back to seek the source of the noise. The gunshot had not panicked them, for it was unique to their experience.

"Hold up!" Vickers said, staring at the Secretary but keying his lapel mike as well. He was too late in both cases. Cardway's rifle boomed again, and the other half-track lurched toward the dinosaurs in a fresh spray of dust. The three animals jerked their heads forward and leaped with the unanimity of a flock of birds.

"Follow them!" the Secretary was screaming. "We'll run'em down!"

The driver let out the clutch without waiting for Vickers' orders. The guide had to jump down from his perch. Only Adrienne's hand kept him from smashing painfully into the back bulkhead.

The driver's obedience caught the Secretary himself by surprise, as it turned out. The half-track had ridden rough at part throttle; opened up, there was literally danger that everyone would be thrown out of the box. The trail they were following would have seemed smooth enough at a walking pace, but at 40 kph it was like going through the rapids in a canoe—sideways. Vickers was clinging to the sidewall with one hand and trying with the other to keep his slung M14 from pounding him to death. Cardway had dropped the Mannlicher and had both arms around the waist of the soldier at the machine gun. The gunner was holding on for dear life to the spade grips of his weapon. When the halftrack yawed, the gun pivoted and made an absurd conga line of the pair.

"Slow down for Chrissake!" Vickers screamed. The vehicle pitched abruptly enough to snap both legs of the ladder just above the topmost braces. Then the half-track broadsided to a stop as brutally abrupt as the previous ride had been.

"Threw the left track," the driver said in the sudden stillness. Vickers and his wife stood up, Adrienne unslinging her rifle.

In their crazy rush, they had gained on the dryptosaurs. Their quarry was forging well ahead now, however. The other vehicle seemed to be on a converging course, but it had fallen considerably behind. Perhaps the carnivores thought they were being pursued by a pair of the biggest ceratopsians they had ever met. In any case, they showed no sign of slacking off.

Adrienne leaped over the cab to the hood of the half-track. "What's she doing?" demanded in

Hebrew the photographer in the front seat. His fellow in the box had unlimbered a holocamera. With a professionalism Vickers could appreciate, he had mounted the stump of the ladder and was rolling tape.

Adrienne's shot was sharp and clean, coming as it did on the heels of a racket so loud that it had been felt rather than heard. Secretary Cardway rose, holding the .458 by the pistol grip. To fire, he would have had to aim through the blonde woman. Vickers' own free hand closed over the forestock of the Mannlicher. He kept the muzzle slanting upward despite all the pressure the bigger man could bring to it.

"Goddammit, she missed!" Cardway shouted.

Five hundred yards down-range, the leading dryptosaur turned a cartwheel and fell. The remaining pair of carnivores leaped its body and continued to run.

Adrienne clicked the safety on as she turned toward her audience. "Not too bad for iron sights," she said coolly. Reslinging her rifle, she lighted a small cigar.

Secretary Cardway's face was a study in gray savagery while they waited for the other vehicle to reach them. Cardway had said nothing more after the dryptosaur tumbled, but to say he had relaxed was to ignore his eyes. Those eyes were directed toward the oncoming half-track, but their focus was somewhere deep in the politician's imagination. Both Craig and Vickers watched the Secretary sidelong, each for his own reasons uncertain how to react if worse came to worst.

They had taken the Rome Plow blades off the half-tracks as soon as the campsite had been cleared. Warren's vehicle might have found the brush-shearing blade handy now, as it cut across the plain to reach its disabled consort. Vickers' driver had already dismounted and was morosely surveying the track. It had been flung from the left-hand bogeys when it skewed on a root at excessive speed. He and his mate, the gunner, would have to straighten the heavy track and then carefully back the bogeys over it before it could be repinned. Vickers felt sorry for the gunner, facing a dirty job that was none of his making. As for the driver, the guide could imagine without a qualm that fool doing the whole job alone in the sun.

The other half-track struggled through the last of the separating brush like a lifeboat in the surf. It turned and stopped on the trail just ahead of the disabled vehicle, the dust it raised still retaining enough forward motion to drift across the passengers. "A bloody fine shot, Mr. Secretary!" Thomas Warren was shouting from the back. Behind him, Stern and Greenbaum were trying to conceal anxious expressions. "I saw the dust fly from its hide at your second shot," the British guide lied enthusiastically, "right over the brisket. That's why it was lagging behind, you see. In fact, old boy—" Warren leaned over the bulkhead matily—"I shouldn't be a bit surprised to find it was your ball alone that put paid to him. They can run quite a distance when hit hard, you know."

"Yes, that's, that's so," Vickers managed to say. He had noticed the other guide salvaging a pair of .458 bullets from the hadrosaur when they butchered it the previous night. At the time, he had wondered why. Now Vickers realized that one of the big bullets would be 'found' in the fresh carcass as proof of the Secretary's marksmanship. Warren really *was* very good—at what he did. Stern had probably made a mistake in wanting Vickers along at all.

Secretary Cardway was blooming like a moon-flower at dusk. "Well," he said, "the way it took

off, you know, I thought it, it was just wounded.
I'd hate to lose a wounded animal that way."

"Bloody sporting!" Warren agreed. "But say, it
still may be thrashing around, you know. Let's hop
aboard this one while your crew puts your own
lorry ship-shape."

Adrienne had jumped down from the hood and
was already stepping to the other vehicle. "Ah,
Adrienne," Vickers said in a bright voice.

She turned to her husband with a genuine smile.
"Oh, I'll be good," she called. "Mr. Cardway's shot
the biggest dryptosaur I've ever seen, is all. I'd just
like to look at it up close before it's mounted."

"Levi, Asch," Stern said to the PR men on
Vickers' half-track, "you will stay here. Two
photographers are enough for our needs."

The vehicle was crowded, but Stern had
obviously directed the driver to take it slowly no
matter what anyone else might say. Several times
Vickers called a halt while he and Warren climbed
onto the hood to take bearings. The dryptosaur
had disappeared when it fell, and its high-striding
companions were already over the horizon. In the
end, it was hearing and not sight that guided them
to their quarry. While they paused, with the diesel
engine only a background whine, Vickers heard
the throaty wheeze of the carnivore.

Both guides turned to the right. In the box of the
half-track, Adrienne and Stern leveled their rifles
toward the noise. A moment later the politicians
followed suit. The holographers capered in the
background trying to get a vantage of what was
about to happen without jostling the line of
gunners in front of them. Vickers felt the muzzle
of the heavy machine gun stir the air past his hips
as its crewman rotated the weapon to bear.

Twenty feet from the vehicle, the dryptosaur
crawled through a clump of mimosa. It hissed

with murderous fury, but its head was barely raised to the level of the knee-high scrub still separating it from the humans. The great jaws champed and ground, clicking the serrated teeth together as if they had flesh between them to shear.

"Its back's broken," Adrienne said. She lowered the butt of her rifle, sure now that there would be no need of a quick shot at a charging killer. "It's just dragging itself along on its forelegs."

"All right, Mr. Secretary," said Thomas Warren, "now remember, you don't want to damage the skull. Anywhere through the body, that's the ticket."

"Luther?" interjected the Prime Minister. He held the double rifle, its heavy barrels looking much too big for his slight form. "Might I join in —finishing the death of your trophy? I would like to think of this as a bond between us, as statesmen and as men."

"Yeah," said Cardway in a drugged voice, looking down the sights of the Mannlicher. Then, more sharply, "Go ahead, goddammit," and fired himself.

The recoil of the Gibbs pushed Greenbaum backward as if the Israeli had caught an over-large medicine ball, but he did not need the restraining hand Adrienne had unobtrusively raised between his shoulder blades. Beside him, the American cabinet official rocked as he fired, lowered his weapon to work the bolt, and raised it to fire again. As before, Cardway emptied the magazine on the struggling dinosaur; but the shots died away sooner this time because he had forgotten to reload after the two distant attempts. His rifle empty, the Secretary swung his leg over the side of the half-track.

"Christ, wait!" Warren shouted in sudden concern. "It may not be—"

Vickers fired his M14 once. After the blasts of the elephant guns, the crack of the military rifle was as sharp as a heartbreak. The ejected case sailed in a flat arc, back over the heads of the rest of the party. The dryptosaur had squirmed under the repeated impacts of the heavy bullets. Now all its muscles relaxed with a shudder, their strain transmuted to the purposeless quivering of dropped gelatine. Everyone stared at Vickers.

The guide lowered his rifle. A little defensively he said, "I pithed it. The little hole this makes in the skull—" he tapped the barrel of the M14— "won't be a problem in mounting. And if you've *got* to get close to a dino this fresh, you've got to destroy the brain first. Or it's apt as not to snap."

Without speaking, Secretary Cardway stepped from the tread to the ground. Stern and Craig leaped down instantly, more in a determination to die at their posts than in any realistic hope of saving the Secretary from whatever danger he might get himself into. Warren, Vickers, and the Prime Minister joined them more circumspectly, while Adrienne and the soldiers kept watch from the vehicle. If the PR cameramen were frightened they submerged their fears in an orgy of concentration on their view finders.

And the dryptosaur was indeed well worth taping. It was a female, lacking the spinal fringe of the males, but it was certainly the thirty feet in length that Vickers had initially estimated. Had it not been in company with two smaller adults, Vickers would have suspected it was of a different species despite the markings. "This is, well, it's unique," the guide said honestly. "I don't believe there's another speciman so fine been taken . . . unless in the past two years?"

"My God, look at the ticks," muttered Craig.

At a distance, the rims of the dryptosaur's eyes and the webbing of its three-clawed forepaws appeared to be red. Close up, the color could be seen to be that of the masses of gorged ticks, each individual the size of the first joint of a man's thumb. The bodyguard looked down and began convulsively to rub at his booted ankles. It was the first time Vickers had seen the man apparently forgetful of the Secretary of State.

"I've never found them to be a problem with human beings," the guide said sympathetically. "As for those particular ones, the stabilization chamber back at the compound should take care of them. The sealant clogs their breathing pores, of course."

"When do you find me a goddam tyrannosaurus, Mordecai?" Secretary Cardway asked.

"Soon, Luther, I am sure," the Israeli Prime Minister responded calmly. "This—mighty creature here that you have felled, this is a magnificent thing too, of course."

"Not what I came for, not what you promised," said Cardway, staring as if toward the horizon. "And it better be soon, old buddy, because this is the last night I spend here." The big Texan spun suddenly, as if to strike Greenbaum. "One thing I learned early—if somebody's got it, he's got it; and if he doesn't, giving him more time or money's just pissing down a rathole. I've pissed away about all the time you're going to see." The Secretary of State marched back to the half-track. "All right," he called over his shoulder, "let's get this show on the road, shall we?"

"Right," said Vickers, not looking at anyone. "We're carrying a collapsible sled in the other track. We'll get that and drag the dryptosaur back to camp—"

"Screw that. Let's get moving," Cardway said.

"May as well have the other crew earn their keep, eh Vickers?" Thomas Warren suggested, his smile fluffing the tips of his moustache. "They can take care of this when they get the lorry running again. We'll take a look where all these trails seem to be going. I dare say that line of trees to the west means water, and that should mean sport."

A shadow razored across the straggling group of humans. All looked up. The pterosaur that had been a dot in the far heavens an hour before was now only a hundred feet above the ground, a monster with the wingspan of an F-86. The fur of its lower surfaces was a dirty blue-gray. The upper side of its wings, visible as the creature banked, was a white dazzling with the sun it reflected. Skimming in a silence that belied its size, the great carrion-eater turned and swept back at an even lower altitude. Its beak was a yellow chisel the length of a man's forearm.

"Titanopteryx," Vickers said. "Saw the dryptosaur go down and wants a meal. Always wanted to send back a living one to see—"

Adrienne's Schultz and Larsen slammed. Both the twenty-foot wings collapsed upward and back as the muscles controlling them relaxed. Inertia carried the heavy reptile over the heads of the onlookers. Its limbs and long neck spun as gravity accelerated what was no longer a glider. When it struck the ground a hundred feet beyond the half-track, brush crackled and a pall of dust rose.

"Nice shot!" said one of the holographers.

"Why on Earth did you do that?" Vickers asked, trying to keep the concern out of his voice.

"It'll be an hour before the other track gets here," the blonde woman said. Her voice seemed calm. She was already reloading the rifle with one of the cartridges from her tunic loops. "I didn't want the flying belly over there chopping up the

. . . Secretary's trophy before then. That dryptosaur is a trophy—" she slung her rifle and stepped
up to remount the vehicle—"to be proud of."

They drove westward toward the trees at the
same deliberate pace that had brought them to the
fallen carnivore. There was much to discuss, but
there was no way to do so while Cardway and his
bodyguard were in such enforced propinquity to
the staff. As a result, the only speech on route was
Vickers' radioed directions to the crew of the
other half-track, telling them how to home on the
beacon he had left and how to load the carcass
when they got there. The Secretary's disinterest
was obvious, though he seemed to have accepted
without question that he had brought down the
dryptosaur himself.

It grew increasingly easy to proceed as they
drew nearer to their destination. Additional trails
forked into the one they were following. After
each confluence, the way grew broader. Clawed
feet had worn the way deeper, as well, so that the
surrounding brush now loomed above the vehicle.
On Earth in a later day, each bush would have
stood on a mound protected by its own roots from
the sculpturing wind. Now only rain and the feet
of passers-by affected the terrain.

One hundred yards from the edge of a meandering stream, the brush had been browsed away and
the ground trampled flat. In the shade of the
broad-leafed cottonwoods and the magnolias
fringing the water rested an incredible profusion
of animals. The PR man in the front was muttering
what seemed to be a prayer, and Mordecai Greenbaum kept repeating. "Superb! Superb!" in
Hebrew. The driver stopped at the edge of the
brush without needing orders.

There were hundreds of animals in plain sight.
The splotches of shade held groups of up to a

score, usually of mixed species. One or more of each assemblage greeted the half-track with a snort or a stiffness and focused eyes; then the sentinal would relax, having determined that the newcomer was not a hunting carnivore. Beyond that, a resting dinosaur had no brain capacity to find interest.

A single bull triceratops paced toward them. Its huge forehead bulged with jaw muscles instead of gray matter. Fifty feet away, the ten-ton beast halted and waggled its horns in sidewise arcs, its beak low. When the half-track did not respond to the challenge, even the triceratops struck it from its short list of significant stimuli. It waddled back toward the shade. Dried mud clinging to the ceratopsian's hide turned it white. Where the mud had flaked off, the scales were as black and shiny as graphite.

"Oh, that I had brought my paints," the Prime Minister murmured. "It is a landscape not of hills and trees but of animate creatures."

In a carefully businesslike tone, Vickers said, "Here's the bait to call down your tyrannosaur, Mr. Secretary. And besides using the carcass for the purpose, there are any number of fine heads. The ceratopsians make trophies that draw attention to themselves in any room they don't absolutely fill. That triceratops that looked us over, or one of those pentaceratops over there—" he pointed—"the spikes are striking and the, the coloration is quite impressive if the shadow didn't hide it."

"And they'll let you shoot, old boy," Warren put in from behind Secretary Cardway. "No need to content yourself with one, not where the game's never been hunted before." He took his left hand from his gunstock to gesture in a wide arc. Though stretches of mud flats broke the stream into a series of connected pools, the line of cottonwoods and magnolias squirmed unbroken as far as the hunters could see in either direction. There was no reason to doubt that the herds of animal life in midday somnolence extended as far as the water-course.

"There must be a dozen species of hadrosaurs in sight from here, crests of every shape and size," the British guide gloated. "Just as many ceratopsians—take one of each. If they spook here, we'll simply cruise a little further up the line to where they—"

"Let me see that," the Secretary grunted, elbowing aside the soldier manning the fifty-caliber machine gun. The startled trooper resisted momentarily, his left hand still gripping the weapon. Stern gave him a quick order in Hebrew. Puzzled, the soldier slid aside. The driver, seated directly below the big muzzle, covered his ears with his hands.

"Pull the charging handle once more," Stern said quietly. Cardway frowned. The Israeli official reached past the politician and drew back the lever on the right side of the receiver himself. When he let the handle go, the breech-block clanged like a horseshoe striking an anvil. "Now it is ready," Stern said. "You press the trigger with your thumbs."

Secretary Cardway's face grew intent while those around him watched with varied expressions. The elephant guns had roared. The blast of the cal fifty was by contrast as sharp as that of Vickers' M14, as loud as a stick of bombs going off nearby. The first three rounds were high. One of them touched a cottonwood and exploded, shattering a branch as thick as a man's thigh. Splintered wood and then the branch itself tumbled down on a trio of duckbills leaping upright from their sleep. Cardway corrected, lowering the muzzle and firing again. This time the explosive bullets raked the tree trunk and the bellies of the dinosaurs as they bolted straight at the gun. The duckbills flopped to the ground, squealing like freight trains slowing.

One of the wounded creatures staggered to its feet again. Cardway ignored it, swinging his gun onto a cluster of ceratopsians. Vickers leveled his own rifle. It was hard to sight on the duckbill's head. It bobbed and dipped as the creature tried with its short forelegs to pat away the coils of its own intestines tangling it. A rush of tears blinded the guide. He cradled his weapon again, whispering to himself.

The half-track shuddered with recoil as Cardway hosed a triceratops standing broadside to them, thirty yards away. One of the beast's long brow horns shattered, then a string of white flashes traversed its side. The triceratops plunged forward, bawling, and collapsed with its beak in the furrow it had plowed. The smokey line of tracers continued to snap through the air which its target had vacated. Bullets walked across the surface of the stream, gouting spray at two-foot intervals. Then they crashed into a gaggle of four pentaceratops staring blankly at the ruin of their fallen kinsman. The nitroguanadine bursting charges slashed the beasts. Two fell, two turned to run. The latter drew with them the panicked creatures to either side. Mud and water sprayed as the line of animals rushed across the stream, stretching away from the gunfire as if it were an arrow drawing a bowstring.

The muzzle blasts ceased abruptly. An instant later the last explosive bullet cracked. The only mechanical noise remaining was that of an ejected case, ringing like a wind chime on the ground among the brass that had preceded it. The stench of propellent, pooling about the half-track in layers, was ripe and cloying. At least it hid the stink of blood and excrement from the dozen wounded and dying dinosaurs nearby. It did not hide their cries. Nothing could have done that, but the crashing gunfire had made even the bellows of pain sound reedy and distant.

Henry Vickers climbed over the side of the vehicle. Behind him, Secretary Cardway was saying, "I've wanted to do that ever since the Convention when those bastards from New York gave me the shaft so deep it clicked on my molars. Yeah . . . ." Without turning around, Vickers could not tell whether the Secretary of State was addressing someone in particular or was just letting his thoughts spray the landscape. Vickers was afraid of what he might do if he turned to look at the man.

The gutshot hadrosaur was still standing. It eyed Vickers' approach as it might have that of one of the scavengers of its own time. Pain and shock kept the beast shackled into place, hooting at the guide through its tongueless palate. Even crippled, it towered above the man.

"Henry!" Adrienne cried.

Vickers shot the duckbill through the roof of its mouth. Soft tissue spattered him. The two-ton dinosaur arched backwards as if it had touched a high-tension line. Both the hind feet left the ground for the instant before the body thudded down on its side. The muscles were spasming under the russet hide, but there was no brain left to register pain.

Vickers walked to the next hadrosaur, sprawled in a heap on the ground. He socketed the slotted muzzle brake of the M14 in the creature's ear and fired. The carcass did not move. The guide stepped toward the third beast, which had begun squirm-

ing in the direction of the stream after the explosive bullets smashed both hip joints.

"Henry!" Adrienne repeated, close at hand. She
caught him by the shoulder. "What are you
doing?"

"Let go of me," the guide mumbled.

"Then get hold of yourself!" his wife said.
Vickers pulled free. The blonde woman stepped in
front of him and brain-shot the wounded hadrosaur herself. Vickers paused at the crash of the
Schultz and Larsen. When Adrienne turned to face
him, he met her eyes.

"All right," Adrienne said angrily, "we'll do
what we have to do. But we don't need to stand on
top of the goddamned things to put paid to them!"

"No, I'm sorry," the guide said. "I didn't—I
won't do something foolish like that again."

The phrase 'do what we have to do' echoed
through Vickers' mind while he and his wife
finished off the wounded animals. He continued to
think about it far on into the night.

In a landscape that had no other light source
than the stars, the propane mantle lantern inside
turned the whole compound of mosquito netting
into a pearly prism. The intrusion vehicles, the
half-tracks, and the individual shelters within
were blocks of shadow. A man, a shadow himself,
stood just inside the zippered gate.

Vickers paused, still in the darkness as far as
the person waiting was concerned. Beside him, his
wife sighed. It was the only sound or sign of
restiveness that she had given during the silent
hours outside the compound. The guide smiled
invisibly at himself and stepped forward again,
fumbling for the zipper. Avraham Stern leaned
toward him from the other side and opened a slit
with a single motion. "Henry," he said in greeting,

"Mrs. Vickers. A pleasant night."

Though the netting could not have made a significant difference, night sounds seemed distanced within the compound. The carnivore snarling at a lesser fellow was suddenly millions of years away. Adrienne lighted one of her small cigars; it belonged to this world, not the other one beyond the nylon gauze.

"Henry, might I speak with you for a moment?" the Israeli official asked. "You are well, I trust?"

Adrienne's face glowed orange beneath the brim of her bush hat as she drew on her cigar. The smoke she exhaled hung in the distant lantern-light like the ink of a squid in still water. "Me for a bath," she said. "There's no point hunting in the lap of luxury if you don't—luxuriate now and again." She sauntered toward the trailers that served as kitchen and showers, part of the cargo from the back-up insertion. Her rifle slanted past her left shoulder, safe and ready to use at an instant's notice.

"I'm all right," Vickers said, both men watching Adrienne disappear into the trailer. "I just—thought it might be a good idea to be outside for a time."

"Certainly," the official said. His right hand was toying with the breech of his rifle. When he noticed the fact, he stopped. "A good night to sit and talk, certainly."

The guide laughed and dropped to seat himself cross-legged on the ground. "Avraham, every word anybody says within three hundred meters of the compound gets routed through the alarm system. Straight into the command post. Now, I'm not going wandering around farther than that into the dark; and do you really think I was going to say the things you're afraid I was saying where the guard is going to run straight to you with them? No, I went out to sit and think; and Adrienne came out to sit with me and I suppose think too . . . or not. And then we came in." He looked at Stern, who could see the outlines of his smile and feel the falseness of it. "We've got a problem that needs solving, you know," Vickers continued softly.

"Henry," the official said.

"No, no." The guide brushed away the unspoken fear with his free hand, the hand that did not hold an automatic rifle. "No, I mean the problem you pay me to deal with, making important clients happy. Getting one a tyrannosaur, in this case."

Stern did not attempt to hide his relief. "And you have?" he asked. "That is . . . is very good. Mr. Warren does not feel there is any certainty that a tyrannosaur will visit the, ah, bait, in the time at hand. And the Prime Minister is equally sure, with which I concur, that the time cannot be extended. Secretary Cardway will hunt tomorrow with us. To keep him longer must be against his will; which would, of course, be even worse than the present unfortunate circumstances."

Vickers rose again in the limber motion of a man younger than he was. "All right," he said, "we'll see. Can you get the others together— Warren and the Prime Minister, that is?"

The official chuckled. "They are waiting in the command post," he said. "I gave the guards—the soldiers—leave from listening to the warning microphones when I realized where you were. Not that I needed to have worried, of course."

The command post was another trailer. It housed the radio, the alarm system, and the banks of nicad batteries on which they could operate when the half-track generators were not present to drive them. The lantern which burned continuously in the center of the compound hung on a pole nearby; but within the trailer, the only light was that from the instruments. In the blue glow, Thomas Warren disappeared behind his moustache and the Prime Minister looked like a skull. The amplified sounds of the Cretaceous night wove a blanket that smothered the words whispered within.

Vickers followed Stern inside. The guide started to close the door, then frowned. He gestured out into the darkness, toward the distant quadrant where the Secretary of State's tent had been pitched.

Stern's smile was a shift of the planes of his face in the dim light. "He was dictating in his tent," the official said. "Now he is asleep. One of the sensors—" he tapped a separate display panel above a larger area screen—"was set within the compound, you see. It will register footsteps, long before they reach us. And his dog is sleeping at his feet."

Vickers grinned back. Craig had been billeted in the large tent with the soldiers. By his own choice, however, the bodyguard had spread his bedroll on the ground a few yards from the entrance to the Secretary's tent.

"That one concerns me, sometimes," said Mordecai Greenbaum. "He is under too much strain. Either they should have sent three or four guards—or they should have been sensible and not sent any."

Vickers shrugged. It was too late to worry about that now. "All right," he said. "I've got a notion of how to get Cardway what he wants. But it's going to be expensive. It'll take one, maybe two round trips of the big intrusion vehicle to do it and to cover up afterwards what we've done."

"The expense of not being successful," said Greenbaum in measured tones, "is the existence of Israel, I am afraid. Tell us what you need."

"All right," Vickers repeated. "There's probably a tyrannosaur in the area . . . and butcher's work like that on the creek bank may bring in more than that in a week or so. Food in that quantity overrides territory, while it lasts."

"That's fine, old chap," said Thomas Warren. His voice had the sharpness of a man who knows he is considered second rate in the instant discussion. "But we don't have a week or so." In the close confines of the trailer, the British guide had not lighted his pipe. He gestured nervously with the stem, like a child holding a revolver. "And besides, you know as well as I do that there may be nothing bigger around here than the dryptosaur we took this morning. You know, I think that with a little better support, old boy, I could have convinced Cardway that it really was a—"

"Horseshit," said Avraham Stern in heavy, careful English. Warren fell silent.

Vickers brushed his hand back and forth in frustration. "No, no," he said, "Warren's right. About being no tyrannosaur near enough, may be. There's only one living tyrannosaur we can locate for sure—and that's the one in a cage at the Institute for Zoology. Topside in Tel Aviv. It's also the one I want returned for Cardway."

The other three men began to talk simultaneously, stopping themselves when they realized that Vickers was still poised to continue. "Please go on, sir," the Prime Minister said. His hinted smile showed his awareness that the guide, too, was smiling.

"We'll leave the compound in the morning," Vickers said, "beat up the bait area. Who knows, maybe there'll be something worth going after there. As soon as the Secretary is out of sight, though, Mr. Stern, here, and Warren carry Vehicle Beth—Aleph isn't big enough for the cargo, and

anyway, maybe the walls on Beth might help if the
dino started to get loose early . . . anyway, they go
back Topside. Avraham does what has to be done
to rig the beast with a radio beacon and get it
loaded." The guide paused, then added, "Ah, you
don't think there's going to be any difficulty getting your orders obeyed ASAP, do you? I mean,
there's not going to be much time, and I know
what bureaucracy can be like."

Stern snorted. "There will be no trouble," he
said. "Those who know me will obey. Those who
do not know me will obey, or they will have a company of paratroopers in their offices until they
have obeyed. I—I do not get much excitement any
more."

"Then it's just a matter of getting Dr. Galil to
drop you a few klicks out," Vickers continued.
"We don't want to turn a tyrannosaur loose in the
compound, after all. That'll take some very close
figuring, but . . . well, it's required. And Shlomo
can do it, he's never failed yet."

"I don't see precisely what I'm supposed to be
doing, old boy," said Thomas Warren. He was
clutching his pipe against the row of looped cartridges over his heart.

"Well," said Vickers, "ah, Thomas, I think it's
going to require more than one man to off-load the
dino. And apart from the security angle, I think it
has to be someone who's familiar with the beasts."

"I'm familiar enough with bloody tyrannosaurs
that I don't share an intrusion vehicle with living
ones!" the Englishman exploded. He either did not
notice or did not care that the trailer door had
begun to open. "*You* can do silly-arse things like
that if you want, but Mrs. Warren didn't raise any
fools!"

"I'll go," said Adrienne Vickers from the doorway.

"You've been listening?" Stern demanded.

The woman spun her cigar out into the darkness, then exhaled in jets from both nostrils before she squeezed into the trailer. She was in no hurry to speak. Though the nicotine had stripped her visual purple so that she could not see by the instrument lights, she knew that she was the focus of the eyes of the four men. "I don't listen at doors," Adrienne said at last, "though everybody in camp's heard Mr. Warren's little outburst, I'm sure."

"Adrienne," Vickers said, "this isn't a game."

"Look, dammit," the tall blonde said. She leaned forward and gestured, her fingernails glinting. "There's only one tyrannosaur we can promise, that's really *promise*. The one Henry and I captured alive. I don't have to listen to you talk to know that."

"You didn't say anything tonight," her husband commented.

"Neither did you!" Adrienne responded sharply, though not in a loud voice. "And we didn't have to, did we? We both knew what had to be done. Anyway—" she drew a breath– "anyway, I'm the one who needs to nurse the baby back. He'll be sedated, but we don't dare have him knocked on his ass, not if he needs to be upright for Cardway the same morning."

"Well then," the Prime Minister said briskly. "We are agreed?" Stern nodded. Warren shrugged.

"Does it ever bother you," Adrienne Vickers asked, "that a—certifiable madman like Cardway has the sort of power you're encouraging him to use? I mean, it's your world. I've found I could do all right without it . . . though I suppose I'd have to get used to a crossbow and smoke banana leaves or something."

"Banana leaves would be an improvement, I'm sure, madame," the Prime Minister said, bowing courteously.

"And we joke about it," the woman continued wonderingly. "Well, it's your world. For however long. Henry, I'm for bed."

"We've said our say," the guide remarked, reaching past his wife to the door catch. "We'll see in the morning. We'll all see in the morning."

Either the sun slanting across their backs was hotter than it had been the day before, or the anger in the box of the half-track made it seem that way. The shadow of the dust they raised stretched ahead of the vehicle, bulking across the scrub like chaos made manifest. Secretary Cardway rode grimly at the front bulkhead, to the right of the cal fifty. The gunner, wedged tightly between the Secretary and Vickers on the other side, looked nervous. He was the same soldier who had manned the gun the day before. What he had seen then had convinced him that both of the men beside him were dangerously insane.

In the distance, flecks spun against the white sky like flakes of cardboard hurled from a giant bonfire. Cardway's face softened minusculy from the stony anger he had maintained since getting up in the morning. Vickers saw the interest and said over the intercom, "Pterosaurs again, sir. For the carrion. What we have to hope is that the bigger carnivores will be there too."

The Secretary of State looked across at Vickers while the soldier between them cringed away. "You goddam better hope so," the politician said. His voice in Vickers' ears was out of synch with his moving lips, because the sound was being picked up by Cardway's throat mike.

In the back of the box, the Prime Minister frowned. Warren, beside him, appeared to take no notice. The Englishman had been morose all morning. When he looked at Vickers, it was with a degree of animation; but the spirit animating his eyes was one of dull anger. Warren had not been pleased to be subordinated to Vickers. It was now evident to him that his employers considered Adrienne also a far more valuable member of the operation than the junior guide was . . . and that made one more factor for Vickers to consider.

Craig and a holographer rode in the middle of the box. The PR staffer at least could be trusted not to actively endanger anyone else.

As they neared the scene of the previous day's slaughter, the circling flecks resolved into pterosaurs descending. There were never fewer than a dozen in sight at a time, even though the lowest continually disappeared at the bottom of the falling helixes. Newcomers, by now from many kilometers distance, replenished the pattern from above. Their fragile wing membranes enabled the great creatures to lift from the ground in air so still that pollen scarcely drifted. The converse of that delicacy was the fact that severe braking forces like those habitually employed by the feathered scavengers of later ages would have shredded pterosaur wings at the first application. Silent and awesomely large, the creatures spiraled down with the gentle beauty of thistledown.

There was something angelic in the descent of the pterosaurs with their dazzlingly-white upper surfaces. Then the half-track rumbled through the last of the masking brush. The ground on which the winged scavengers were landing was a living Hell of previous arrivals.

Thirty meters in front of them, a dryptosaur glared up from the carcass of the duckbill it had finished disemboweling. The carnivore was probably one of the pair that had escaped the day before, a smallish male with scar tissue ridging the left side of its head including the eye socket. Not a choice trophy, but closer than Vickers cared to see a carnivore to one of his clients. "Go ahead, sir," he said, aiming at the top of the beast's sternum himself.

"It's smaller than the other one," Cardway muttered correctly. He sighted and fired anyway.

The dryptosaur was facing them astraddle of the herbivore's neck. Its head and body were raised higher than they would normally have been. Like a dog on a morsel, the carnivore was trying to look as threatening as possible to drive away its competition. The half-track was probably equated in the beast's limited mind with an unusually large ceratopsian—not a creature that a dryptosaur or even a tyrannosaur of several times the bulk would normally have charged. Still, the beast lived by killing, and a wound could be expected to bring a response. The guide tensed.

And promptly felt a fool, when the Mannlicher blasted and the dryptosaur crumpled like a wet sheet. Cardway had placed his bullet perfectly, shattering the carnosaur's spine after wrecking the complex of blood vessels above the heart. The beast flopped over on its back, the hind legs kicking upward convulsively. A drop of blood slung from a talon spattered coldly on Vickers' wrist, but the danger was over. "Perfect!" the guide said with honest enthusiasm. "Now—"

Secretary Cardway cut off the instructions with another thunderous shot. Beside himself, Vickers started to curse. Then he stepped back. There was no point cursing an avalanche or a waterspout. The Secretary was as ungovernable as those forces of Nature when he once began firing. The muzzle of the .458 jumped three more times, each thrust preceded by a momentary spurt of orange

as the last of the powder charge burned outside
the barrel. The reports lessened in apparent intensity, though only because they were literally
deafening to the listeners. After the fifth shot, the
ringing that persisted was loud enough to
challenge the myriad squalling of the scavengers
remaining on the scattered corpses.

There were no herbivores in sight where there
had been hundreds the preceding day. Possibly
that was a reaction to the carnage itself, the
slaughter and the stink of blood. More likely, the
plant-eaters would avoid the area only so long as
the sharp-toothed throng were bolting the carrion
like locusts on Spring wheat. "Pull up a hundred
meters or so to the right," Vickers ordered the
driver. "Dead slow." The guide squinted though
the sun was behind him as he surveyed the crop of
vermin. Usually the presence of the pair of dryptosaurs—the second was slashing at a pentaceratops
which had died on the far bank of the stream—
would mean that nothing bigger had found the
kill. A tyrannosaur would drive away the one-ton
dryptosaurs, though it was likely to ignore anything smaller. Here, however, the volume of flesh
was so great that Vickers hoped against hope that
the clanking of their treads would lift the dragon-
like head of the greatest of the carnosaurs into
sight from where it rested behind a fallen triceratops or the like.

Nothing of the sort happened. Even the lesser
meat-eaters, which *were* present, ignored the
vehicle. That was just as well. There were at least
a score of dromaeosaurs visible, half-ton
predators with the habits and vicious
temperament of hyenas. The slaughter had drawn
several packs together, some of them surely out of
their range. When the food had been bolted down
to the last scraps, the bush would be the scene of

fighting which nothing human could equal in savagry. For the nonce, all were fully occupied with stuffing down gobbets of meat. Their mouths expanded like snakes' to accept larger pieces than rigid jaw-hinges would have permitted. The number and proximity of the carnivores still made Vickers nervous, even with the heavy machine gun to back him up in an emergency.

Smaller than the toothed dromaeosaurs but still potentially lethal to a man were the ornithomimids, beaked omnivores in appearance much like the ostriches for which some were named. Their normal diet was of seeds and insects. But as when the lemmings swarm in Norway, the reindeer feed on them, here a similar abundance of flesh had summoned the swift runners from far across the plains to feast. They pecked and squabbled, darting in to seize a strip of meat and dragging it back to a distance of a few meters. They bolted their food, defending it with glaring eyes and legs whose kick could rip sheet metal.

The least of the scavengers were feathered, though only a few of them were true birds in the sense that they or their ancestors could fly. Many of their descendents would, however. Warm-blooded creatures like dinosaurs needed either bulk or insulation to prevent their high metabolisms from outstripping any possible food source. The smallest of the dinosaurs crawling over the bloating carcasses were no bigger than chickens. Like chickens, they could not have survived without the dead air space provided within their layers of feathers—the feathers being modified scales, as was the fur of mammals and the pterosaurs. Some few had made the insulation do double duty, adding wing beats to the powerful thrust of their hind legs when they wished to climb a carcass or escape to a nearby bush with a chosen morsel. The high skies were still the province of the great pterosaurs now descending, however, their delicacy more efficient until the storms of the coming age swept them into oblivion.

There were no mammals visible save the occupants of the half-track. The night would bring them out again from the holes to which they had been driven tens of millions of years before by the ancestors of the dinosaurs. So long as Earth hosted the dinosaurs, the mammals would grub for insects in the dark and would fall prey to the least of the swift-striding creatures with whom they in no sense competed.

The vehicle halted as Vickers had ordered. Craig, the bodyguard, said, "You did this as an insult, didn't you?" His voice was high, on the edge of control.

The guide turned in surprise. He had become accustomed to thinking of the bodyguard as a tool rather than a human being, an object with a programmed set of responses to stimuli ... rather like his own Uzi sub-machine gun. It was disconcerting to hear Craig volunteering statements that had no bearing on his duties. It was more than disconcerting that the statements made no sense. Vickers wondered if the strain had in fact pushed the younger American off the deep end, ready to spray all those around him with bullets too small to be useful except on men.

Perhaps Secretary Cardway had the same thought. "Craig, what the hell do you mean?" he demanded with something less than his normal assurance. Greenbaum edged backward, trying to get behind the bodyguard without being obtrusive about it. Adrienne and Stern had been 'left in camp with the vehicle that wasn't running right' according to the story the Americans had been told. They would have been comforting companions at this juncture. Thomas Warren merely watched with a glimmer of a smile.

"He's trying to shame you with this filth, sir," Craig said. He gestured with his left hand at the landscape, the slaughtered dinosaurs lying like hillocks completely covered by the mass of creatures feeding on them. "This, this—disgusting . . . he'll make you out to be a butcher to the world, sir. He's just brought you here to discredit you!"

Vickers was very still. There was an instant's fear within him that perhaps Craig had seen within him a truth that the guide had hidden even from himself. There was nothing unnatural about the scavengers, any more than the sight of maggots festering in a dead rabbit is unnatural. But it was true that this circus of carrion and corruption would affect many voters with the repugnance with which the machine-gunning had affected the guide himself.

But Secretary Cardway blinked incredulously. "Oh, for Christ' sake," he said, "I had to bring you but I don't have to listen to crap. Keep your mouth shut if you still want a job when we get back." He turned to Vickers, utterly ignoring the bodyguard whose insight he was unable to credit. "And we're going back right now," he said. "I've wasted enough time." Rotating his head to fix the Prime Minister, he added, "If this is your idea of fun, Greenbaum, you must love campaigning. Heat, dust, rubber food, and idiots."

The responder on Vickers' wrist looked like a watch. It now gave a tiny chime and tickled his skin with just enough current to get his attention. The guide glanced down, certain that God must answer prayers in the Cretaceous. The device was tuned to the radio beacon Stern and Adrienne carried to tag the tyrannosaur. The responder's face had lighted dull orange, meaning that the beast had popped back into the Cretaceous within two— or three, at the outside—kilometers of the responder. That was almost too close, since it would take some minutes to unload the tyrannosaur and ride the intrusion vehicle back Topside. But Vickers could easily kill time on route until Adrienne radioed with the coded message that gave him the all-clear.

"Well, this is a wash-out, it seems," Vickers said, beaming at the others, "but there's a spot I noticed just a—a few minutes from here where I'll give you my word there's a tyrannosaur."

Even Greenbaum and Warren looked askance at the senior guide. Vickers' enthusiasm had carried him momentarily out of the present setting. The incongruity of his triumphant tone did not strike him until he saw everyone else in the vehicle gaping as if he had lost his mind. "Ah," he continued, in a more reserved fashion, "I'll sit beside the driver there and guide him. Mr. Secretary, if you'll stand ready but not, not shoot until Mr. Warren or I say, say to shoot, that is, we'll put you in the best place."

As the guide clambered down to exchange places with the holographer, he surreptitiously set his responder on search mode and swept it in an arc. The lighted face glowed green until the guide's arm pointed within one degree of the beacon. There it flashed red, giving Vickers the bearing. Setting the little device back on ranging, he said to the driver, "We're headed northeast, friend." He gestured. "Take it easy. One of these trails to water should lead us back the way we want. When it branches, I'll give you directions."

The soldier frowned in puzzlement, but Stern had made it clear that morning that Vickers was to be obeyed no matter what he ordered. The

vehicle shuddered into gear, then swung wide so
that the driver could steer it into what looked like
a suitable gap in the brush.

This time, no one had suggested salvaging the
dead dryptosaur. Vickers wondered silently
whether even bagging a tyrannosaur would affect
Secretary Cardway as Greenbaum and Stern
hoped it would. Very possibly it would not—
which was probably to the world's benefit.

Branches flapped toward Vickers' face and
sprang away as the half-track crawled through
brush that was growing denser. Occasionally a
cluster of stumps would appear where some ceratopsian had sheared off a thicket near the ground
and spent the next ten minutes stuffing it all down
his gullet. More often, an alcove had been stripped
of leaves and bark by some hadrosaur's enormous
battery of teeth. The naked white branch-cores
splayed skeletally toward the beaten trail, then
were gone and past and replaced by similar signs.

Twice at a forking, Vickers checked his
responder and pointed the driver on. Above and
behind him, Secretary Cardway's expression
showed an increasing impatience for something to
happen. The guide in turn was concerned that he
had not yet received clearance from Adrienne. He
was planning a delay—taking the next wrong
turning should be enough—when Nature
accomplished the desired end herself. Brush
crashed to the right of the trail and a huge
ceratopsian head loomed over the half-track.

"Hold it!" Vickers cried. The driver's foot,
poised between brake pedal and accelerator,
slammed down on the former. The juddering halt
sprayed dust forward, but their speed was low
enough to avoid injuries. It was a triceratops,
snorting a dozen feet in the air. Its beak was open,
displaying rows of knife-edged shearing teeth

behind it. "My God, Mr. Secretary!" Vickers cried as he swung his door open, "I think we've got a pair mating! I don't think any clients ever had a look at this before!"

"Nail the blighter right through the throat!" said Thomas Warren in the box above.

Vickers, shocked and furious, spun around. *"Wait for Chrissake!"* he shouted. Cardway had already leveled the Mannlicher and it was doubtful that he even heard. The guide leaped, trying to get out of the cone of shock when the big rifle fired. He was partly successful. The muzzle blast sledged him but did not knock him down with a nose bleed, as would have resulted from slightly closer proximity. Leaves trembled in an arc to either side of the gun. The triceratops lurched upright with both its broad front paws lashing at the sky.

Vickers snapped off two shots at the dinosaur forty feet away. From his angle, all he could see beyond the brush was the creature's weaving skull —but a shot anywhere else would be useless at this point anyway. Then a hawthorn thicket splintered toward the half-track to pass the female, charging with her head down and her black-tipped horns aimed at the cab.

If the two ceratopsians had stayed coupled, they would have been harmless even to spectators approaching close enough to touch them. Violently dismounted by her mate, the female's certain reaction was to run in the direction she was facing. While that was not a charge, technically, the effect was the same on anything that happened to be in the path of the ten-ton missile. It was really the first time the heavy machine gun could have been useful. It was not useful, of course, because the range was too short and the gunner was unprepared for a target appearing twenty feet below the rearing head he had trained on. Vickers, leaning over the hood of the half-track, fired.

The tiny uranium penetrator, moving at 3,500 feet per second and no more affected by skull bones than it was by the air between muzzle and target, took the dinosaur just behind the right eye. Eight feet away, the bullet exited behind the left shoulder. The exit hole gaped momentarily like a hungry mouth, but flesh is plastic at hypersonic velocities: the wound spasmed back to normalcy almost as suddenly as it opened. Within the skull, however, the shock waves of the penetrator's passage were still reverberating. The lump of nerve tissue serving the triceratops as a brain was scrambled as thoroughly as an egg dropped from an airplane.

The female's hind legs continued to drive her, as a headless chicken's will; but the thrust was no longer forward since the forelegs had buckled and the creature's beak was gouging the soil. The right brow horn struck the frame under the vehicle's left fender and pierced it with a crash like an anti-tank gun firing. The tip broke off. The dead triceratops came to rest with its eyes open and its vertical nose spike touching the bumper.

Vickers stepped to one side and smashed the sacral thickening of the spine to end the thrashing of the corpse's hind legs. Then he looked up at the men in the half-track. Everyone else had been too startled to shoot. "Warren," Vickers said, speaking loudly over the tinny ringing in his own ears, "if I ever hear you intend to go on a time safari again, I'll came back from wherever I am and beat you within an inch of your life."

The three faces peering at Vickers over the front bulkhead of the truck were a study in contrasts. Secretary Cardway looked bemused. His rifle was raised. He had recocked it too slowly for a second shot at the male triceratops, and in his focus on the male, the Secretary had not noticed the rush of the female until it was over. The soldier in the middle gazed down at the dead female, well aware that he had been too slow to stop it with his cal fifty. The gunner knew that he had not prevented disaster himself, and that had disaster occurred . . . shit rolls down hill, and he was on the bottom.

Thomas Warren was smiling, apparently because he did not know what else to do. It dawned on Vickers that the Englishman really was not aware that his advice to Cardway had almost gotten them all killed. Had Vickers been a hair slower or a hair less accurate, the ceratopsian's charge would at best have left them stranded in the bush with no vehicle and no radio. The worst . . . a search team would have been hard put to find human traces after a creature larger than a pair of elephants had trampled them all into the ground. Warren's own rifle had slumped back to high port—but like Cardway, he had been aiming at the male triceratops. It was as if the female of the pair, by being unseen, had become non-existent.

Mordecai Greenbaum laid a hand on the shoulder of the machine-gunner, rotating him out of the way to make room. "I do not think that will be necessary, Mr. Vickers," the small Israeli said. His voice penetrated easily the sounds of the male triceratops dying close off in the brush. "When the beasts were mating, shooting one was sure to provoke the other, was it not? I do not think the Ministry of Tourism needs employees who exhibit such bad judgment. I will speak to Avraham."

"Say, hold hard a minute," said Warren. The fatuous smile dripped away as full realization of what was happening struck him. "We're supposed to be entertaining the client, right? And he's not a bloody photographer, he's a gunner, so I—"

"Are we ready to proceed, Mr. Vickers?" the Prime Minister asked.

"*I* damned well am," said the Secretary of State. He had lost the open-eyed stare he wore over his sights, relapsing into the arrogant impatience which Vickers found only a touch less intolerable.

"Now listen!" Warren shouted. "You sods aren't going to do this to me! If you think I'm going to keep quiet while you—"

"Mr. Warren!" said Greenbaum. Listening to the snap of his voice, Vickers for the first time realized how the man could rule his coalition cabinet as if it were a drill team. "I will remind you that breaches of security can be viewed as treason; and treason trials may be held *in camera* if the need warrants."

"I'm not a Jew," the guide said, gray-faced and too stunned to edit the words bubbling from his subconscious.

"You need not be Jewish to be tried for treason to the State of Israel," Greenbaum said crisply, "nor even a resident to be tried. Eichman was not a resident either, you may remember, . . . Driver, let us go on."

"Mobile Two to Mobile One," the radio said in Adrienne's attentuated voice.

"Thank God," said Vickers aloud before he thumbed his lapel mike. He raised his index finger unnecessarily to quiet the others before saying, "Go ahead, Mobile Two. Is everything all right?"

"More or less," the radio hissed. Then, "Yes, it's all right. We're proceeding to join you. We're on a pony, not the half-track."

The guide blanked his face. Cardway probably did not know that the expedition had brought none of the four-wheeled utility vehicles, so Adrienne's appearance on one would not give the deception away. Still, the initial plan had been for her and Stern to ride the intrusion vehicle back Topside after they had dropped the tyrannosaur in the bush, then to be reinserted at the compound. That way, everything at the camp when Cardway returned would look the same as it had when he departed. Instead, Stern and Adrienne had brought back a pony along with the tagged dinosaur; and they were obviously proceeding from the drop site rather than the camp if they expected to join the hunters before they made the kill. The change in plans concerned Vickers as much as did his wife's initial 'more or less' on the radio.

"We could name this one," Warren said in an odd voice. Vickers looked up. The British guide's face was stiff and his gesture toward the triceratops, dead under the wheels, was broadly theatrical. "We could call her Adrienne, do you think? And the other one, maybe we'll name it Stern?"

"Warren," Vickers said. His left hand touched the receiver of his rifle, but the fingers sprang away again as if the metal were afire.

"Or maybe Washman, I hear he was one," Warren continued. His eyes were unfocused and his voice had no inflection. "Of course, we could scarcely find all the names for—"

Vickers sprang upward, his left hand closing on the Englishman's tunic and his right whistling in a punch that would have smashed his knuckles had it more than grazed the other's head. Warren's snakeskin-banded hat fell off. The barrel of the heavy machine gun was in Vickers' way, blocking him from a closer grapple. His feet were on the seat and he was trying more or less unconsciously to climb through the gun and the bulkhead on which it was mounted. Prime Minister Greenbaum shouted an order as he and the soldier dragged Warren backward. The British guide had thrown

an arm across his face. His expression was that of
an awakened sleepwalker.

Under the pressure of the two Israelis, Warren
surged back and over a chest of camera equipment. Vickers' anger broke when his grip did. He
steadied himself against the machine gun, panting. John Craig's Uzi was six inches from Vickers'
left eye. The safety was off. "Put that goddamned
thing away," said Vickers wearily. "I'm no danger
to you and yours." He flexed his right hand. He
had skinned the back of it somehow, probably by
brushing the cal fifty when he swung at Warren.
"I'm no danger even to that shit, it seems," he said.
"Mr. Prime Minister, if you'll keep him where I
don't see him for a while, I'd be obliged. We can go
on now." Vickers sank back into his seat. "We've
had enough dirty laundry."

The driver backed, ignoring the crunch of brush
buckling under his treads. He cramped the front
wheels sharply, steering toward a wall of thorns
and vines to clear the triceratops dead across half
the trail. As the soldier engaged forward again, a
little utility vehicle with two persons aboard
swung around a bend in the trail ahead. The man
at the machine gun almost fired by reflex.

Everyone was cursing. The half-track clashed to
a stop, more from unexpectedness than real
danger of running over the aluminium pony. Stern
was at the tiller guiding the vehicle awkwardly.
Adrienne was far more experienced with the
ponies, but shots had been fired and there was a
triceratops making the earth shudder as its
muscles continued to die. The blonde woman
squatted behind Stern, trying to look in all directions at once and ready to respond instantly with a
bullet from her Schultz and Larsen.

Stern jerked the tiller. To the men on the half-
track, the smaller vehicle disappeared behind the

bulk of the female triceratops. Moments later Adrienne and the Israeli official scampered around the great carcass. "Came by a trail that put us ahead of you," the woman explained loudly as she opened the door to the cab. "Move over." In a voice that Vickers saw on her lips rather than heard, she heard, "We need to move fast. That dino isn't going to last long."

Stern was being handed into the back by one of the holographers. Secretary Cardway was speaking in a cold rage, though Vickers did not turn to see who the recipient might be. As the half-track moved forward again, he mouthed to Adrienne, "An overdose of dope? We could dick around in the brush and hope it'll wear off."

"Left at the next fork!" Adrienne shouted to the driver. Then, to Vickers under the rising whine of the diesel as they plowed through brush, "We brought it back in shackles, no drugs at all. You know, Avraham may be a desk jockey but he's got enough guts for two."

Vickers smiled, calmed by the scent and touch of his wife in the cramped cab. "I think he's seen his share of field work of one kind and the other," the guide said. "He's . . . a good soldier. Jesus, a good German. I think . . . I'm afraid that's what we all are, good Germans, doing our jobs and keeping quiet."

The flash of lights and shadow as the half-track lurched down the trail was a perepheral distraction to Vickers and Adrienne as they faced each other in the close quarters. "Well," she said, "the tyrannosaur's about to become a good dinosaur. In the sense of being dead as one. They've figured out what the problem is when dinos come Topside: parrot fever . . . or bird fever in general, I guess. This one's caught it just like the rest, and its lungs are already hemorrhaging."

"What?" Vickers demanded, certain that he had not understood his wife correctly.

"Bird fever," she repeated. She put a hand on her husband's shoulder to steady her as the wheels bounced on a head-sized rock. "Ornithosis. It's not a serious disease in birds today, ah, Topside. But dinos are close enough genetically to catch it, and they have no natural immunities. It's like small-pox and the Pacific Islanders to them."

Everyone on the half-track ducked involuntarily as the dappling of the vegetation blackened momentarily into solid shadow. The driver steadied on the wheel again. Vickers let out his breath and lowered the rifle he had been trying to clear with too little room to do so. The titanopteryx sailed on, barely faster and barely higher than the half-track. The straggling limbs of the brush hid the pterosaur again.

The responder on the guide's wrist pinged twice, flashing red. They were within one hundred meters of the beacon and—God willing—of the tyrannosaur. Of the end of this charade of a safari. "Stop, stop!" Vickers ordered, touching the driver on the forearm. They slowed to a halt with barely a quiver. As the driver thumbed dust from his instrument dials, the guide stood on the seat facing back toward the other men. "We've sighted fresh spoor," he lied. "The trophy is very close. For the, ah, remainder of the stalk, one of the holographers and W-warren will ride in the cab. Mr. Secretary, you'll stay where you are, if you please, and I'll ride in the front on the other side of the machine gun. Adrienne, Mr. Stern, if you will take the back corners and watch your quadrants—"

"No," said Secretary Cardway, bracing a hand on the bulkhead. "I'm not going to shoot it from a tank. I'm getting down."

"Sir!" Vickers blurted, trying to come up with a

suitable lie. He had almost said the truth, "That's too dangerous to allow—"; and that would have made the big Texan's decision irrevocable.

Adrienne, swinging lithely out of the cab, supplied the right words before her husband or anyone else could use the wrong ones. "It's not a matter of safety, Mr. Car—Mr. Secretary," she stated matter-of-factly. "It's visibility. That extra four feet of height gives you a shot the bush can't block." She began to climb into the back, her right foot on the fender and a hand raised to the one Stern outstretched to meet her. Warren and a PR man were getting out over the rear bulkhead as the Prime Minister watched with steel points in his eyes. "And besides," the blonde woman said with an apparently absent glance at Cardway's bodyguard, "on the ground you'd be between a charging tyrannosaur and all the other guns, that one—" she flicked a thumb at the cal fifty as she stepped over the bulkhead—"included. Standing in front of one of those when you know somebody's going to fire it isn't the sort of courage that . . . brings back elephants."

Craig leaned forward to whisper to his principal. His knuckles were white on the grip of the sub-machine gun. Cardway brushed him back with a scowl, still poised to climb down. The bodyguard's face contorted. He shouted, "I won't have it! I swear to God, I'll blast the first man that aims near you! If you step down, *everybody* gets down or else disarms!"

Stern and Adrienne both shifted their stance, a change more mental than physical at the moment. Craig's outburst appeared to bother even Secretary Cardway. The cabinet official opened his mouth for a curt retort; but he swallowed the words unspoken a moment later. He frowned. "All right," he said, "goddammit. Let's get this show on the road."

Vickers used the gun mount as a grip to lift
himself over the bulkhead. Not only was it faster,
it kept him away from the sullen Warren standing
by the cab door. The box of the half-track was still
more crowded than Vickers liked when they were
facing dangerous game, but he did not feel that he
could safely unload the supernumeraries so near
to a carnosaur either. "Real slow, now," he said to
the driver, settling the fore-end of his M14 in his
left palm. "Dead slow."

The squeal of bearings in several of the bogeys
was high-pitched and in keeping with the alien
atmosphere. Inevitably, the noise would announce
them to the tyrannosaur, but Vickers was not concerned that it would frighten him away. It was the
tyrannosaur's world, and he was king in it. Perhaps the beast would stalk down the trail to
investigate. That would give them the appearance
of danger and a simple, no-deflection shot that the
Secretary could be expected to make.

The half-track brushed through a slight kink in
the trail. They were on the edge of a sharply-
defined clearing. The guide recognized it as being
cut by the boundary of the intrusion field when a
vehicle snapped back Topside with its immediate
surroundings. Directly across the clearing, twenty
meters away, sprawled the tyrannosaur in a field
of white-leafed wormwood. The beast had probably not moved since Stern and Adrienne dragged
it from the intrusion vehicle with a tractor. It lay
on its belly, facing three-quarters of the way away
from the hunters. Its hind legs were stretched
back along its tail like those of a huge tadpole.
Pulmonary blood had painted the beast's jaws and
muzzle, drawing a black mist of flies.

"It's asleep," the guide said sharply. "Quick, Mr.

Secretary, put one through its chest and be ready for the charge!''

The titanopteryx was skimming toward them so low over the field of wormwood that the tyrannosaur's haunches hid it. It pulled up to brake its flight like a parachute opening. The huge pterosaur seemed to lower its hind legs as it hung in the air, gripping the dinosaur's hide as if its wings rode on something more tangible· than air. The maneuver was so effortlessly graceful that Vickers would have gasped in delight—if it had not just made an obvious liar of him.

For a moment, no one said anything more. The diesel clattered. After glaring at the half-track, the pterosaur arched its neck and slammed its chisel beak into the haunch of the sprawling tyrannosaur. The flesh beneath the mottled scales rippled away from the impact, but the dinosaur as an entity did not move.

"You sons of bitches," Secretary Cardway said. Deep-throated venom was thick on his voice. "You shot it yourself and dragged me here to make a fool of myself." Cardway's voice rose. "Did you have pictures of yourselves killing it, is that the idea? Wait till I was all over the national press with 'my' tyrannosaurus and then blackmailing me into supporting you? Was that it?"

No one was answering. Vickers turned toward his furious client, not because he had a response but because the anger had to be faced like any other catastrophe. The soldier between them at the cal fifty was shrinking away, disassociating himself from a rage as inexplicable to him as an astrobleme was.

Cardway reached across the receiver of the big gun and slapped the guide with his right hand. "Go ahead and laugh, you bastard!" the Secretary shouted. "Laugh at how you played me for a fool."

Vickers could not see for tears and the bloody rage that pulsed behind his eyes. "Look, here's something for you to tape!" the Secretary was shouting. He raised the Mannlicher and fired. The bullet slapped dust from the tyrannosaur's haunch, near the bloody gash the pterosaur had already torn. The winged creature screeched and hopped to the ground. Its beak quested for an adversary.

"You sons of bitches!" Secretary Cardway repeated. He jumped to the ground, stumbling as he hit. He used the butt of his rifle to brace himself and began to stalk toward the fallen dinosaur.

In the cab of the half-track, Thomas Warren was grinning like a madman. The two holographers were rolling tape, though they must have known it would probably have to be wiped. "Sir!" Avraham Stern cried, "you mustn't—"

For an instant, Vickers saw everything with the clarity of inclusions in a crystal lens: the Secretary's hunched shoulders; the incised margins of the wormwood leaves; the flicker of the tyrannosaur's right eyelid. Then the whole world shrank to the front sight of the M14, with everything beyond it as blur as it was supposed to be when the guide's fingers squeezed the trigger. He paused.

"I warned you!" Craig shouted.

Adrienne Vickers did not fire. There were too many people in too confined an area, and a 250-grain gilding-metal bullet from her rifle would penetrate everything it hit except perhaps the engine block. Instead, the tall blonde dropped the Schultz and Larsen and leaped a five-gallon thermos of water to tackle Craig as he shot. Adrienne's right hand gripped the bodyguard's throat, her left seized the Uzi at the juncture of barrel and front sight. Together, the pair of them cannoned into Vickers. Craig fired a six-round burst through the bed of the truck before Adrienne's leverage broke his finger against the trigger guard. His screaming stopped a moment later when Avraham Stern leaned forward. With a short, axial blow as if he were playing billiards, Stern brought the butt of his rifle down on Craig's skull. The Israeli official kept the muzzle of his FAL vertical, just in case the shock jarred the hammer off its sear.

Vickers was jammed forward against the bulkhead while 9mm bullets blew splinters into his shins. He had not fired. The tyrannosaur's head lifted an inch on its bed of wormwood. Its tail swept in an arc like a scythe, catching first the titanopteryx, then Secretary Cardway. The great pterosaur squawked and spun, hurled toward the carnivore's thorax by the impact. That was accidental, however. The tip of the tail took the Secretary of State across the buttocks as the dinosaur had intended and flung him forward. The four-foot jaws were already open to receive him. When the jaws closed, they thudded like a casket dropping. The Secretary's left arm flew off. His hand and chest disappeared into the carnivore's mouth.

The Israeli driver stood up in the cab, waving a short-barreled grenade launcher. The gunner in the back of the half-track was gripping his weapon, despite the group struggling at his feet. Neither soldier shot. Mordecai Greenbaum leaned over the side of the vehicle and fired the cast-off Gibbs double twice into the chest of the tyrannosaur, still belly-down in the white-dusted foliage. The dinosaur stiffened. A tiny, two-clawed forefoot flicked up, too short even to pick the beast's great teeth. Then the carnivore relaxed, its head falling back sideways to the ground. The jaws lolled open. The Secretary of State, impaled on a score or more of four-inch teeth, did not spill out. His body above the rib cage lay within the dinosaur's mouth. The left arm and the borrowed Mannlicher, dropped when the tail struck, lay on the ground like storm wrack.

Henry Vickers straightened. Stern and Adrienne were dragging away the unconscious bodyguard. The official looked up. "Is there a chance?" he asked.

The guide grimaced. "Not even if it had happened in the operating room of Walter Reed," he said. He turned and fired a single round through the carnosaur's skull, aiming between the jaw hinge and the ear hole. The beast did not move as its brain was destroyed. "But I suppose it's safe to drag out what's left now," he said quietly.

The Prime Minister was in a whispered conversation with the holographer who had been beside in the back. Greenbaum looked at the heavy rifle he still carried and set it down. "We have holographic tape of—what has happened, Mr. Vickers," he said. "You attempting to finish off the animal before it harmed the Secretary, and the, the American bodyguard preventing you by his attack. The blame is clear." The little Israeli paused, shaking his head. "It will not gain us the —end for which this exercise was planned, of course. That has become impossible. But at least we can apportion blame."

Vickers jumped down from the half-track, holding his rifle at the balance in his left hand. Adrienne glanced at the unconscious bodyguard, now being trussed by Stern with a rifle sling. Seeing Craig was safe, the blonde woman poised to follow her husband. Before she could do so, Vickers looked back. "Adrienne," he said, "there's a net in one of those chests. Would you bring it, please?"

Adrienne blinked. "Why?"

Vickers gestured toward the titanopteryx. The creature mewled as it struggled back toward the shelter of the tyrannosaur's carcass. Its left wing, injured by the sweep of the dinosaur's tail, dragged behind it like the train of a troll-queen. "We're taking that back with us," the guide said. "Alive."

"D-darling," said his wife, her mouth more dry with fear than it had been when she saw Craig aiming his Uzi at her husband, "I don't think—"

The guide's face contorted. "I'm through with killing-for-a-business!" he screamed. "Through with it! This is alive and I'm sending it back alive! And if I never see another tourist hunter, it'll by *God* be too soon!"

The two soldiers and the older cameraman—the one who had served in the Golan—retrieved Secretary Cardway's body. Greenbaum watched them grimly, holding the reloaded .470 with its muzzles an inch from Craig's face. The bodyguard remained unconscious, slumped away from the stanchion to which he was bound. The younger PR man thought of taping that too, but the look on the Prime Minister's face deterred him. Thomas Warren remained seated in the cab. Occasionally he would spit out another fragment of the plastic stem of his pipe.

It took Vickers, Adrienne, and Avraham Stern half an hour to capture the injured titanopteryx and load it onto a cargo skid. That was respectable time. The creature was half again as heavy as any of the three of them, and it was capable of ripping the armored hide of a dinosaur with its beak. They made a good team, the blonde woman thought. All three of them were willing to do whatever was necessary to accomplish the task at hand.

"Ah, there you are, Mr. and Mrs. Vickers," called the pudgy man with the clipboard. He began trotting toward them across the busy traffic of the hangar.

Avraham Stern paused in mid-sentence and turned from the Vickers' to whom he had been talking. "Professor Wayne," he said loudly, "we will have completed the final briefing in a few moments, if you please." He managed a smile as he looked back at the American couple. "I should not be harsh with him, should I?" Stern said. "He was extremely helpful about releasing the tyrannosaurus to us when we came back for it. For all the good that that did."

The Israeli official's voice was surprisingly mild as he spoke the last words. Adrienne narrowed her eyes and said, "That's over with now? The—the plan isn't being carried out without US support?"

Stern shrugged. "The frigate *Gromky* docked in Tripoli seven hours ago," he said. "Such cargo as she carried—a number of large drums—was immediately escorted by an armored convoy toward El Adem. The air base, you know. Where the containers go from there will be the question, of course."

"They may stay there till the cans rust away," said Vickers. "And . . . and anyway, it's better than World War III, I think."

Stern looked around. He was back in a dark business suit, a dumpy, balding man who might have chased ambulances or sold used cars for a living. "Among the three of us," he said quietly, "I also think it is better. However, I do not think it is good." He stretched out a hand to Vickers, paused, then gave his left hand to Adrienne as well. "God be with you," Stern said. He began to walk away.

"If the Holocene gets too hot, Avraham," Vickers called after the departing official, "you're always welcome in the Cretaceous."

Professor Wayne, head of the Zoology Section,

had been waiting tensely a dozen feet away. Now he stooped like a hawk on the couple. He moved so suddenly that he almost collided with a quartet of turbine pumps whining toward the intrusion vehicle on fork lifts. The plump American professor scuttled safely through the equipment, his clipboard tight against his chest as if it were a poker hand he was hiding. "Ah, good, good," he bubbled. "The committee—the Biological Oversight Committee—only now reached a decision. I was very much afraid that I would have missed you with the message."

Adrienne smiled, more tolerantly than she would have been able to do a few years before. "We still have half an hour, Doctor," she said. "Though I hope it won't take that long, since we've got other business to attend to . . . ."

"Oh, of course, of course," said the zoologist, sounding shocked. "It shouldn't take anything like that. It should—" he paused. "Well, it will take less time if I say it, of course. Very simply, we want you to hold the size of individual living specimens you send, ah, Topside, to two hundred kilograms apiece. Until we inform you otherwise. It's a matter of space, you see. We hope to expand the facilities shortly, but for the next six months we can no more care for an adult ceratopsian than we could—eat one at a sitting." He grinned brightly to emphasize his joke.

Adrienne responded with a frown as her fingers toyed with the sling of her rifle. "But you have thirty acres, don't you?" she asked. "I mean—I was there just, well, ten days ago to bring back the tyrannosaur."

"Oh, of course, but I mean *secure* space," Wayne said. His tone was that he would have used if he had been accused of faking experimental data. "That is, an area not only free of birds and bird droppings, but sterilized. It's quite amazing how virulent the least trace of ornithosis has proven to the higher Cretaceous life forms. It seems to be no exaggeration to say that every archosaur you sent back from the previous base was killed by the sparrows in our compound here."

Adrienne laughed. Vickers smiled, though it was through an unwillingness to dampen his wife's good cheer than from any humor he himself saw in the wasted effort. Still, he and Adrienne had accomplished their own tasks. That was the only thing they would have had to be ashamed of . . . . "How's the pterosaur coming along, then?" the guide said aloud. "It's within your size limit, I suppose?"

"Yes, yes . . . ," the zoologist said, frowning. He tapped his clipboard with the hinge of his glasses. "Frankly, I don't understand that at all. To begin with, I would have thought that the Order Pterosauria had diverged from the main stem of the dinosaurs—and birds, of course—so far back that they would not be susceptible to diseases of the latter. Of course, humans can catch ornithosis too, under extreme conditions . . . . But still, I'm quite sure we kept the titanopteryx in a sterile environment from the moment you returned with it. And—"

"Wait a minute," Vickers said, waving his free hand palm down. "You mean that it died?"

"Yes, this morning, that's what I've been saying," Wayne responded. "Technically we'll have to wait for the pathology report to be sure, but there's no real doubt that it was ornithosis again. The surprising thing is that the pterosaur must have been infected before we received it. Infected in the Cretaceous, that is. Which ought to be impossible."

Vickers and his wife stared at each other.

"Christ," whispered the blonde woman, "the tyrannosaur. It had the bug, God knows, and we carried it back—"

"You took the tyrannosaur back to the Cretaceous?" the zoologist exclaimed. "Oh, my goodness—why did you do that?"

The guide shrugged away the question. "What's going to happen?" he demanded. "I mean—back where we left the carcass. In the Cretaceous."

"At the end of the Cretaceous," Adrienne said, her eyes staring out beyond the walls of the hangars and the present time. "As close as Dr. Galil could place us to the boundary between the Cretaceous and the Cenozoic. Where the dinosaurs were the biggest, and just before they all disappeared."

"Well, I don't know, exactly," the zoologist said with a look of increasing concern. "Introduction of the bedsonia-chlamydia organism causing ornithosis could radically reduce a non-resistent population, of course. But even myxomatosis didn't wipe out hares in Europe and Australia, just reduced their numbers to a few percent of what they had been before the, well, plague. And that was only until natural increase built up the—oh, dear!"

"Yeah," Vickers said. "Rabbits breed like—rabbits. But some of the bigger dinos aren't sexually mature until they're thirty years old."

"And the small ones, the ones that *do* breed quickly enough to build up an immune population," said Adrienne, the distant expression still in her eyes, "they're the ones that don't have enough body weight to depend on for insulation. The ones that have already grown feathers . . . . The birds are the only . . . dinosaurs to survive Secretary Cardway's safari."

"Oh, dear," Professor Wayne repeated. He

started backing away from the conversation,
oblivious to the final loading operations still going
on. "I really must discuss this—" A workman with
a cartload of steel framing shouted an angry
warning. Wayne stopped, turned, and walked
quickly toward a door. The plump man was almost
at a run when he disappeared from sight.

A technician called something unintelligible
across the volume of the hangar. He reconsidered
and spoke into a microphone. The speakers on
Vickers' and Adrienne's lapels rasped, "Insertion
Group? We will be ready for final countdown in
ten, repeat, one-zero minutes."

Vickers keyed his mike. "Acknowledged," he
said. To his wife he added, "I suppose we can
board now. It'll be . . . good to get back, I think."

"Cardway brought the end of the dinosaurs,"
Adrienne said. Even next to her, Vickers could
barely hear the words. "If he'd lived, he would
have ended . . . human civilization, wouldn't he?
Perhaps not over Avraham's little plot—"

"It wasn't his."

"Whosoever. Cardway would have had four, eight
years of his own soon with his finger on the
button. He·wasn't going to make it that long
without stepping into the deep end, was he?"

"Adrienne, I think we'd better board," Vickers
said. The hangar was growing quieter as the last of
the workmen filed out through the doors to the
storage bay.

"Henry, I was watching you," his wire whispered. "I don't think anyone else could tell, not
even Craig. But you weren't aiming at the tyrannosaur. You had your sights in the middle of Cardway's back. And you didn't fire."

The guide's face was as calm as a saint's. He
took Adrienne's left hand in his own, but he was
looking toward the loaded intrusion vehicle. "It

wasn't that he slapped me," Vickers said, as softly as his wife had spoken. "I could have taken that. But it made me think . . . . I don't want to die, not any more—" He squeezed the tall blonde's hand, the pressure reassuring to him at a level below consciousness. "I thought for a moment that there were things more important than whether I lived or not, though. And there are. But I couldn't pull the trigger, not on a man. Even a man like Luther Cardway."

"You were wrong about your life not being more important," Adrienne said. She broke into a bright smile and began leading the guide toward the intrusion vehicle. Her left arm crossed her chest to reach him. "The world can take care of itself," she said. She laughed aloud and added, "As it did, you know. As it did."

"It didn't if you were a dinosaur," Vickers replied bleakly. "And I was responsible for that, not the world."

His wife sobered. "Henry, no one is responsible for what happens sixty-five million years before he's born. Not even if he's there. We *can't* change the past—whatever the bloody-minded dreamers in the Ministry of Defense may hope. The Cretaceous *now* Topside is exactly the same way it was when Stern and I left here with the dino to go back."

"Even if I didn't change it," said the hunter, "I made it happen." In his mind the tyrannosaurus still lay dying, its lungs destroyed by the disease; and the scene was multiplied millions, billions of times across the face of the Earth in ripples spreading from his action.

"All right then," snapped Adrienne, "but think of *what* you made happen. You made a world that mammals could grow and evolve in. Are you going to be sorry about that? Are you sorry that you're

—that *I'm* not two inches long, snapping up bugs that blunder by in the dark? Because sure as Hell that's what we'd be if something hadn't wiped out the dinosaurs!"

Vickers looked at his wife. After a moment he squeezed her hand. "No," he said, "I'm not sorry about that." Together, they began to walk slowly toward the intrusion vehicle.

THE SIXTY-FIVE MILLION YEARS
AFTERWORD

    Charles Dickens' megalosaurus waddled on four legs like a lizard; Arthur Conan Doyle's hopped like a toad instead. L Sprague deCamp's sauropods walked on the bottom of lakes, snorkeling air through their long necks. And my dinosaurs—well, you've met my dinosaurs. All four of us described our dinosaurs in accordance with the best scientific thought of our respective days. The other three writers were dead wrong, and I am not so great a fool as to doubt that I am dead wrong also. The best someone writing on dinosaurs can hope for is that it will be a generation or so before it is obvious just how wrong he was: paleontology is not a science in which the official truth is graven on stone, albeit the data are.

    What degree of change in the official truth about dinosaurs can one expect in a generation? Well . . . I started taking an active interest in dinosaurs in about 1950. The most widely-known dino-

saur in America at that time was certainly the
brontosaurus, the trademark of Sinclair "Dino"
Gasoline. Though Sinclair is defunct, I think the
brontosaurus will be familiar still to most readers
and thus will make a good example.

The brontosaurs of 1950 were among the largest
reptiles ever to live. They were reptiles because
they were cold-blooded. They lived in swamps and
marshes like hippopotamuses, eating the soft
plants found there. While brontosaurs were
capable of staggering out on land, they did so at
the risk of rupturing the cartilaginous pads
cushioning their knee and ankle joints. Their great
bodies had to be buoyed up by water except on
rare occasions. The brontosaurs used water for
protection as well; their nostrils were set high
atop long necks, which permitted the animals to
breathe while standing thirty feet deep in water
where predators could not follow.

Today's brontosaurs (so to speak) are still big,
but they probably were not reptiles. That is, their
ancestors were warm-blooded, and there is no real
reason to believe that brontosaurs had lost the
capacity that gave their forebears domination of
the land. Brontosaurs occasionally walked
through or died in rivers, but their teeth were not
adapted to eating aquatic plants. As a matter of
fact, the short-faced head that you are used to
seeing on restorations of brontosaurs is not based
on a brontosaurus skull at all. O C Marsh (one of
the founders of modern paleontology) put together
a brontosaurus skeleton from a quantity of
jumbled bones which did not include a skull. He
secretly stuck on a loose skull from another site to
complete his specimen. In 1915, brontosaur
remains were found with a quite different skull in
place. Marsh's successors showed a regard for

awkward data known to more professions than theirs: they suppressed the find for sixty years.

It is certain that brontosaurs—or very similar beasts—walked through water; a number of trackways are preserved in mud that hardened to stone before the tracks were erased. On the other hand, elephants and human beings walk through water also without living at the bottom of lakes. Brontosaurs did not live under water either—because they floated. Some of the tracks prove *that*, as well. There is a trackway consisting of a double line of dabs where one of the beasts touched the bottom with the tips of its forefeet to pole itself along. The rest of the body—porous bone, fat, and yards of intestine—must have been bobbing along on the surface like a cork or it too would have left some sign in the bottom mud. Brontosaurs were no more able to stand on the bottom of deep lakes than are men without lead belts or concrete overshoes.

What was the purpose of the long neck, then? Presumably the same purpose as that of a giraffe's long neck: it permits its owner to browse on vegetation that nothing else can reach. Brontosaurs' legs were pillars like those of elephants, not bandy arcs like those of heavy water-dwellers like hippos. Since it is now admitted that there was nothing abnormal about the brontosaurs' joints either, forests rather than swamps become their evident habitat.

Oh—and they officially aren't brontosaurs any more either. It seems that another specimen was given the scientific name apatosaurus before Marsh got around to describing his (slightly-edited) specimen as brontosaurus. The earlier name has scientific precedence.

All this points up the basic problem which faces people who wish to study dinosaurs today: there are no dinosaurs today. What we have are fragments: almost always fragments only of the hard parts; almost always partial even then; and at best, only a tiny fraction of the number of species which presumably existed during any given time horizon. No one can properly be blamed for making the best guess from the available data. For that matter, no one can be blamed for making an honest mistake where there were no data. Marsh's sin was not that he added a conjectural skull to his brontosaurus, but rather that he concealed the fact that it *was* a conjecture.

Luck and sophisticated techniques have given us increasingly-detailed glimpses into the beasts of the Mesozoic. We have the outline of the soft parts of icthyosaurs, fur from a pterodactyl's wing, small running dinosaurs with feathers, and —incredibly—fossilized mummies of anatosaurs (trachodons, if you use an older text; duckbills). The mummies are complete enough that gullet contents can be analyzed (evergreen needles and similar dry-land vegetation). Obviously the beasts did not dry out after dying in a swamp, which used to be described as their normal habitat; but authorities can still argue as to whether anatosaurs' feet were shod with horny hooves or with webbed toes.

And of course one can not determine even from a mummy whether a creature was warm-blooded or cold-blooded when alive: a dead crocodile and a dead man both reach ambient temperature after a few hours. Incidentally, I am using the terms "warm-blooded" and "cold-blooded" throughout this essay because they are generally familiar. In the technical literature, these common terms are generally replaced by "endothermic" and "ecto-thermic" respectively.

The hard evidence that dinosaurs were warm-blooded is skimpy. First, dinosaur bone marrow seems to have been geared to the rapid production of blood corpuscles, like that of modern mammals and birds but unlike that of modern reptiles. Second, dinosaurs flourished in regions which are believed to have been cooler than modern large reptiles could inhabit today. Reptiles are torpid and therefore vulnerable during cold weather. Third, warm-blooded predators must kill more frequently than must cold-blooded predators of similar sizes in order to fuel their bodies. There are thus relatively more predators to prey animals in a cold-blooded ecosystem. Predator-prey ratios among dinosaur populations seem to approximate those of mammal populations rather than those in which the predators are known to be/have been cold-blooded.

These data are real but not conclusive. First, warm-bloodedness may require rapid production of blood cells, but the reverse is not necessarily true. Second, modern reptiles which must compete with large mammals may be limited to warmer latitudes than were the dinosaurs. And third, the samples which we have of fossil com-munities are far too limited to permit hard statis-tical analyses of the biomass.

Still, such hard data as there are imply that dinosaurs *were* warm-blooded. The circumstantial evidence in support is overwhelming. For instance, an animal requires a great deal of energy simply to hold its body off the ground. Anyone who has chased a skink knows how quick a lizard can be—in a brief dash. But most of a skink's life —or a crocodile's—is spent motionless, belly to the ground, legs splayed . . . waiting. The ability to stand upright for long periods and to exert maximum effort for a matter of minutes instead of a matter of seconds requires a high metabolism and a sophisticated method of regulating body temperature.

The factors which require warm-bloodedness to support a mammalian life-style hold true for dinosaurs as well. The ancestors of the dinosaurs were Triassic carnivores called thecodonts, reptiles similar in appearance to crocodiles. Some thecodonts departed from the normal lizard posture by rising up onto their hind legs alone to chase their prey. This proved to be a hugely effective adaptation. Later thecodonts—proto-dinosaurs—carried the adaptation a stage further and became bipedal at all times. The result was the most successful class of land vertebrates the world has ever known. The thecodont proto-dinosaurs not only swamped all competition in the carnivorous niches from which they arose, they also radiated into the herbivorous niches until they filled all the latter as well. As their size increased, the largest herbivorous dinosaurs slumped back into a four-legged stance to carry body weights of up to eighty tons or so. But the ancestors of even these great sauropods were bipedal herbivores, and the ancestors of the ancestors were swift-running, bipedal carnivores.

A wolf requires a high metabolism to live the way it does. A thecodont like saltoposuchus (the 'leaping crocodile') which balanced on two legs rather than four, required at least as high a metabolism. A bipedal body design would have been as useless as daVinci's ornithopter had it not been powered by a high metabolism and all that implies in the way of internal temperature control.

The final evidence that some thecodonts and

their dinosaur descendants were warm-blooded comes from the mammals themselves. By the end of the Permian Era—or say, some 250 million years ago—mammal-like reptiles called therapsids had appeared. The therapsids were *very* mammal-like. They were warm-blooded and furry, and they dominated the world until the expansion of the thecodonts. The common belief that mammals appeared as tiny insectivores living in darkness under the domination of the dinosaurs is false. Proto-mammals had appeared millions of years before the earliest dinosaurs. They had developed into a number of large forms, carnivores and herbivores both, which weighed upwards of a half ton apiece. The expansion of the thecodont proto-dinosaurs, however, blew the therapsids out of every eco-niche above the size of a possum. The tiny, cowering insect-eaters were all that was left of the mammals after they faced the dinosaurs and were found genetically wanting, right down the line.

Certainly the bipedal stance of the dinosaurs was superior to the quadrupedal sprawl which the earliest mammals retained from their reptilian progenitors. Still, warm-blooded mammals would have had a great advantage over reptiles which could only be active during the heat of the day. The proto-mammals proved in fact to be totally inferior to the proto-dinosaurs; and this is the most convincing evidence of all that the dinosaurs as well as the mammals were warm-blooded.

Early restorations showed dinosaurs flopped on their bellies in the mud, which was all their metabolisms would have permitted if they really had been cold-blooded. A closer study of the way dinosaur joints were constructed, and the discovery of dinosaur tracks preserved in stone, proved that the dinosaurs stood erect and that they strode with their feet under them. The restorations were therefore revised (though the assumption of cold-bloodedness was not). As a result, the recent theories about dinosaurs do not change their popular appearance as much as they change the backgrounds against which the dinosaurs should be painted.

But one pair of changes dealing with musculature does greatly modify the look of some of the animals themselves. The hadrosaurs, the "duckbilled" dinosaurs, have generally been restored as if they had had no cheek muscles. Their huge batteries of grinding teeth (around a thousand teeth per individual) required cheeks to hold in the mass of pine needles, et cetera, that was being crushed. A "duck-bill" restored with cheeks differs as strikingly from the popular conception as a cow would differ from reality if it were restored *without* cheeks. As I mentioned earlier, the problem in studying dinosaurs is that there are no dinosaurs to study.

And that is even more true of what happened to the ceratopsians, the frilled quadrupeds generally typified by the three-horned triceratops. The bony frill is usually shown covered only by a layer of skin and is described solely as a defensive device. The bone surfaces, however, show scarring from the muscles attached to the frill on both the front and back sides. The muscles attached to the back of the frill moved and supported the weight of the enormous head. The muscles in front closed the beast's jaws. These jaw muscles change the appearance of the frill to which they were attached from a bare hollow to a bulge like a weight-lifter's biceps. The leverage provided by their frills enabled the ceratopsians to shear material like nothing else before the advent of the hydraulic press. That ability no doubt compensated the animals for any problems it caused by preventing them from looking like their restorations.

I began this essay by denying that TIME SAFARI was the truth in any absolute sense. It isn't, it can't be. But neither is there anything in the backgrounds I have used which I know or believe at this time to be false. In one particular, the background proved to be more accurate than I wish it had been. "Boundary Layer", the final portion of the volume, was completed two months before the Israeli air strike on the Baghdad nuclear facility.

I expect the 1975 Dinosaur to supplant the 1950 model of the same beast during the remainder of my lifetime. There have already been a number of good, general books on the subject. In a decade or so, popular texts will relegate discussions of "cold-blooded dinosaurs" to the introductory chapter, along with a picture of the sprawling Megalosaurus of the 1851 Crystal Palace Exposition. If there is a delay in the replacement of the Old Dinosaur, it will occur (I believe) because the old-style restorations of artists such as Charles R. Knight and Zdenek Burian deservedly have a life of their own. Burian's eery painting of brachiosaurs snorkeling from the bottom of a river is no more "false" than is Duchamp's NUDE DESCENDING A STAIRCASE; but neither painting should be taken as a statement of physiology.

There are still a few years for you to be able to amaze your friends with the New Truth about Dinosaurs, however. I can whole-heartedly recommend three books on the subject:

THE HOT-BLOODED DINOSAURS by Adrian J. Desmond; 1976; Dial Press/James Wade.

ARCHOSAURIA by John C. McLoughlin; 1979; Viking.

THE WORLD OF DINOSAURS by Michael Tweedie; 1977; William Morrow.

Note that I said I was recommending three books. I do not recommend any of the texts alone, at least not whole-heartedly. Compare what the writers say, contrast their viewpoints, and from the montage of statements construct your own picture of the Mesozoic world. I found that the reseach for this book taught me considerably more about thinking than it did about dinosaurs.

After you have read the recent texts, go back and read:

DINOSAURS by Edwin H. Colbert; 1961; Dutton.

This is a scholarly and well-written statement of all the things you have just been told are wrong, plus a great deal of uncontroverted material. Whether or not Dr. Colbert convinces you that perhaps it's still too early to trade in the 1950 Dinosaur after all, he should make you realize that the 1975 Dinosaur—sparkling now in the showroom— is going to be battered and rusty also by the year 2000. So whatever you decide, do so in a spirit of good humor and the knowledge that however worthwhile the search for answers is, absolute truth remains the domain of Religion and not Science.

—David Drake

Here is an excerpt from the new collection "MEN HUNTING THINGS," edited by David Drake, coming in April 1988 from Baen Books:

IT'S A LOT LIKE WAR

A hunter and a soldier on a modern battlefield contrast in more ways than they're similar.

That wasn't always the case. Captain C.H. Stigand's 1913 book of reminiscences, HUNTING THE ELEPHANT IN AFRICA, contains a chapter entitled "Stalking the African" (between "Camp Hints" and "Hunting the Bongo"). It's a straightforward series of anecdotes involving the business for which Stigand was paid by his government—punitive expeditions against native races in the British African colonies.

Readers of modern sensibilities may be pleased to learn that Stigand died six years later with a Dinka spear through his ribs; but he was a man of his times, not an aberration. Richard Meinertzhagen wrote with great satisfaction of the unique "right and left" he made during a punitive expedition against the Irryeni in 1904: he shot a native with the right barrel of his elephant gun—and then dropped the lion which his first shot had startled into view.

It would be easy enough to say that the whites who served in Africa in the 19th century considered native races to be sub-human and therefore game to be hunted under a specialized set of rules. There's some justification for viewing the colonial overlords that way. The stringency of the attendant "hunting laws" varied from British and German possessions, whose administrators took their "civilizing mission" seriously, to the Congo Free State where Leopold, King of the Belgians, gave the dregs of all the world license to do as they pleased—so long as it made him a profit.

(For what it's worth, Leopold's butchers *didn't* bring him much profit. The Congo became a Belgian—rather than a personal—possession when Leopold defaulted on the loans his country had advanced him against the colony's security.)

But the unity of hunting and war went beyond racial attitudes. Meinertzhagen was seventy years old in 1948 when his cruise ship docked in Haifa during the Israeli War of Independence. He borrowed a rifle and 200 rounds—which he fired off during what he described as "a glorious day!", increasing his personal bag by perhaps twenty Arab gunmen.

Similarly, Frederick Courteney Selous—perhaps the most famous big-game hunter of them all—enlisted at the outbreak of World War One even though he *wasn't* a professional soldier. He was sixty-five years old when a German sniper blew his brains out in what is now Tanzania.

Hunters and soldiers were nearly identical for most of the millennia since human societies became organized enough to wage war. Why isn't that still true today?

In large measure, I think, the change is due to the advance of technology. In modern warfare, a soldier who is seen by the enemy is probably doomed. Indeed, most casualties are men who *weren't* seen by the enemy. They were simply caught by bombs, shells, or automatic gunfire sweeping an area.

A glance at casualties grouped by cause of wound from World War One onward suggests that indirect artillery fire is the only significant factor in battle. All other weapons—tanks included—serve only to provide targets for the howitzers to grind up; and the gunners lobbing their shells in high arcs almost never see a living enemy.

The reality isn't quite *that* simple; but I defy anybody who's spent time in a modern war zone to tell me that they felt personally in control of their environment.

Hunters can be killed or injured by their intended prey. Still, most of them die in bed. (The most likely human victim of a hungry leopard or a peckish rhinoceros has always been an unarmed native who was in the wrong place at the wrong time.) Very few soldiers become battle casualties either—but soldiers don't have the option that hunters have, to go home any time they please.

A modern war zone is a terrifying place, if you let yourself think about it; and even at its smallest scale, guerrilla warfare, it's utterly impersonal.

A guerrilla can never be sure that the infra-red trace of his stove hasn't been spotted by an aircraft in the silent darkness, or that his footsteps aren't being picked up by sensors disguised as pebbles along the trail down which he pads. Either way, a salvo of artillery shells may be the last thing he hears—unless they've blown him out of existence before the shriek of their super-sonic passage reaches his ears.

But technology doesn't free his opponent from fear—or give him personal control of the battlefield, either. When the counter-insurgent moves, he's likely to put his foot or his vehicle on top of a mine. The blast will be the only warning he has that he's being maimed. Even men protected by the four-inch steel of a tank know the guerrillas may have buried a 500-pound bomb under *this* stretch of road. If that happens, his family will be sent a hundred and fifty pounds of sand—with instructions not to open the coffin.

At rest, the counter-insurgent wears his boots because he may be attacked at any instant. Then he'll shoot out into the night—but he'll have no target except the muzzle flashes of the guns trying to kill him, and there'll be no result to point to in the morning except perhaps a smear of blood or a weapon dropped somewhere along the tree line.

If a rocket screams across the darkness, the counter-insurgent can hunch down in his slit trench and pray that the glowing green ball with a sound like a steam locomotive will land on somebody else instead. Prayer probably won't help, any more than it'll stop the rain or make the mosquitos stop biting. But nothing else will help either.

So nowadays, a soldier doesn't have much in common with a hunter. That's not to say that warfare is no longer similar to hunting, however.

On the contrary: modern soldiers and hunted beasts have a great deal in common.

APRIL 1988 * 65399-7 * 288 pp * $2.95

To order any Baen Book by mail, send the cover price to: Baen Books, Dept B, 260 Fifth Avenue, New York, N.Y. 10001

Have You Missed?

DRAKE, DAVID
At Any Price
Hammer's Slammers are back—and Baen Books has them! Now the 23rd-century armored division faces its deadliest enemies ever: aliens who *teleport* into combat.
55978-8 $3.50

DRAKE, DAVID
Hammer's Slammers
A special *expanded* edition of the book that began the legend of Colonel Alois Hammer. Now the toughest, meanest mercs who ever killed for a dollar or wrecked a world for pay have come home—to Baen Books—and they've brought a secret weapon: "The Tank Lords," a brand-new short novel, included in this special Baen edition of *Hammer's Slammers*.
65632-5 $3.50

DRAKE, DAVID
Lacey and His Friends
In Jed Lacey's time the United States computers scan every citizen, every hour of the day. When crime is detected, it's Lacey's turn. There are a few things worse than having him come after you, but they're not survivable either. But things aren't really that bad—not for Lacey and his friends. By the author of *Hammer's Slammers* and *At Any Price*.
65593-0 $3.50

CARD, ORSON SCOTT; DRAKE, DAVID; & BUJOLD, LOIS MCMASTER
(edited by Elizabeth Mitchell)
Free Lancers (Alien Stars, Vol. IV)
Three short novels about mercenary soldiers—never before in print! Card's hero leads a ragtag group of scientific refugees to sanctuary in Utah; Drake contributes a new "Hammer's Slammers" story; Bujold tells a new tale of Miles Vorkosigan, hero of *The Warrior's Apprentice*.
65352-0 $2.95

DRAKE, DAVID
Birds of Prey

The time: 262 A.D. The place: Imperial Rome. There had never been a greater empire, but now it is dying. Everywhere its armies are in retreat, and what had been civilization seethes with riots and bizarre cults. Against the imminent fall of the Long Night stands Aulus Perennius, an Imperial secret agent as tough and ruthless as the age in which he lives. But he stands alone—until a traveller from Earth's far future recruits him for a mission so strange it cannot be disclosed.

55912-5 (trade paper) $7.95
55909-5 (hardcover) $14.95

DRAKE, DAVID
Ranks of Bronze

Disguised alien traders bought captured Roman soldiers on the slave market because they needed troops who could win battles without high-tech weaponry. The leigionaires provided victories, smashing barbarian armies with the swords, javelins, and discipline that had won a world. But the worlds on which they now fought were strange ones, and the spoils of victory did not include freedom. If the legionaires went home, it would be through the use of the beam weapons and force screens of their ruthless alien owners. It's been 2000 years—and now they want to go home.

65568-X $3.50

DRAKE, DAVID, & WAGNER, KARL EDWARD
Killer

Vonones and Lycon capture wild animals to sell for bloodsport in ancient Rome. A vicious animal sold to them by a trader turns out to be more than they bargained for—it is the sole survivor of the crash of an alien spacecraft. Possessed of intelligence nearly human, it has two goals in life: to breed and to kill.

55931-1 $2.95

DAVID DRAKE

"Drake has distinguished himself as the master of the mercenary sf novel."—**Rave Reviews**

To receive books by one of BAEN BOOKS most popular authors send in the order form below.

AT ANY PRICE, 55978-8, $3.50 . . . . ☐

HAMMER'S SLAMMERS, 65632-5, $3.50 . . . . . . ☐

LACEY AND HIS FRIENDS, 65593-0, $3.50 . . . ☐

FREE LANCERS, (ALIEN STARS #4), 65352-0, $2.95 . . . . ☐

BIRDS OF PREY, hardcover, 55912-5, $7.95 . . . ☐

BIRDS OF PREY, trade paper, 55909-5, $14.95 . . ☐

RANKS OF BRONZE, 65568-X, $3.50 . . . . ☐

KILLER, 55931-1, $2.95 . . . . ☐

Please send me the books checked above. I have enclosed a check or money order for the combined cover price made out to: BAEN BOOKS, 260 Fifth Avenue, New York N.Y. 10001.

ENTER A NEW WORLD
OF FANTASY . . .

Sometimes an author grows in stature so steadily that it seems as if he has always been a master. Such a one is David Drake, whose rise to fame has been driven equally by his archetypal creation, Colonel Alois Hammer's armored brigade of future mercenaries, and his non-series science fiction novels such as **Ranks of Bronze**, and **Fortress**.

Now Drake commences a new literary Quest, this time in the universe of fantasy. Just as he has become the acknowledged peer of such authors as Jerry Pournelle and Gordon R. Dickson in military and historically oriented science fiction, he will now take his place as a leading proponent of fantasy adventure. So enter now . . .

AUGUST 1988 65424-1 352 PP. $3.95

DAVID DRAKE
THE WORLD OF
CRYSTAL WALLS
BOOK I

THE SEA HAG

BAEN BOOKS